EYE
OF THE
HAWK

NEAL R. SUTTON

EYE
OF THE
HAWK

A TED CHESTER NOVEL

atmosphere press

For John and Susan, for making me the person I am today. Alice, for being as strong and determined as you have been throughout your life. For being there for me through good times and bad times, for which I'm forever grateful. And Monty, for that newfound joy.

PROLOGUE

MABEL WAS IN A DAZE AND HAD THE FEELING
of nausea and sickness. Her eyes felt heavy, and she couldn't manage to open them with all the strength she had. The darkness was the unknown of reality—in the distance were the sounds of dripping and metal clangs. There was a mixture of smells that had the ingredients of damp and must.

Last night was hazy. She remembered being in The House of Weekend club with Hafwen and meeting those two men on the rooftop bar. Eventually, after more drinks, conversations at the club, and indoor dancing in the main dance room, all four of them went back to the apartment the girls had booked to stay at in Berlin for their trip. The rest was a blur, but she knew deep down she was in desperate need.

A heavyweight sensation was felt around her right wrist as she tried to lift her right arm to rub her eyes. She couldn't lift it more than a few inches before it fell back down again. She saw a silver metal chain around her wrist attached to a wall mount through the obstructed view of her daze. Her mind raced to the possibilities of her situation. Had she been arrested, she thought? Her thoughts then came to her friend Hafwen; where was she? She began to pierce the light through

3

her eyes as she started to muster some strength and con-sciousness. She was starting to gain a sense of her surround-ings. The damp must become more potent in the air, and everything still seemed blurry to her eyes.

"Hey. You," someone said.

Mabel turned her head towards the voice. She still felt lightheaded as she manoeuvred her body, slightly nauseous still as she turned.

She saw the figure of another person across the room from her. From the outline of her long blonde hair, which seemed to be the brightest object in the gloomy room, she knew it was another girl by the voice.

"Hey," she said again.

Mabel tried to speak, but she couldn't project any more than a mumble, which she didn't even understand herself. She had now alluded to the fact that she was drugged last night. She had never felt like this before and tried to get up, but she was stopped. She looked down to her arm through the foggy stare and saw the outline of a silver chain keeping her locked in her seated position on the floor.

"Hey, stop. You can't go anywhere," the girl said.

Mabel surrendered. She tried to speak again but felt sick with her lack of energy.

"Save your energy. You will need it".

Mabel leaned forward and vomited. She wasn't sure if she had thrown up on herself but felt the odd splatter on her arm as she projected. She thought whatever the poison was; she threw up; it was better out of her. She used her free hand to place two fingers on the back of her throat to make herself heave. She vomited again in any direction she could away from her.

"Better out than in," the voice said again. "I'm Amanda."

Mabel heard the English accent from Amanda. Simul-taneously, she placed her free hand's index and middle finger into the back of her mouth to make herself heave and vomit onto the floor again. She stopped after three more attempts with nothing projecting but a nasty cough. She felt a cloud begin to lift over her body, and she was starting to feel a slight sense of balance now. Mabel began to speak back to Amanda through the coughing.

"What was that, sorry?" Amanda spoke.

"You're English?" Mabel said.

"Yes, and it seems you are too?" Amanda spoke.

Mabel nodded and let her head fall back against the wall.

"Yeah, Wales. Where are we?" Mabel returned.

"Hell. Far from the Green, Green Grass of Home."

"Where are you from?"

"Liverpool."

Mabel stared back at her hard as her vision started to clear. She tried to read Amanda's eyes to see whether she was scared or not. Amanda was pretty with her bright blue eyes and cleanish bright blond hair, and she seemed composed and possibly accepting to the fact of whatever her fate was. Mabel leaned forward to gain a visual of the room. It was spacious, old, and frail. The room had colossal grey building blocks and a few white pillars whose paint was peeling off in big flakes. She counted nine other girls in the room, making ten, and slowly realised the situation.

"They've kidnapped us, haven't they?" Mabel asked.

Amanda only nodded in acknowledgement. There was a sound of crying coming from another corner of the room. The post restricted Mabel's view of who was making the sound. There was a whisper through the crying, which was hard to hear. The person spoke again much louder, and the words were more precise.

"What's your name?" a person whispered.

A few seconds passed as the crying girl cleared her nose and composed herself.

"Hafwen," the girl said.

Mabel felt a sense of relief but also horror that someone

she knew was in the same situation as her and didn't manage to escape their predicament. She then remembered her wrist; she still had her bracelet on, which her mother had given her before she left, she shook her wrist, which was tied, and the silver coin flicked up on her wrist and into view, revealing the wording. "The eye will protect you," it still said.

The silver coin had the engraving of a hawk flying. Her mother gave her the bracelet before she left to go travelling. It gave her a sense of hope, but no one had any idea she was missing, and she thought it would be too late when someone eventually realised. Her last memory of her mother was the night before she left to travel. Her mother was a respectable parent and a hard worker, too; working twelve hour shifts on various days and nights as an ITU nurse and her father as a policeman.

Mabel was catching up on some TV shows before she left for the continent. Her mother came in after a long and emotional shift to find no laundry or cleaning had been done while she was at work. Her mother took out her frustrations on Mabel, saying she was lazy, and Mabel returned the favour by stating she hated her and hoped she died. A mother and daughter relationship can be complex, and emotions can run high quickly, but love is often shared. Mabel would have the opportunity to apologise and, likewise, the mother would too in an ordinary world. However, this wasn't an everyday world. This was potentially going to be the regrettable thought going through her mind as she either succumbs to her death or worse. She may not have the opportunity to rewind time and make things better with her mother. It looked destined that their last interaction would be negative and in both of their minds forever.

AMSTERDAM

CHAPTER ONE

THE SIRENS OF AN AMBULANCE ROARED PAST the fleet of unmarked vehicles. They were both rushing in opposite directions, with the ambulance's beacon lights reflecting beautifully upon the Amstel Canal. Although beautiful at first glance, it had a grim realisation of the scenario those paramedics and the tactical unit team may face as they head towards their destinations.

Ted Chester was leading the operational unit as its vehicles roared through the streets of Amsterdam. A joint task force of Europol, The Dutch National Police Korps, Dutch National Crime Squad and Ted Chester had collected intel and evidence on an Organised Crime Group. Ted was an International Liaison officer from England who had resided in Amsterdam for just over a year. He had worked cases in the capital related to fraud, money laundering and gun crimes. He had predominantly worked out of Schiphol Airport during his time, leading operations against drug trafficking by organised crime groups. He joined the National Crime Agency at the age of twenty-four and worked his way up to ILO after six years, where he got his first posting in the Netherlands.

However, this was bigger than he could imagine. He had

come across it from time to time in his career in the Netherlands, but it had never directly affected his case. He had always reported it to his Korps superiors in the Netherlands but never led operations on it specifically. The Netherlands has the highest level of registered victims of human trafficking; he knew it wasn't surprising to be aware of it. More specifically, the problems around sex trafficking, in which prostitution is legal in the Netherlands, leaves victims, primarily females, exposed to sexual exploitation.

The tactical team was close, just a couple of streets away now.

"ETA one minute," someone chirped over the radio.

"Remember your position," Ted replied.

The convoy of vehicles separated down different routes when approaching a junction near the apartment. Some of the SUVs carried on, which included Ted's vehicle. The speedometer dropped as they quietly pulled up into a small car park next to the Canal. Across the road was a gated walkway that led to a courthouse with a surrounding high-rise building, including some apartments and workspaces closed by the city council due to safety concerns. Two cars secured the car park, whilst four others occupied possible exit routes and avenues down the apartment's side streets.

"Car three in place." Ted radioed.

"Car five in place," another agent responded.

As the remaining cars gave all clear on their positions, Ted announced Operation Hawk was in place.

The evidence gathered over the last eight months from Europol, and other agencies was that a group of Hungarian OCGs had moved at pace across Central Europe, exploiting and trafficking women for sex slavery. There was specific evidence from a source, Ted's, that these OCG members were stalking and hunting down women, capturing them and transporting them to Eastern Europe to profit millions from their sales. Evidence from the source included names and addresses of meeting points where men, who were assumed to be part of the OCG, would meet at trendy coffee bars in the cycling streets of Amsterdam. The next step was to uptake the surveillance from all agencies, using microphones from fellow agent members who would sip on their Nespresso whilst reading 'De Telegraaf'. Fellow agents would disguise in cleaning vans or fake taxis parked a couple of side streets away, the hub of the information being reported back to a seedy hotel room with Ted and members of the Europol task force on operation Hawk.

Although the OCG members spoke in their mother tongue, translators were hired to convey the two and sometimes three-way conversations. The men would discuss pleasantries about their wives, their children and, more importantly, if Amstel were better than Dreher. There were conversations about football, the prostitutes they'd paid for the night before from their evening of window shopping. They'd, of course, slip in the discussions about work life. These conversations resulted in why operation Hawk was at the apartment complex that night and sitting across the road from the gated passage. The men had left the café shop unsuspecting and went straight to the address to check on their cargo, leading the team to the address.

The work conversation discovered that they had hidden thirteen girls under the courtyard's basement itself. You could access the storage basement from two points inside the building complex. One entrance was across the yard and down a set of steps. The other was inside the apartment with a set of stairs. The team took the apartment plans from the city council archives, which they had on file from when the building was closed for refurbishments, but these refurbishments didn't take precedence and became delayed. Cracks and sinkholes appearing on the Amsterdam streets and walkways took most of the city councils' budget. The OCG stumbled across this building and called it home temporarily as the base for their illegal activities.

Upon discovering the address, agents would conduct walk-throughs to see who entered the complex. Establishing how many members there were for when they decided to invade. Luuk Visser and Fenna Berg, who worked at Europol in the Hague, joined Ted and Sander Meyer, the chief of police for the Dutch Korps, in the operation. Members from the National Crime Squad in The Netherlands and the unknown agent inside the apartment complex tipped off the initial information for the meeting at the café shop. With the dangerous complicity of the situation, Ted and the team knew they were on their own and needed to move fast. They quickly established over eighteen hours that six members came in and out continuously. Time was ticking as to what would happen to the girls in captivity. Through the photographs taken during the surveillance, three men became established as Hungarian and Romanian OCGs with previous links to drug smuggling, money laundering and human trafficking. The operation was in place; they had the address linked to OCG; they knew that girls were being kept at the address thanks to the coffee shop conversation. They estimated how many members occupied the derelict property. The plan was set.

Ted, Luuk, Fenna, Sander and other members of the National Crime Squad met at a secluded HQ earlier in the day to discuss the plan. They were going to go in quietly and armed, that very night. They couldn't waste any more time with those girls in the basement. The complex was square-shaped and had roads on each of its four sides, following the infrastructure of the walls symmetrically. Ted and Fenna's cars were in the car park at the front, across from the gate. Luuk and Sander's cars were on one of the other side roads surrounding the apartment complex. The remaining vehicles were at the back and to the right of the complex, were full of National Crime Squad Officers.

Ted stared intensively at the gate, waiting, and seeking any signs of movement. The vision of the car was slightly blocked when a car drove past on the main road, but Ted didn't miss anything at that moment. He saw someone cross the court-yard; Ted took out his telescope to look closer. Marius Deme-trescu was one of the three men identified as OCG members.

"Alpha 2 spotted," Ted radioed.

During their planning, Stefan Agarici and Luca Manu were the two other men recognised on the Europol database, who again had links to Hungarian and Romanian OCG. They were down as Alpha 1 and Alpha 3; the other unidentified men were called Delta.

The man went out of his vision and inside the building. A few seconds later, adrenaline coursed through Ted's body. He saw Marius swiftly move across the courtyard to the stairs which led to the girls. Another person must have been at the bottom of the stairs because Marius seemed to be barking orders at him intensively.

Fenna Berg, who was in the same car park as Ted, could see the same scene unfolding.

"They seem unsettled," she spoke.

"I'm getting the same impression; everyone get ready in case we need to move in quickly. Anything happening near you one, two, five, six?" Ted asked.

"Nothing yet," Luuk replied.

"Nope, silent," another agent responded.

The other two cars updated that there was no movement around the back or side of the complex. Marius proceeded down the steps moving out of view of the courtyard. It was now a waiting game.

"Lost visual on Alpha 2."

Suddenly, Marius and the mystery person reached court-yard level again. The mystery man had his back turned to talk to Marius, both in frantic conversation, gesturing and pointing with their hands. They started to look around in different directions, high and low.

"Alpha 1 confirmed," Fenna informed.

Stefan Agarici was the other man as his body turned to look towards the gate. They both started to pace around, and it seemed that Marius took out his mobile to make a call. Stefan descended back into the basement.

"All units set. It's time," Ted said.

Luuk urgently responded, "We have a door opening at the back. Delta stepped out. Currently looking around. Delta now back inside."

"You remain covered?"

"Yeah, we have parked cars in front of us; we're hidden."

They were aware that the gate to the courtyard was locked. Researching the door type and experimenting earlier at a local dealership, the team figured out how to open it. Brute force being the winner, they had a thick short metal pole commonly known as a key to knock down doors, and it did the trick on the practice run.

Suddenly, Ted saw two men run across the courtyard in and out of view from the gate. Ted bolted upright and had one hand on the door handle when he saw a figure being escorted up the steps with a hood over their head by an unknown man, then another and another, three in total.

"We have three hooded persons with two, possibly three men – unknown status. Going across the courtyard, possibly towards your location Luuk. Go, go go!"

In the car park Ted and Fenna's car doors flung open. Ted had his gun holstered whilst running over to the gate with the key. Ted took the gate off its hinges with the force of the key. Gunshots were fired from the left and right of the compound. Ted, Fenna and the remaining team cautiously entered the courtyard with raised weapons looking for signs of movement. The sound of thunder through the apartment block to the right piqued Ted's interest.

"Fenna, clear the courtyard and the basement."

Fenna ordered two agents to cover the left-hand side of

the courtyard, and two more followed her to the basement. Ted moved towards his right with caution but could feel his heart beating out of his chest. He entered the doorway and saw legs lying on the floor.

"Gun down, Ted, it's Luuk."

Ted gave him the nod while still holding his gun up, ignoring instruction.

"It's Stefan Agarici; I got him," Luuk said through heavy breaths.

"Any more come your way?"

"One more with maybe two girls, other agents have pushed on, but we got one of the girls who was with Stefan; the agents have got her outside," Luuk said.

It must have been one of the girls that came up the courtyard steps as Ted noticed the head bag on the floor next to the body. What about the other two girls and men, he thought? His thoughts immediately changed when he heard noises coming through the apartment, but seemingly towards the other end of the complex, opposite to Ted and Luuk's position. They went back into attack mode, swiftly moving from room to room along the corridor, which turned left towards the courtyard. Thunder rifled through the air again. Ted saw up ahead, across the courtyard, agents moving in from the doors to the left and the right. They both upped their pace as they reached the other side of the yard. The agents seemed to be in a standoff position on approach but were still alert. On the floor was another Delta OCG member.

"Turn him over," Ted instructed Finn, one of the stationed Korps officers.

"What?"

"Turn him over, now."

Finn did as instructed and Ted recognised the dead man as Marius. Who was one of the men carrying the two other bagged persons. Another body occupied the floor, a National Squad agent.

"What happened?"

"Mees came in from the street through the door, and when I saw him, I saw the Delta member come up through the basement stairs. He saw Mees and shot him three times. One of the girls is alive in that room there; Zoe is with her, consoling her, paramedics are on their way, but Mees got one or two shots off when he was shot. He got Marius, and a second girl got caught in it, too, sadly. She fell down the stairs," Finn said.

Bartel Fitz, an agent watching the left, walked in from the street, stared at the scene, composed himself and lowered his weapon.

"They've gone."

"What do you mean they've gone?" Ted shouted.

"They knew we were coming. They've..."

"How?"

"I don't know."

"For fuck sake... tell me what happened." Ted pointed at him.

"We were watching the door... and this car was coming up the street... and when you gave all clear to go, the car stopped on the other side of the road and started firing at us. These two white vans pulled up and flung everyone into the back like trash, the girls, you know, and off they went. Luca and three more people went in the back, and God knows how many were in the van's front seats or the car that was with them. We were trying to keep covered and aim our guns back in their direction; we just saw glimpses from above the dashboard."

"Where did the car go?"

"It drove off at speed; Zoe managed to get the plate."

"Waste of time, it will be a fake. We can run it and see where it leads. Get cameras on the van and ANPR on the car. Where's Fenna and Sander?"

Fenna appeared from the courtyard into the hallway and looked at the bodies; her face was full of sadness as she saw

Mees' eyes staring helplessly into the ceiling. She straightened herself up when she heard her name as Ted spoke.

"You're going to want to see this," Fenna said.

CHAPTER TWO

FENNA LED TED DOWN THE STAIRS FROM THE
courtyard to the basement. Fenna was mid-twenties with dark
brown hair and a small figure but an athletic build. Ted filled
Fenna in briefly on what had happened with the two OCG
deaths, the mixed fortunes of the dead girl and the one Mees
saved. Fenna explained that there were two more girls' bodies
to account for if the numeric count was correct from the coffee
shops conversations.

"Do the girls know what happened to them?" Ted asked.

"Too soon to ask. Let's get the girls checked out, and I'll
get some of the agents to ask questions. If they're any good,
they will do it anyway."

Ted nodded.

The basement was grim, the smell of body odour, urine
and gone off food with the lingering smell of what was
desperation and depression. There was light from a single
bulb exposed hanging from the ceiling, but it seemed on its
last life. There were tables at the edges of the room and chains
running along the walls with cuffs attached to them to keep
the girls in place.

Sander walked over to them; she had come into the

complex with Luuk, pushed on and found the steps from the courtyard. She had surveyed the area with Fenna initially, and Ted also filled in Sander on the upstairs events, and she became emotionally struck by the news of Mees, one of her own Korps.

"Sorry for your loss, Chief."

"Thank you; he had such a bright future. I'll take over the process once we've cleared up here."

"Understood, sorry."

"It's not your fault, Ted; that's just the way it played out. How did they know we were coming? That's what I want to know."

"Me too."

Silence overcame the group, apart from the rustling of papers from the agents investigating the contents of tables, which brought Ted to break the silence.

"So, Fenna, what did we find? You said two bodies?"

"Yes, over here."

They walked over to the bodies. A sudden dose of anger and harsh reality flowed through Ted's veins. He knew the world was a dangerous and challenging place at times, but this was a new level, a personal level. He imagined the two teenage girls being his two daughters, who he loved dearly—an unforgettable moment in which the image, he knew, would be imprinted into his mind forever as he glanced upon their dead bodies. The lifeless eyes of the girls haunted his very nightmares before he even slept. The dark red blood pooled around their bodies, and their innocent faces were dirty and full of deprivation.

"So yes, Fenna found these two here," Sander filled in the silence.

"Yes, this one is estimated seventeen or eighteen years old—gunshot wound to the chest. And two shots with the second girl, shoulder and cheek, estimated fifteen or sixteen. Some bruising on the arms and legs, but marks around the wrists show they were tied up".

"No belongings, ID?"

"No, nothing at all on these."

"I'll get onto the missing lists with our own country and Europe and start there," Sander replied.

She turned her attention to one of the agents searching the tables.

"Anything?"

"No. There are loads of drawings. Must have been how they passed the time. Drawings of families, I think. Holiday drawings, a Few old newspapers, like months old."

"Nothing? There must be something," Fenna said with a tone of desperation.

"There must be something," Ted echoed.

Luuk entered the basement, followed by Bartel and Finn. All three of them held their nose and made a face, affected by the sights and smells of the room.

"Jesus," Luuk gasped.

Ted defeatedly walked over to the three agents who had just entered.

"Any news on the girls? They say anything?"

"Nothing with mine; she's in shock. She hasn't spoken, not even nodded, or acknowledged anyone. But the medics say she is going to be fine, needs fluids."

Finn stepped forward proudly.

"Zoe's been talking to the girl; she talked. She's with the medic now getting looked after; want me to radio her down?"

"Please."

Whilst Finn radioed Zoe, Sander asked to be excused from the room to see the whereabouts of Mees and inform the next of kin. Ted nodded and looked around, wandering over to the drawings on the table. The crayon drawings varied from the type a proud parent would put their five years old's drawing on the fridge and some had more detail and were better in quality and definition. Some included drawings of houses, holidays, and family members, including mum or dad on them. Some pictures were crumpled and ripped; some even crumpled into a ball. One of the spots on the table had a crumpled piece of paper, and once unfolded it was in a few parts. When placed together, the puzzle pieces turned into horror. "LET ME GO" was written, and pictures of death. Maybe the OCG members had reviewed the drawings and taken some away if they exposed names or were more threatening. Suddenly Zoe made her way to the basement.

"Sorry, I was with the girl."

"She talking?" Bartel asked.

"She wasn't at first, as you'd imagine."

"What's her name?" Ted asked.

"Francesca Garnier."

"What did she say?"

"Enough to give us something helpful, I hope. Francesca is from France, Bordeaux. She was on a trip with her friend, just a bit of a getaway. She talked to these boys in Escape's club, and they went back to the apartment Francesca rented for their trip. She doesn't remember their names, maybe Claude, she said. She doesn't remember much about when they got back to the apartment. She vividly remembers being in a car, but they had bags on their heads; they couldn't see anything. Then woke up here".

"Was her friend one of these girls lying here?" Ted said, pointing at the bodies.

Zoe paused and shook her head but didn't take her eyes off the girls.

"No, her friend Avril Monet was one of those taken in the van. She didn't want to fight; Avril was scared. Francesca said she and three other girls wanted to fight; they talked about it for days when they were alone. Some tried to talk them out of it because they thought they would get killed."

"How long had they been down here?"

"About a week, but they said they didn't know when it was

day or night. There were three other girls when they arrived, and they kept on coming."

"What happened tonight?"

"Yes, well... they were being fed by one of the men. Then someone shouted down the stairs in an eastern European accent, she said, and they started to get annoyed and frantic. Some other men came down, untied them all, and told them to get up because they were leaving. She and four other girls stood and looked at each other, wondering if this was their chance to escape. The other girls just went willingly with the men. But she identified Marius and Stefan as the ones who took her up through the photos we showed her"

"But only three girls came up?"

"She said they just stood there shaking. One of the men ordered something over the radio and left them and took the three girls up."

"Okay, and Luuk took down Stefan, and we have Marius dead too. They can't talk, but we will try what we can with what we have from Francesca."

Ted had a mixture of hope and disappointment that they didn't know why they decided to leave. Did they choose to up tools and go, or did they get spooked? He thought it but didn't want to believe that his undercover agent had turned against him already. Ted was contemplating leaving the basement and regrouping with the other teams, getting updates on the girls and maybe even having a conversation with them himself. Luuk turned around from the table and held up two of the drawings, holding them up like a child their teacher ignored.

"Am I missing something here? Do these girls like Germany?"

"Maybe they're German," Bartel said.

Ted heard the conversation, and a hint of adrenaline kicked in. He strode over to Luuk, and the rest followed.

"I thought that, but there are no family drawings or happiness to them. It's bleak. Random even," Ted said.

Someone was rapidly making their way down the steps; it was Finn.

"Sorry, my radio isn't working. Erika is talking."

"Erika?" Luuk said.

"Your girl. Erika Bartek, who was with Stefan."

"Fantastic! What did she say?"

"She's on route to the hospital. But the doctors said she had been talking. She said she heard conversations in Romanian. She is from the Czech Republic, but her mother is from Romania. They were allowed to use the toilet in the apartment blocks when they got fed. She overheard a conversation yesterday afternoon. She said afternoon because the sun seemed high in the sky when she looked out the window into the courtyard; it was the first time she had smiled in days seeing the sun. She heard a man saying they would be leaving in a few days; she said she heard Germany."

The feeling of optimism lifted in the lifeless room and on the faces of the agents in the grim basement.

"It looks like we have our lifeline. These girls were trying to leave us clues and they're working with us. Please make sure we get these bodies out of the basement and the apartments appropriately. Call Sander; she will help with the searches for family. Search the rest of the apartments. Ask the neighbours if they heard anything. See if we've got anything on the van and car," Ted said.

"I'll help Sander," Fenna said.

"Very good. We will meet in the morning at HQ after we've done here. We're going to need cameras and ANPR footage."

Luuk, Bartel, Finn, Zoe and Fenna all nodded and left the room as the forensic officers arrived to test the bodies. Ted felt he needed justice for the girls who lay motionless in that complex. Although it could never be equalled by what they had been through before their deaths. Some could give up and wish to die, which adds to the ticking clock imprinted into his thoughts. They had to do it for those still living in fear, and the hope they would be saved gave him a new purpose.

There was a personal and sympathetic thought that his daughters, if older, could be in the same scenario if they were travelling alone, but knowing that other parents' were living through the trauma was an horrific thought for him. There was a different motivation from the previous cases he worked on with drug trafficking, money laundering, and cybercrime. At the start of the night, he hoped this would be the end of the case; however, now he knew it would only be the beginning.

BERLIN

CHAPTER THREE

NAUSEA BEGAN TO WEAR OFF BECAUSE THE contents of her stomach were drying on the concrete floor. Mabel had fallen back asleep in her upright position, using the hard wall as comfort to lean on. Lack of energy was the next concern as the contents of food and liquid mixed within a cocktail of smells. She thought back to how she got into this position and happier times. Only a few days ago she was at her home in Wales. She began to fall into a trance of sleep again, reimagining her steps. She felt excitement and panic coursing through her body as she frantically moved around the bedroom. She searched in her drawers and cupboards for what she was seeking but couldn't find it. She exhausted the bedside tables wardrobes and moved over to the chest of drawers in front of her bed. She slid open each drawer, starting from the top, rummaging through her different drawers that contained clothes and other garments. When she reached the final drawer, she was near distraught, but then her heart stopped as her eyes focused on what she was looking for under a cluster of trainer socks. She picked it up to check the details printed on one of the inside pages. She let out a deep breath as the stress and anxiety dispersed from her body.

"I've found it!" she screamed.

She lifted the passport like a sports captain would when presenting a trophy to its supporters. She began to jump up and down, keeping it lifted on display in her empty room. Suddenly, she reached for her mobile device to message Hafwen, with whom she was sharing her European adventure. She messaged her that the panic was over, and she had found her passport. It took a few months of planning in the spring, and she had used her passport to purchase flights and book apartments but had forgotten where she had buried it for safekeeping. The cocktail of emotions returned as she had the most important thing for her trip, but the panic of needing to be organised overwhelmed her. She stared at her empty suitcase needing the motivation to pack for the trip in two days. She found her Bluetooth stereo on the TV stand, turned it on and searched her music device for a song to play through to lift her motivation. She selected "Always Like This" by Bombay Bicycle Club.

They were one of her favourite bands and she had seen them live on multiple occasions. She often reminisced on her only chance of interaction with the band; when she was asked in the queue for the concert by its very own band members where Nando's was. She was so starstruck she couldn't muster the directions for them. Their music activated her muscles to dance and navigate around the bedroom. She became focused on what items she would need for her trip and started to fill her suitcase. There was a knock on the bedroom door. She told the person on the other side to enter as she turned down the music a couple of decibels. An older man came in, followed by an older woman in their mid-fifties.

"Here are 500 euros for you," her father said as he handed her an envelope.

"Thank you, Dad. Love you!"

"Love you too," as they exchanged a hug.

"Your mum has something too," he said, nodding at the

women.

She looked at her mum, who was holding a paper gift wrap in her hand. When she passed it to her daughter, she un-opened it carefully. It was a silver bracelet with a silver circle attached to the chain. The circle had two sides to it, one of which had a raised emblem of a hawk in flight. The other side had written content that featured 'The Eye Will Protect'.

"Keep it safe, and you will be safe. I know I've said it multiple times, but I don't want anything to happen to you," she said.

"It's beautiful; I will wear it all the time. Don't worry, Mum, I will be careful."

She took the bracelet and undid the clip to wrap it around her wrist. She flicked the chain around her wrist and caught it to connect the pin, and then linked it together. She flickered her wrist to check the tightness of it, but it fit perfectly.

"So, what do you need to pack?" her father asked.

"Everything!"

"Make sure you pack only things you need; don't you have baggage allowances?"

"Yes, do you still have the bag weight I can use?

"It's in the attic; I'll get it for you now."

"We will leave you to pack. I'm going to get changed because I'm going to work. Your Dad will be out too, so if you can do any work around the house, I would appreciate it," her mother said. Mabel hugged her Mum again just before she left. She would be alone in the house, which usually meant having house parties, but it wasn't necessary with the rush to pack for her trip. Both parents left her in the room, closing the door behind them. She opened her mobile device and sent a mes-sage to Hafwen.

Have you started packing? X

She looked at the empty suitcase, then down at the bracelet her mother had given her. She loved its look, and not just from a sentimental value. Her phone vibrated, and it was Hafwen's reply.

No! I'm freaking out, haha x

As she read the message, there was a pitter patter along the carpet floor, and then suddenly, it leapt onto her bed. A Jack Russell puppy was investigating the suitcase on the bed, sniffing the contents and proceeded to step inside it and lay down.

"You can't come with me, Pip!"

The dog let out a sigh, and he rested his head forward on his front paws.

She awoke from the beautiful dream of home; and remembered the grim surroundings she was chained to. She looked down at her bracelet and read the words engraved there. She remembered when she told her Mum that she would be careful and safe. It wasn't her choice to be captured, but it was going to be her choice to try and escape from the dark reality she was facing.

AMSTERDAM

CHAPTER FOUR

THE BOARDROOM IN THE POLICE STATION

overlooked the Amsterdam central train station. Ted pondered while looking out the window, spotting the people walking across the river and noticing the gothic buildings he knew so well. His thoughts were overloaded with the events of last night and a desperation to move quickly with the operation. Sander was sitting quietly in a chair at the head of the long table, filling out paperwork. Ted and Sander had been there thirty minutes before the meeting was due to start at nine o'clock, discussing the apartment complex operation and how to proceed

Sander proceeded to talk about the updates she had on the identity of the girls. A Polish national called Maria Kaminski was discovered to be the dead girl caught in the crossfire. She was reported missing seven days ago by her parents back in Warsaw, who said she hadn't answered calls or responded to any text messages, nor had her friends received communication from her. The information had already filtered through to the Dutch police from Poland. So to the girl who survived near the hallway and stairs, Francesca. Her parents had reported Francesca missing five days ago when she wasn't on her flight home. Both Maria and Francesca's parents had been notified by Sander, with different hopes and fears confirmed. The two girls from the basement hadn't been identified. No missing reports had been released, nor was there any identification of the girls found at the scene. Presumably, the OCG members had confiscated them or destroyed evidence of their previous lives.

The boardroom door opened, and it started to fill up with Luuk and Fenna from Europol, followed by Finn, Zoe, Bartel and other members of the Korps and crime squad who were there the previous night. Sander told everyone to take a seat, and Fenna took a sip of her coffee and looked up mid-sip when Ted spoke.

"Any news on the car plates and CCTV Fenna?"

Fenna pulled a face. Not due to the question but because the coffee was too hot and burning her throat.

"Yeah, sorry, here is the report. We got something," Fenna said, passing over a file.

Sander prompted everyone to sit down and get the briefing started. Ted picked up the folder from the table and studied it whilst Fenna spoke.

"We got a match on the plates and have been collecting the ANPR cameras data. We've followed it across The Netherlands and Germany through the night. The last hit on the car was on the Bundesautobahn 2 at Helmstedt, near Magdeburg. The plates are false; they belong to a seventy-one-year-old man in Nijmegen. The vans we followed through CCTV near the apartment. We took the plates and tracked the ANPR just outside Emmen, near the German boarder, but we lost them.

"Changed the plates, probably. See if we find another same make or model cars on that Autobahn," Ted said.

Fenna nodded.

"We lost the other van in the city near the complex, changed the plates, we think... but Luuk," Fenna said, offering a hand out in Luuk's direction.

Fenna looked at Luuk, and so did Ted and Sander intently. Luuk cleared his throat.

"Yes. As you said, the other van was spotted near Emmen on the ANPR, which is on the other side of this country; we think they're taking different routes. The other van that changed near the complex, we think, was at a petrol station near Beckum, Germany. The cashier said he grew suspicious of them because one of the guys opened the back of the van and shouted something. The guy who paid for the gas was edgy and looking around, so they called it into the German Police. We've got the plates on the van using CCTV, trying to track ANPR on them now from the gas station."

"So where are they going?" Sander asked.

"We can't say for certain. The map seems like they have taken different directions, not keeping to the same roads. It looks like east, and it could be Hanover. However, the car was spotted after that location. Maybe Hamburg? But that's too far north. Maybe Berlin?"

Finn straightened up and checked his Rolex watch to check the time.

"Anything from you, Finn?" Sander asked.

"No, nothing. Erika and Francesca don't know much more. Their parents are on their way here to see them."

Sander nodded and spoke next, giving a full update on Mees. There was a momentary pause whilst a few bowed their heads. She gave everyone updates on the next of kin's contact and the appropriate steps for his post-mortem and funeral service. Sander then asked other officers for their updates. Some of the Korps and Crime Squad officers in the room said they'd questioned some of the local neighbours during the night. Bartel said his round of questioning included a few neighbours confirming people were on the property the last few nights. Their descriptions were of eastern European men, but they assumed the city had finally found the funding and the workers to restore the apartment. However, Zoe's update included that some residents saw girls arriving three or four a night, coming in for the last week or so. Zoe clarified their appearance and whether it seemed they were under duress. The residents confirmed they thought they were prostitutes and there didn't seem to be any violent altercations. One of the other Korps officers, Martin Pieters, said one of the neighbours was walking his dog one night and investigated the opening to the courtyard where the gate was—he was confronted by a man identified as Luca Manu. The resident decided to walk away from the interaction and head back home straight away but didn't report it.

"So do we go to Berlin?" Luuk interjected.

"Looks that way. Fenna? Do you think you can get someone from their state's police to the petrol station in Beckum to ask the cashier more questions before we arrive?" Ted said.

"Yes, no problem."

Fenna pulled out her phone and stepped out of the room to make the call. Ted stood up and walked over to the view from the window earlier. He was looking down at the people in the street walking across the bridge. His thoughts wandered back and forth between the case and his two daughters at home. He was relieved that two girls were safe, but they had lost three girls who had died. He felt a drop in his stomach for the girls kidnapped and taken away in the various vehicles. What seemed to be an effective plan to capture and detain the OCG members had gone wrong in some way. He knew this would start a journey across the continent to follow the case. He knew he would be away until the case came to a terminus, whatever line that might destine. He had to do one thing. First, he had to see his daughters before he went.

The agents in the room looked around at one another as Ted became distant from them, staring out the window. He was brought back into focus when someone spoke.

"I'll call the Federal office in Germany and Zoll about our Jurisdiction with this... they'll want to work with us on this,"

Sander said.

"Of course. Let's see what Fenna gets back from the officers at the petrol station. Pack up everyone, pack your suitcases, and not in the holiday type of way, pack light," Ted said.

Everyone stood up, collected their coffee cups, and left the room. Sander was the last one to go and looked back at Ted from the doorway.

"We have something in common, you know? We both have daughters. It shouldn't be personal, but it just is. That means we will fight."

She closed the door behind her.

This left Ted on his own. He would head home before his wife took their daughters to the Magna Plaza shopping centre on Saturday afternoon. He would be on the road for a few days at the very least, maybe even more. He would need a couple of changes of clothes. He suspected his news of travel wouldn't go down peacefully with his wife, but she knew the nature of the job. You marry your husband, but you also marry their job.

His daughters were twins and both aged seven, nearly eight. They'd been living in Amsterdam for around a year now. After this, Ted thought about stepping down from this post as ILO already, because of the distance from their family and friends back in England and giving the children the upbringing they wanted with their old friends. Ted's wife was struggling with living abroad as Ted was hardly ever home due to the high nature of his job and the long hours he was working. There would be a new posting in another country in less than a year on the horizon too, as the contract only dates for two years. Leaving the thoughts of that decision for another day, he dreamed of hugging his daughters before he left, and never letting them go.

CHAPTER FIVE

THE JOINT INVESTIGATION TEAM WAS IN PLAY, and the operation was moving forward at speed. Ted was riding with Luuk and Fenna from Europol; the other car included Finn, Zoe and Bartel from the National Crime Squad. They were about twenty kilometres from Beckum. The town gains its name from the nearby Beckum Hills sitting in the northern part of North Rhine-Westphalia.

Sander had stayed in Amsterdam to greet Mees' wife and family members. The agreement to process death in the line of duty came with a beneficiary readied for his wife and family. She was also overseeing the operational clean-up of the apartment complex. The bodies of Stefan and Marius only included their passports, five thousand euros between them, and two CZ75 Pistols. The whole apartment provided no evidence or trace of the OCG members; they were either thorough with their clean up, minimalistic or had intel they had to leave. The premature joy of finding two cell phones in the apartment was left deflated by the removal of the sim cards.

A girl called Lucy from the suburbs of Amsterdam later that morning walked into the police station in Amsterdam, claiming she had been stalked yesterday afternoon by the man whose picture was broadcast on the RTLZ news. This man was Marius, shot dead in the apartment complex. She couldn't offer much else from her experience because she swiftly went into a nearby coffee shop after a foot race with the man. Marius walked past the café, went out of sight, and wasn't seen again. CCTV in the area could confirm this when Sander arranged that part of the investigation. Sander had also dealt with the press conference and impending Dutch Media shortly after the debriefing in the boardroom. She gave her audience updates on the death in service of one of their officers, the outcome of the girls saved, and those found dead at the scene. In addition, she updated the media on two unidentified members of the gang they were pursuing. It was agreed she wouldn't expose the failure of the operation but stated that this was only the start of the investigation and they had further leads to explore. She used the TV appearance to appeal to witnesses of the apartment complex or to anyone who had seen the mens' pictures that she shared. Lastly, she prompted the public to be vigilant for everyone, particularly those of a certain age and female gender. This was the main headline in The Netherlands for that day. Media outlets received footage from residents who had filmed the accumulation of police cars outside the apartment complex through social media, which heightened the media's demand for answers.

A German public prosecutor approved the immediate crossing of the operational task force into Germany. Before the legislation was passed, police were required to abandon criminals and investigations at the borders. After its approval, the pursuing country would continue its pursuits with neighbouring authorities' support. In this case, approval was gained when Europol shared the intel leading up to the Amsterdam apartment pursuit and the updated information with the location of the vehicles on the ANPR cameras. There was one condition to the approval; officers would join them from the

Customs investigation Bureau (*Zollkriminalamt*) and the State Police North Rhine-Westphalia, the new norm in international police cooperation and with member states of the European Union. In recent times Europol and police forces regularly exchanged information and collected intelligence and analysis with other parties when cross-border investigations occurred.

There was a vibration in Ted's pocket; Sander was calling.

"How're things going?"

"Good. Twenty minutes from the petrol station. How was the press conference?"

"Good. The media are like vultures, but I guess we should have known they'd be on to it with the noise made on social media. Anyway, we got an ID on the two girls in the basement..."

"Let me just put you on loudspeaker."

"They are both Russian nationals. We had a missing report come in for one of the girls this morning after our briefing. We have Anya Semenov, sixteen years old, from Rostov-on-don. She was on holiday with her parents. She went out for a walk yesterday afternoon and didn't return; they tried her number and got no answer. They waited for her to return, but she didn't. The other, Inessa Petrov, eighteen, from St. Petersburg. Studying at the University of Amsterdam as an international student. She didn't turn up for her last two days' lectures and did not return contact from friends and family."

"How did you identify Inessa?"

"Well, she had a series of numbers on her arm. It was faint from crayons but was enough for us to read it. Someone here at Korps thought maybe it was a Student ID number because they went to Amsterdam University and knew the length of digits. It turns out they were correct, and we identified her that way."

"How are Mees' parents and wife?"

"Shocked and upset. Nothing more I can say."

"Sure, yeah. I'm sorry again."

"Don't apologise, Ted. Please don't beat yourself up about it. Let us do our jobs now."

There was a brief silence in the car as progressed a few hundred metres Luuk nodded his head towards the road sign on the front that read: *BECKUM 5 (kilometres).*

"Best of luck; keep me posted with anything."

"Will do, Sander."

Ted disconnected the phone and held it in his hand as they drove on. It was now Fenna's phone vibrating, and Ted turned in his seat to face her as she answered.

"Fenna speaking... ah yeah... okay... brilliant. Yeah, I'll keep them posted when we meet them there."

Fenna disconnected and felt the presence of everyone looking at her.

"Good news and bad news. Bad news, no luck on the van lost in Emmen. Needle in a haystack, so many vehicles of a similar description, too many to track. The Mercedes Car, same situation. However, the van at the petrol station, they picked up the plates on the CCTV and we got a hit on the ANPR. It seems like they've been trying to keep off the Autobahn and main roads. We had hits on ANPR going through Michendorf, just south of Potsdam, but nothing has been hit on the system again since."

Ted felt the surge of adrenaline kick into his veins. He now had a decision to make, should they press on as the investigation deemed to have its following location or thoroughly interview the petrol station staff member. They were already four hours behind the OCG and had no idea of the exact location they could be heading. Indeed, Berlin was one of the possible destinations which seemed likely. Even so, with the city being over 890 square km in size and 4.5 million people living there, the chances of finding them was still remote.

The radio chirped from the other car, and it was Bartel.

"We're ten minutes out from the petrol station."

Ted was still pondering whether to leave the cashier to the

state police and move towards Berlin.

"Who is your source, by the way?" Bartel questioned.

Fenna and Luuk were looking at Ted, so would the officers in the other vehicle if they could see him.

"I'm not going to reveal my source, Bartel."

"Come on. How did you know about the complex? Are you holding anything back from us that can help us? We don't even know what he looks like; what if we shoot him by accident?"

"I'm not going to hold anything back, Bartel. We are here to help these girls; and besides if we need to use self-defence, then we take them down. He knows not to react when we see him."

"He must be a guardian angel to you if you're keeping him quiet."

"You could call him that if he helps us."

"Could he not tell you about them leaving last night? What they were going to do or where they are going now?"

"Brilliant questions, Bartel. However, he needs to keep a low profile. If he can't communicate with me, it's not safe."

"Okay, Ted. What are we doing then? Taking the petrol station?"

Ted decided, in the end, he would ignore his heart. He would speak to the cashier and see what information they could get from them and anything that the CCTV could reveal. On the other hand, they wouldn't know where to start when they got to Berlin, so he prayed the ANPR would bring some new life to the case. Additionally, Fenna was in touch with the Berlin Police, who knew the registration plate of interest, and she would be the first to know if there was a hit on the plate recognition cameras.

"We are here," Luuk said.

Both cars pulled into the petrol station. Ted hoped this wasn't a waste of precious time.

CHAPTER SIX

THE STATE POLICE HAD TEMPORARILY COR-
doned off the petrol station to members of the public. One of
the officers lifted the tape so the two cars from Operation
Hawk could enter the forecourt. There was a search of the
grounds and a review of the CCTV underway to find additional
discoveries. Ted got out of the car, and Luuk and Fenna
followed. The National crime squad members, Finn, Bartel
and Zoe, also exited the other vehicle. They met together near
the car's bonnet to construct a plan that would be thorough
but effective. Luuk said he would review the CCTV and
communicate with the state police about anything they've
observed on it so far. Bartel suggested joining him whilst Ted
told Finn and Zoe to search the grounds, restrooms, or
anything the men may have used. A phone sound pinged
within the group, and Luuk pulled out his phone and read his
text. He studied it for a few seconds, scrolling through the
screen as he read it.

"I've had a message from the surveillance team at HQ.
They've not got a match on any vans of the same description.
That's here or from Emmen. They must have gone off the
major routes." Luuk said.

Frustration was visible on everyone's faces as they were over twenty-four hours into their operation. It was disappointing to nearly have them pinned in at the apartment complex and just to disappear completely.

"Come with me, Fenna; we will ask the attendant a few questions," Ted said.

"No problem."

They walked through the petrol pump stand to a chair where the garage worker was sitting outside. Ted offered a hand to the man who looked around sixty years old, with short grey hair and a grey kept beard. The man took his hand in exchange.

"Afternoon, I'm Officer Ted Chester, and this is Fenna Berg from Europol; what's your name?" Ted asked.

"Leonard Wagner."

Leonard shook his head in confusion.

"Europol?" Leonard questioned.

"Yes, we are investigating a criminal group who passed through here," Fenna said. "What's been explained to you so far?"

"I've been asked different questions about looking at CCTV, anything odd from the men I saw. What they did or said, what they bought from the counter," Leonard said.

"What did they buy?" she continued.

"A full tank. Loads of water bottles, two crates of twelve Gerolsteiner water. Some bags of pomsticks and sweets."

"Okay. Did they say anything?"

"They said nothing. Didn't even say thank you. I was brought up with manners, they weren't."

Fenna nodded.

The man continued, "They spoke with their faces, their eyes. They looked mean."

"What do you mean?"

"They were up to no good; that's why I called it into the police. The guy standing outside of the van was nervous; he kept looking at the back of the van. Something or someone was in there, I'm sure of it. I've worked here for thirty years, my father before that. I learnt to people watch and read people." Ted looked at Fenna with a 'this is worthless' look. The man did the best thing for the team in reporting it; it led them in this direction, but the stop wasn't bringing anything new to the operation.

"Is there anything else you can tell me, Leonard?" Ted asked.

"No, I'm sorry. Just the CCTV is probably all I can give you."

"That's good enough. You did the right thing in calling it in, Mr. Wagner. Thank you for your time. Things will be back to normal soon; we won't be long."

"Thanks, I'm losing business here. It's a busy autobahn, you know?" Ted and Fenna stepped back onto the forecourt, where they had parked their cars. He was trying to see if there was an angle he could gain, but he had a feeling of negativity with the pitstop they made.

"Let's see if Luuk got anything with the CCTV, Ted." Fenna offered.

Ted straightened his face so it wouldn't show his feelings.

"He's here now," Ted said.

Luuk walked out the shop door with Bartel, offering a small crumb of optimism. Luuk explained they got photographs of the men who came through here, and he would send them to his team and Sander for further analysis. Luuk played the narrator to the CCTV from what the shopkeepers' story was. The van pulled up in the forecourt and stopped by a petrol pump. One of the guys went into the shop to collect the purchased groceries. One of the other men filled the fuel using one of the pumps, maxing the petrol intake to the cost of seventy euros. There wasn't anything additional within the CCTV that suggested further investigation. The men's posture and gestures did cause suspicion, which the shopkeeper detailed.

A group of armed officers appeared from the rear of the petrol station shop, immediately noticed Ted and walked over in unison. With dark black hair and a chiselled face, the group leader, a tall man, offered a hand in greeting.

"I'm Karl Weber of the German National Crime Squad. This is Hans Meyer and Emilia Schneider."

"Very nice to meet you," Ted said, looking at each person as they shook hands.

Hans was very tall, maybe six foot five, with a slim build and dark brown hair. Emilia had brown hair kept in a ponytail with an average build and height.

"We have the North Rhine-Westphalia police securing the area, but we left the important matters to us. Anything you need, let us know; we will be working with you on this case as you've crossed borders. We've also sorted accommodation for us all in Berlin too."

"Thank you," Ted said.

The German crime squad exchanged greeting with Luuk, Fenna and Bartel. She excused Finn and Zoe's absence, they were searching the grounds at the rear of the shop's property.

"I don't think we have much to do here," Karl said.

"No, we don't. I'll make sure we fill you in with what we know so far on the way," Ted said, defeated.

"Great. We'll contact the Berlin state police for you. Local police here won't cross lines to help." Hans said.

Ted wasn't sure about Hans and his crime group's introduction and wondered if they would be hard to work with, but so far, they seemed helpful and approachable, which was important. In previous cases, when he worked for the National Crime Agency in England, he saw too many egos from various local police boroughs tarnish investigations.

"Can you check-in to see if the Berlin police have had anything come up on the plates? I know we will get updated ourselves through Europol, but just in case they have anything we don't see," Ted said.

Karl nodded and told them about the address for the hotel in Berlin near the Jewish memorial. Karl also asked Hans and Emilia to tell the state police to reopen the petrol station and get ready to rejoin the autobahn east. Luuk told Bartel to let Zoe and Finn know they were heading off now.

Ted headed back to the car with Fenna, followed by Luuk. They were disappointed that nothing new was discovered except for the photos of the men at the petrol station, but he hoped something would come back positive. They got back into the SUV, and Luuk put the hotel address in the sat nav device and pressed search.

"How long is it saying?" Ted said.

"It's four and a half hours to Berlin," Luuk said.

"Make it four."

Luuk nodded, turned the engine on, let the handbrake down and hit the accelerator.

BERLIN

CHAPTER SEVEN

THE BEAUTIFUL SERENITY OF THE LAKE WAS TO be seen for kilometres around. The faint shadow of towering trees engulfed the edges of the vast lake in the distance. The summer sun covered the lake and the stretch of artificial beach where visitors bathed and rested. The lake was a charming spot full of different visitors. There were tourists, those who lived in the country-side exercising their right to use their local lake, and those escaping the complexities of city life. Lake Wannsee was most popular for those wanting to get water on their skins during the summer months. Behind the soaring trees across the lake was a momentous building standing proudly. Now a memorial museum, it once was the meeting place for senior government members of Nazi Germany. It was deemed the site where the proposal of the destruction of the Jews was set.

Mabel was floating on her back like a piece of driftwood. She left her body to move in the direction of the wind. Her dark brown hair swirled in the water just behind her as she drifted upon the lake. She became almost transcended by the sounds of the rippling water around her. She lived near Ogmore-by-Sea in South Wales on the Glamorgan heritage home coast. At a young age, she joined the lifeguards and became an avid swimmer. She fell in love with the water as she began to swim, often towards Tusker Rock, named after a Danish Viking who colonised the local area, which is completely visible at low tide.

Suddenly, something broke her trance; she heard a slashing noise come closer. A force was felt on her shoulders, pushing her under the water. She felt for the ground beneath her, but it was too deep. She managed to find some leverage on a large boulder underneath her and pushed herself up with a gasp of air. Hafwen met her with laughter as Mabel coughed up some of the water she had inhaled. She smiled and joined in with the laughter.

Mabel and her friend Hafwen were embarking on a backpacking trip to cities in Europe. They started in Berlin, and their travel order was to Copenhagen, Munich, Rome, Lyon, Paris and Amsterdam. After finishing her last year of sixth form at Brynteg Comprehensive School in Wales, she was going on to study German and History at Chester university. Teachers had told her that she was excellent in German and that languages were influential bonuses in any future career. She became very interested in the complexity of the German language in early secondary education but found it simplistic in her mind. Hafwen had attended the same college but was attending another university to pursue medicine from September. With the hope of not losing contact or their friendship when they departed after the summer holidays, they arranged the summer trip.

Once they swam back to the beach, they both collapsed on the towels they had laid out by two beach-style huts. They put on their sunglasses and allowed the powerful sun rays to embrace their skin. The day was moving into the late afternoon, knowing they would need to head back to the city shortly. They were both staying in an Airbnb apartment in Kreuzburg near U Kottbusser Tor Station. They arrived yesterday morning, taking in some city sights, Brandenburg Gate, TV Tower, Reichstag and the Jewish Memorial. They'd sampled some of the nightlife in some of the local bars in Kreuzburg where they were staying. With tonight being a Saturday, it was all about house music and techno, which was one of the reasons they chose Berlin as one of the weekends of parties on the continent. House of Weekend was the club of choice for the evening, with rooms full of music, a rooftop bar that took in the Berlin skyline. "I hope there are some nice boys," Hafwen said to Mabel.

They both laughed.

"Yeah, it would be good. Maybe a German millionaire!" Mabel said.

They both exchanged laughs again.

"Where we going to eat before we go out?" Hafwen asked.

"I know a good place near the apartment that does good pizza. Zola, it's called. Proper Neapolitan style pizza."

"Brilliant, shall we dry off and go? The train is in thirty minutes." Hafwen said, looking at her phone.

"Yeah, let's go."

Whilst Hafwen stood and grabbed her towel to shake off the sand. Mabel lent up on her arms, closing her eyes to the sky and taking in a deep breath. She was happy; she was by the water, which she loved, and was about to have the best month of her life.

CHAPTER EIGHT

THE TEAM CHECKED INTO THEIR HOTEL JUST off the Brandenburg Gate. The hotel was located across the road from the memorial to the Murdered Jews of Europe. Ted had visited Berlin before with his wife and seen the memorial. It was a beautiful memorial but had an eerie edge to it, and it was a powerful tool for future generations to understand its significance. He acknowledged its rows of grey concrete slabs of different heights as he got out of the car. He went round to the boot and collected his bags from the back of the SUV. The valet in front of the building offered to take their bags, but the team felt more than capable. However, the help from the valet taking the car to park was much appreciated. The sun was starting to set on the city, covering the memorial in the last beacons of light before nightfall.

Ted walked into the hotel with the original Operation Hawk task force. Hans joined them, Karl and Emilia, too, from The German National crime squad. They arrived in their vehicle just after the first two cars disembarked at the front, accepting the offer of valet too. Another vehicle included the City State Berlin Police, who took over from the North Rhine-Westphalia once the petrol station investigation was closed.

There was a debate on whether they should be given accommodation with working in the city, but Ted and Luuk insisted on having the operational team together. They would use the room as a base to rest up and continue their preparations and pursuit. Twenty hours ago, they were making the final preparation on the Amsterdam apartment block, and now, four hundred kilometres later, they were starting to connect the separate pieces of the operational puzzle. The petrol station hadn't brought anything fruitful to the investigation, but something suggested they were heading in the right direction.

Ted checked in first and made his way up to his room on the second floor. He placed his case and bag on the side table and looked at the view out of his hotel room window. It wasn't a direct street view that overlooked the Jewish memorial, but it overlooked an alleyway offering a view of more bricks from the adjacent building.

"Paid no expense," he said, which was from a line from one of his favourite films as a child. He went to his bed and sat down on the edge of it, pulling out his phone to call Sander.

"Hey, Ted, how's it going?"

"Not bad, we've checked in."

"I'm going to travel through the night once I've done here."

"When will you be here?"

"Early morning. Breakfast?"

"Yeah, we will be up bright and early."

"How is it going?"

"Okay. I've got the deputy on media duty now. He comes back from his holiday today, so straight into it."

"Does he know?"

"If he's read the news, he would have called me. So I guess not."

"Bet he will enjoy that phone call."

"He's retiring soon; he can holiday all he wants soon. Lucky sod!"

They both exchanged a laugh over the phone.

"No news on any movement yet with the vehicles?" Sander said.

"Not yet, no, but we are ready to go when they do. We've got Berlin state police on it".

"No problem, I'll let you get your sleep for tomorrow."

"See you soon, Sander."

Ted ended the call and pressed the power button on his phone. However, Ted's phone screen lightened up. It was a text from Luuk saying they were going down to the hotel bar for one drink and asked him to join them. He wanted to carry on working, thinking the investigation over, but the thought of one beer brought temptation to alleviate some of the stress he had built up. He needed to get his head out of the investigation, if just for ten minutes before he went crazy. He texted back saying he would be down shortly.

Ted found his wife's contact details under 'Rose' and hit the green button. She answered the call after only a few rings.

"Hey," she whispered.

"Hey, I've arrived in Berlin now safe and sound."

"Good. The kids are asleep; I'm just catching up on housework."

"I know it was my turn this weekend; I'm sorry."

"It's okay. Maybe you will be back in time for next weekend?"

"Maybe."

"I forgot to ask you, did you see if there were any jobs back in England?"

"Listen..."

"Sorry, I know it's not the right time."

"It's okay. I won't speak about it now. I'm going to head down to the bar to talk with the team."

"Okay, I'll speak to you soon. Maybe during the day so you can speak to the girls?"

"Of course, I'm sure I'll be able to tomorrow."

"Okay, see you soon. I love you."

"Love you too."

The phone disconnected. Ted felt a heaviness in his chest from the prospect of thinking about his family difficulties back home with his workload already. He knew the best thing was to take his mind off it. He rose from the bed to undress. He planned to shower and put fresh clothes on from his suitcase to go down to the bar.

Ted saw Luuk and Fenna on stools at the bar, each nursing a glass of beer. Other Korps and German operational officers were scattered around the room in groups. Ted exchanged head nods with some of them who were drinking espressos and the occasional person taking the alcoholic option. Upon approaching the bar, Ted noticed an unattended glass on top of a napkin.

"This for me?"

"Yeah, enjoy. Weihenstephaner. It's meant to be one of the oldest breweries in the world. Brewed in this very city," Luuk said.

"Thank you. Only one though for me." Ted smiled.

"Of course."

Ted, Luuk and Fenna exchanged glass clinks and exchanged conversations about home life. Ted spoke about his family, life back in England before becoming an ILO and some of his previous cases in Amsterdam. Luuk discussed he had been with Europol for four years, and Fenna said she had done three. They'd both joined the sex trafficking department last summer after working in border control, from where their careers started. Fenna was petit with brunette hair and moderately built due to her love of kickboxing which she had trained for as a child. Ted placed her around twenty-four years old if she started her career at Europol three years ago, and he knew not to ask her age. Ted noticed that Luuk had various tattoos on his arms in the car to the petrol station. He had blond hair, blue eyes and was built for playing hooker for a rugby union team.

"When did you get your tattoos?" Ted asked.

"Just before I started at Europol. This one on my forearm is a cross. My mother was religious, and we went to church every Sunday. I'm not into God now or anything, but it's a tribute to her. She passed before my twenty-first birthday."

"Sorry to hear that."

"It's okay, you didn't know me then. I have a snake on the other arm; I just like snakes."

"Fair enough." Ted said, taking a sip of his beer.

"On my chest, I have the logo of Ajax football club. I can show you if you want?" Luuk offered, looking back and forth at Fenna and Ted.

"No, it's okay," Ted said, holding up his hand.

"You got tatts?" Luuk continued.

"No. I don't want any, but I've always been intrigued by them. They always mean something to someone, but I wouldn't get one, I don't think."

Luuk raised his beer.

"They do have meaning to the holder."

All three of them took a sip of the cold beer and placed it down on the counter.

Bartel, sitting with the Korps officers, got out of his seat and walked over to the bar to get a drink.

"Hey, you want a drink?"

"No thanks, Bartel; I'm going up when I finish this. Which looks like now," Ted said, pointing to his empty glass.

Fenna and Luuk declined the offer, stating they were retiring for the evening. Bartel leaned over the bar to get in closer to Ted so he could whisper.

"So, you know any more from your... guy?" Bartel inquired.

"No. What's it to you? You keep asking."

"Just want to get these guys, you know. The same as you."

"We will get them. But stop asking me about 'my guy'. And

don't drink another beer after that one," Ted said, pointing at him.

"Sure, Boss," Bartel said with an army salute.

Ted turned back to Luuk and Fenna, who were still sitting with near-empty glasses.

"I'm going to go to bed and get some sleep, see you in the morning. Call me if anything happens." Ted said.

"No problem, I will be calling it a night soon too." Fenna said.

Ted pointed at Luuk.

"Don't be raiding the minibar."

Both laughed as they turned their stools back to face the bar.

"Good night," Luuk said.

"Night both," Ted said as Fenna waved back.

Bartel faced the bar again to get the barman's attention. Ted's mind focused on his curiosity about Bartel, and he wondered if he may have to tread carefully around him.

Ted lifted out of his stool and started to walk through the bar area back to the lobby; he pulled out his phone, unlocked the screen and opened up his pictures. He was scrolling through images of his daughters and wife as he moved through the screen. The photos gallery suddenly became obscured as he received a message notification on his phone.

Guess you've tracked us. Meet me at Angel's Club at 11.

Ted felt a bolt of energy in his body. Ted looked at the time at the top of the phone, which read 10:09 pm. He opened google maps to check his location in relation to the Angel Club and saw the route he needed to take. The journey included two underground train rides with the connection to be made at Alexanderplatz.

Ted hit the elevator button in the lobby. He was going back

up to his room to get a jacket as he hadn't planned on making an outdoor visit this evening. Ted got out his phone on the ride up in the elevator. He closed the google app down and opened his photo gallery again. He scrolled to the image of his two daughters jumping in the air together on the beach, which made him smile. The elevator door opened when it reached his floor, and the signal bar was whole again. He opened the messaging app, selected the unknown number, and typed a reply.

See you there.

He was about to press the send button when he realised the message would never be delivered as it was an unknown number. He flicked the screen off, put the phone back into his pocket, and stepped out of the elevator.

CHAPTER NINE

MABEL AND HAFWEN WERE STRAIGHT INTO THE club's interior once they showed confirmation of their VIP status on a QR code on their phone. Although, the entrance didn't lead directly to the destination of the nightclub. There was an elevator at the far end of the lobby, across from lockers containing mail for the apartment complex residents in the high-rise building. A man dressed in skinny black jeans, a white top and a black cap pressed the button for the elevator doors to open. He was much more casual and trendier than the suited security guards at the entrance.

Once they entered the elevator with a dozen other people, the trendy man reached inside the elevator and pressed floor fifteen. The doors closed, and a jolt of movement came from underneath them as they rose the building block. The elevator was full of German, French, Polish, and English conversations with people of different ages.

"You're going to love this, you know. I can't wait to get out on the rooftop," Mabel said.

"I know; I just hate elevators." Hafwen replied.

"It's not that; it's just that it's crammed in here. Don't worry."

They rode up in the elevator for a few more seconds and felt the speed of the lift slow down, leaving a queasy feeling in their stomachs.

"We're here," Mabel said.

Before the elevator doors opened, you could hear the faint thud of a musical base getting louder. The genre was either electro, house, or techno music. Once the elevator hit the designated floor, the music overwhelmed the flow of conversations throughout the elevator doors. They opened and the elevator filled with strobe lights and sound—an integrated light show blinded them as they entered the dance room. The music submerged all sound and blocked any attempt to hear or hold a conversation. Mabel tried to seek a dialogue with Hafwen, but she could listen to nothing. Mabel pointed over towards another doorway behind the bar Island in the middle of the room, and they manoeuvred their way through the crowd.

The door's entrance led towards a stairway leading up to the seventeenth floor, the rooftop area. The spectacular views covered the Berlin skyline, with a rooftop terrace and bar to match. They walked towards the rails surrounding the rooftop for a better look at the TV Tower and Alexanderplatz. They sat down at the back of the terrace on a sofa accompanied by a table and two chairs opposite. Their position was raised from the bar area across the deck. There were a few steps to climb to make it more secluded and private. There were already a few people sitting at tables drinking and relaxing. They took in the view of the deck, which had a bar running along its left-hand side, with a DJ in the far corner. The DJ was playing a chilled playlist compared to the one inside the club. There were rows of seats along the right, running along with the barriers, with most people standing due to the number of people taking in the outdoor drinking.

A barman noticed the girls walking onto the terrace and to their seats. He approached them and asked if they would like a drink, and they both ordered a cosmopolitan. The barman left them and said he would bring them right away.

"Top service here, mind." Hafwen said.

"Yeah, great service. Let's get a photo," Mabel said.

Hafwen leaned in closer to Mabel on the sofa side, and they angled their bodies to take in the backdrop of the city. They both smiled, and Mabel clicked the button to make it flash and set the timer to three seconds. They posed and smiled in the photograph to capture the moment of happiness. After a few minutes, the barman returned with two drinks and two napkins. He placed the napkins on the table and set the Cosmopolitan glasses on top to stop any condensation or spillage. They asked the Barman if he could take a picture of them at a different angle to take in the moment and the landscaped night sky. The barman returned the phone and left them to their drinks. Mabel sent the pictures to Hafwen, and they agreed to post them on social media.

They noticed that two guys had sat down at the table opposite. Hafwen smiled at Mabel and made an eye movement toward the boys. In their mid-twenties, the two boys were well kept and dressed in bright casual clothes. Mabel heard their conversations in German and gathered they were local to the area due to their dialect. The same attentive barman came over to the raised deck and asked the boys for their order. They both ordered half a litre of Berliner Kindl, and the barman left them. Hafwen began to move to the music and asked Mabel what was playing. Mabel took out her phone and opened a music app that told her what track was playing: "C O O L" (Ben Pearce Remix) by Le Youth.

Mabel turned her phone, so the screen was facing Hafwen.

"Never heard of it before," Mabel said.

"I like it," Hafwen replied.

Mabel smiled and moved her eyes towards the boys.

"They're looking at us, you know," she whispered.

"I know," Hafwen said.

The barman returned the two draught beers to the table for the men, again accompanied by two napkins. The girls turned to peer over the rail as they sipped their drinks. The view down was queasy for anyone scared of heights; thankfully, both were fine. They looked down at the queue for the entrance, which was now stretching around one side of the building. The girls turned back to the deck view and started to discuss their plans for the next day. They were leaving Berlin behind, moving to their next destination, and catching their early train to Copenhagen on Sunday. The girls had almost finished their drinks and were feeling slightly drunk. This was because they'd had a bottle of white wine with their Margherita pizzas at the restaurant and drank predrinks of Gin and Tonic at the apartment before that.

One of the boys engaged in a welcoming greeting to Hafwen, and they both started a conversation about their names, what they thought of the rooftop bar and other small talk. The other boy looked at Mabel with confidence.

"What's your name?" the man asked.

"Mabel, you?"

"Mable? Nice name. I'm Elias. So, what brings you to Berlin?"

"We're travelling around Europe. Are you from Berlin? I can tell by the accent. I'm studying German at university in September."

"That's cool. Yes, I'm from the city."

"Cool."

Both smiled at each other. There was a brief silence as the other man began a flowing conversation with Hafwen. The man was the first to speak after the lull.

"So can I buy you and your friend a drink?"

CHAPTER TEN

TED GOT OFF THE TRAIN AT U ROSE-LUXEM-burg-Platz and walked up the steps to the street level. The pavements were busy with people starting their nights and some ending in their drunken states he observed. Some of those people made their way into a Turkish takeaway to make their hangovers slightly manage-able in the morning. Ted noticed the sign for Angel's Club across the street and approached. Before entering the Premises, he observed around him to ensure he hadn't been seen by anyone on the train or following him on the street.

A large muscular man held the front door, he nodded at Ted. Ted nodded back, walked into the darkly lit entrance, and greeted an older tattooed woman who asked for Ten euros for entry. He paid the fee and walked through the double doors to the main room. The interior seemed much more significant than the street's shop front. The front of the building was run down and had signs of neglect on its exterior. However, the inside was refurbished and had a modern look to it. An extended bar area that took up most of the building's wall was left. A stage with a pole in the middle was at the back of the room, presumably for the live performances. Seats and round tables for drinkers and watchers were in the middle of the room. A few men sat at the various tables with dancers pretending to be interested in their average jobs, lifestyle conversations and below-average looks. There were rows of booths with leather couches to the room's right, which seemed to be for more private viewings or relaxing for the punters.

A young blonde lady confronted Ted upon entry, who seemed to have an Eastern European accent.

"You are looking for a dance?"

Ted stumbled with his words upon the shock of her fast approach.

"Not yet; I need a drink first."

"Okay, come find me. I'm Veronica."

"Okay, no worries," he said as he swiftly manoeuvred to the bar area.

He looked back towards the booths and seating area as he made his way to the bar looking for the man he was meeting. He ordered a bottle of Becks from the barman to blend into its seedy establishment. He thought there was a sense of unwanted irony in being in a strip club when he was on a mission to save victims who had fallen to abuse before. As he wasn't the meeting organiser, he removed it from his mind. He noticed two men next to him at the bar, not to question their suspicion but solely due to their English accents, possibly from northern England, where he was from. One of them pulled out his phone and opened a music listening app, which told them which song is playing: "Wicked Games" by The Weeknd.

He knew the singer from his music collection on Spotify but wasn't aware of the song. He assumed it was from his earlier music before he became mainstream and gained a wider audience. The lyrics to the song captivated its type of setting, bringing an aura of sexiness but a harsh edginess to it.

The barman placed a napkin down on the bar and set the bottle of Becks on top, exchanging a thank you in German. Ted turned around to survey the room, placing his elbows on the bar as he leaned back. He took a sip of his beer and wanted to message the man to find out where he was, but it wasn't possible. As he finished his sip of beer, suddenly, he felt a vibration in his pocket. He leant forward to stand up, using his free hand to reach for his phone out of his pocket and read the message.

> Booth, next to the blonde who was talking to you when you arrived.

Ted looked towards the row of booths across the room and noticed the blonde Russian woman dancing on a table surrounded by four men in smart attire. To the right of them was a man sitting alone. He was twiddling a small glass of Coca-Cola, it seemed, but untouched. Ted walked over, swerving between the tables in the middle of the room. He looked uneasy as the blonde woman performed for the men at the table. Those thoughts from the case made him question whether the stripper had made this her decision or she was forced to participate in this employment.

Ted slid into the booth across from the man.

"Shit, Vladimir, you look like crap," Ted said.

Ted searched all over his face as he said it, to look for any signs of stress. There weren't any marks or blows, so he looked okay apart from the bags under his eyes. Ted noticed a black crucifix tattoo that he hadn't seen before to the right of his right eye. Ted assumed it was new, from his previous meetings Ted had found out that Vladimir was Christian, with a majority of eighty per cent of Romanian nationals identifying with that religion.

"Hello to you too," Vladimir replied.

"Sorry," Ted said, raising his hands. He continued, "Thank you for getting in touch."

"I've only got a few minutes; then I have to go back before

they question my break."

"How are you?"

"Okay. Amsterdam has changed things, you know. Sorry I couldn't warn you. I was in the thick of it."

"That was going to be my first question. What happened?"

"We were meant to be in Dam for another five days and then move on to Berlin. I don't know the next steps after that, but something spooked the bosses."

Neither of them had touched their drinks; they didn't need to drink; it was there for show now.

"How did they know?"

"The stupid neighbours maybe. They knew the building was derelict, and they knew there was activity going on. An older man walking his dog said he didn't see much work going on the day before your operation. So, we had a few people take watch outside to see if anyone else was looking from the neighbourhood, you know."

"So how did they know we were coming? Did they see us? You were already pulling out of there just as we arrived! It can't be the neighbours. We interviewed a few of them, and none of them said they reported anything before what happened."

Vladimir looked down at his glass, turning the glass around on top of the napkin.

"That I don't know."

"Don't bullshit me. Come on!"

Vladimir looked back up at Ted. Ted stared at him intently like he was in a police station interview room.

"I think someone tipped us off, like let us know you were coming. We started moving that night, about one hour before you arrived. No one knew what was going on, and we were just told to move."

Ted leaned back. His face showed he was processing the information. He blamed himself for the way they approached the apartment complex, but the more he reflected on it, the more he knew he did things right. The Operational task force followed the correct process. There had to be another factor that led to the criminals being pre-empted about the arrival of the impending task force of officers.

"Stefan said to start packing. Put all passports, phones, and any of the girls' stuff into bags, take everything," Vladimir continued.

"What would you do with the documents?"

"Destroy them all. No trace."

"That your job?"

"I've done it, but no, or I'd have some passports for you here. It's too risky anyway. They search when you leave and search you when you come in too."

"What have they got you doing?"

"Just general babysitting, thankfully. Make sure they have food, water, the security, you know."

"Tell me what happened to the dead girls in the basement?"

Vladimir's eyes started to turn dark. Ted noticed he put pressure on the glass using both hands, gripping it hard.

"I was told to do it. They weren't listening and they were fighting back, not coming with us."

"Did you do it?"

"No!" he shouted as he slammed his fist on the table.

Vladimir composed himself and apologised for raising his voice. They were whispering initially but the outburst projected over the club music within the booths. On surveillance of the room, it seemed that no one took an interest in Vladimir.

"I was told to do it; I didn't do it. We started to move after being told to leave. Marius and Stefan took the girls up the stairs to the courtyard as they thought it would be quicker to take a few up the courtyard stairs instead of the stairs that led to the exit on the left-hand side of the building. Many of the girls were going up the apartment stairs and holding things. Luca and I were at the back of the long queue. Two girls were just at the bottom of the stairs, the last girls we had. They were Spanish, I think. They said they knew we were going to Berlin. Luca turned to me and told me to go down to the bottom whilst he told the rest to continue moving up. He came down to the basement too and started shouting at the girls. 'What did you say?' Then he turned to me and said they were too much of a liability; they knew too much. He told me to shoot them. The only thing I'm thankful for is that my gun wasn't loaded. I knew it wasn't, so I pulled the trigger well, knowing it was empty. The fear in their eyes still haunts me as they looked at me when I pulled it, knowing at that moment they should have been dead. Luca saw my gun wasn't functioning, and he fired his instead. I heard gunshots, and they dropped to the floor like pieces of garbage being tossed out. That must have spooked your officers, as I heard gunshots from the courtyard and building above too. We moved up the apartment side stairs and heard more gunfire from up above. A girl fell down the stairs, and Marius was dead, and one of your agents. We just exited out onto the streets and moved into the van. Our second cars arrived and gave us cover fire from your agents, and we left for Berlin".

Ted registered the missing pieces to the puzzle of what had unfolded in Amsterdam, but he still had questions.

"So some girls knew about Berlin?"

It was the first time any positivity filled Vladimir's face during the conversation or for the time Ted had known him.

"Yeah, I knew one of the girls was going to the toilet. I was outside the door when we were meeting. The room was full, and I saw her and said Berlin loudly in the flow of the conversation. She looked at me whilst the guy unlocked the toilet door. I went down later that afternoon to check up on them. The same girl made eye contact with me whilst they were all tied up. They had paper and pens in front of them, which we gave them to help with their boredom. Some criminals have a heart, you know...."

The attempt at humour was lost on Ted, and Vladimir pressed on.

"I noticed they had drawn pictures of either their family or very creepy bleak words. Some had drawn about Berlin. The girls were cautious of me, but the girl who went to the bathroom said to the girls I was a good guy. I don't know her name, one of the girls asked if I was a cop. I said no, but I was there to help, but it would take time.

"Vladimir, you could blow your cover like that."

"I know, but if you see what I'm seeing, it plays with your mind. It would help if you gave yourself some purpose, or you'd go crazy. It will be like Stockholm Syndrome, where I just become like the captors, and I don't want that. I hid the pictures away from them, so they didn't see it."

Vladimir stopped in mid-flow, looking down at his glass again turning it slowly. He then looked up at Ted again with an unhappy face.

"But I got those two girls killed."

"We got Erika. The one who heard you in the bathroom. She is safe with us. She said she heard Berlin from one of the guys and guessed that it was you. We've also got another girl."

Vladimir smiled again through the sombreness.

"What are the gang saying now we have killed two of their men?"

"They're pissed off and worried. The senior members don't tell us much, but I think they're working with someone. I'd be careful. From what you've said and what happened. They were tipped off, and don't blame me; I swear it's not me!"

"It's okay, Vladimir. I know what you have riding on this, and I trust you."

They both nodded at each other in acknowledgement. Their conversation was interrupted by another half-naked woman with dark down hair who had a German accent.

"Want a dance, baby?"

Vlad put his hands up in a no thank you signal. The women pulled a face and walked off along the booths to find another party.

"I don't know where the girls are now, and they're not taking any chances. Do you think they know there is a rat?" Vladimir said.

"I don't know, but I'll find out. Just keep yourself safe there."

"I thought I would be free by now."

"You will be, Vladimir, I promise."

"I know you've helped me, but I don't know how long I can last. I'd rather be in a shit hole in prison in Romania with my brothers," he continued.

"We both know you don't want that, Vladimir. That's why you're here in the first place."

Through Ted's previous operations in drug trafficking, intel had become available that an OCG was trafficking drugs into Amsterdam from Bucharest. Over a series of months, they had tracked and gathered evidence of their dealings to prosecute and execute a lawful arrest. Vladimir's brothers were the big dealers in the group, plus other various OCG members. Vladimir's role was a minor piece in the puzzle, a follower, an introduction to the family business. The group was looking at a long time in prison back in their home country of Romania. Ted saw that he had a potential asset in Vladimir as an undercover operative in exchange for information on the OCG. Unlike his brothers, Vladimir would be spared jail if he wanted to cooperate and behave. Vladimir agreed and gave evidence on the OCG dealing and the other members, including his brothers. In the testimony, Vladimir said he was forced into working with the gang at twelve years of age. His eldest brother Marko Tarnicerui took care of him when his parents died, visiting their own family in Serbia at the height of the Balkan war. His brothers, after the prosecution, were sent to prison on the compounding evidence gathered through joint opera-tions from Ted, the Korps Dutch Police and Europol.

The conviction began the assignment as a covert human intelligence source for the British government for the next case. Vladimir wasn't called Vladimir Balan previously as he went by the name Alexandru Tarnicerui. The following step to fully integrate him back into society as an intelligence source was to change his ID so that groups couldn't detect him. Alexandru had long black hair and a kept beard, but he changed his appearance to short hair and clean-shaven by becoming Vladimir. Typically, his first task would have to become a source for drug trafficking groups that were oper-ating and integrating himself into the OCG. However, the force filed several missing person reports in Amsterdam over one month. There were indications an OCG group was carrying out human trafficking and sex trafficking operations. Vladimir was sent to Hungary for two months to contact OCGs about joining their groups. This was where Ted had lost contact with him, and the operation halted until the team made new ground. Ted thought he had either joined the group purposely, breaking trust with the authorities, or the OCG had killed him.

A week ago, from the Amsterdam apartment raid, Vladi-mir contacted Ted on a burner phone about a meeting place by the river Amstel in the city. This led the task force to be assembled and Ted led Operation Hawk the night before. Vladimir hadn't betrayed Ted's trust with the lifeline given to him, he had taken it, and the operation was in play.

Vladimir looked down at his watch.

"Look, I've got to go. Don't follow me. All I know is some guys are scouting the park tomorrow. Mauerpark."

"Scouting?"

"Yeah. They do all the hard work, the stalking. They pay pretty local guys on the ground to meet girls, get to know them, take them back to an apartment, drug them, and they tell us to come to get them. Then they text us to come pick them up."

"You've taken them away?"

"Yeah. Look, if I don't do it, they'll get suspicious."

"Of course. How many have you taken?"

"I've lost count. It must be close to fifty. I almost remember their faces at sleep time."

"All right, Vladimir. So Mauerpark?"

"Yeah. I'll see if I can text a time, but the park is busy from midday."

"One last thing before you go. Do you know the names of the other members? We have Luca Manu alive, Stefan and Marius dead."

Vladimir looked tentatively at his surroundings to ensure no one could overhear him.

"Yeah Vlado Petrovic, Miroslav Ilic and Zivko Dordevic.

"Thank you, Vladimir."

"I think there is a sale happening. I don't know if it's here or somewhere else, but I heard them talking about buys from Russia, Hungary, and Asia. I heard them say they needed to get rid of the girls and make money now they know they're being followed. Look, I got to go now. Take care of yourself, Ted."

"You too, Vladimir."

Vladimir nodded, slid out of the booth, and put his baseball cap on. He left his untouched drink on the table. Ted left enough time for Vladimir to exit the building before sliding out of the booth himself and heading for the front door, ignoring another woman's approach as he left, making his way outside to be left with his thoughts. He knew he would have to move faster if they looked to offload quickly. All he had was the hope of the ANPR camera and the following day's location at Mauerpark. Ted was starting to believe he wouldn't have much time to sit around and drink coffee, and this was going to be a fast-paced investigation that he needed to keep up with, or he would be left in the dust.

CHAPTER ELEVEN

THE ALARM CLOCK WAS SET FOR SIX AM, BUT Ted was disturbed by an incoming call on his phone. He reached over for it on the bedside table, noticing it was four-thirty on the digital alarm clock on his bedside too, and it was Sander calling.

"Hello," Ted croaked.

"Heavy one?" Sander said. "Did I disturb you?"

"Well, it's early, but I'm okay. Never enough hours in the day anyway."

"That's the spirit. Anyway, I'm on my way; I'm about twenty minutes away from your hotel."

"You drive through the night?" Ted asked as he straightened up in bed.

"Yes, the deputy is back and got straight into it. So, therefore, it freed me up."

Ted shot up out of bed to reach for his work shirt and jeans. He lifted his arms and thought he would take a quick shower after the phone call. Still on the phone, he walked over to the kettle, switched it on, and poured an instant packet of coffee into a mug.

"I feel like you've got news for me, Sander?"

"Yes and no," she replied.

Ted sat back down on the edge of the bed and rubbed his eyes with one hand whilst his other elbow was on his leg to keep him propped up.

"The girls we saved in Amsterdam were kind of vague on what happened before being taken. However, both remember speaking to some young men they met on a night out. It looks like they are targeting girls out for the evening who are intoxicated. We brought her back in for some questions before their flights home. We got her to look back at the CCTV, and we've identified two men on the footage, but they aren't in the system. We're working on that back at the station, and the deputy is taking the lead on that."

"Okay, great. Do you think these young men can lead us to the OCG?"

"Unsure. If I were a criminal, I'd want to cut ties with them if they got caught, and I wouldn't give too much away to them.

"Very true."

"Any news on your intelligence?"

Sander was referring to the newly named Vladimir Balan. She was aware of his existence and even supported his role to work for the British government in the Dutch territory.

"Yeah, I met him last night. He Just gave me a location on where their scouts are meeting today. It must be similar to the ones the girls identified for you on the CCTV, and they've already got them working in Berlin."

"Unfortunately, these probably aren't the only gangs operating like this out of major European cities. It's too vast to stop it all, sadly. We just need to work on this one."

"Yeah, sure. He also said they're looking to move quickly. They know they're being followed. I think someone is tipping them off."

"Who?"

"I don't know."

"It can't be anyone from Korps. Could it be Vladimir?"

"I don't think it's him. He didn't know our plan to attack the apartment the other night."

"I don't like where you are going with this, Ted, but I understand. Okay, we will work on this one together."

"Can I make an assumption Sander?"

"Yeah."

"Bartel."

"Why?"

"I don't know. He seems generally interested and pumped up for this operation, which is great. However, he is very nosey or something else. He is very interested in our guy."

"He may not come across that well to you, but he is a straight guy. A good officer. I've seen him raise from his initial application, training to the officer he is now."

"I know, and I'm sure he is good; just call it a hunch. Let's just have our eyes peeled on this one."

"Okay, I'll keep an eye on him for you too."

"Thank you. Not just him, though; it needs to be everyone."

"Noted. I'm ten minutes away. See you downstairs. Wake Luuk and Fenna for us; I'll call the rest. As you said, they're moving fast. We best do too."

Ted nodded, although she couldn't see it as the phone disconnected. He walked over, picked up the kettle, and poured it into the coffee cup. He was watching the boiling water turning its dark substance. He pulled up his phone again and called Luuk, and told him to pass on the message to Fenna to get downstairs for a meeting. The call ended, but Ted noticed two notifications on his screen. One was from his wife late into the night, saying to stay safe. He read it but didn't reply as the message may wake her up from her sleep. The subsequent notification was from Vladimir.

1pm @ the park

Ted felt a boost of energy that hit him like no coffee could ever accommodate, and it tracked his thoughts back to the possible leak in the operation. He reflected on his journey to and from Angel's Club last night. When Ted left the club, he was sure that he wasn't being followed and back in the hotel's bar area, a few people were on the sofa seats, but none were officers or anyone who raised concern. He finished the rest of his coffee and jumped into the shower briefly. Once he finished, he changed into a fresh shirt from his suitcase, jeans and casual shoes. He pulled out his phone to call Sander. When he was in the shower, he had a plan from the racing thoughts around his brain.

"Hello, are you here?"

"Just pulling up. Is there valet here?"

"There is, but I'm not sure at this time in the morning."

"Don't worry; there is one here."

"Just quickly. Today's location is Mauerpark, which is a public park just north of the city."

"Okay. But couldn't that wait until I'm here? I'm parking now."

"I'm thinking of bringing something up in conversation today. After you mentioned those men you have on CCTV in Amsterdam?"

"Okay. What is it?" Sander hesitated.

I've also got names on the other OCG members."

"Jesus Christ. Vladimir came well then?"

"Yeah, but I think if I say the names, it may cause suspicion amongst the leak if there is a leak in the team."

"True, it could well do. Listen, give me the names; I'll run them back at Korps HQ. I'm sure Europol will when you announce it too."

Ted gave the names over the phone to Sander, who said she would call HQ when she got into the reception area to feed the information back—hoping that the results would be back in time for the morning meeting to discuss. As the conversation between the two continued, they decided they would need to expose Vladimir's name within the intel of newly named OCG members. It would be too risky if the leak passed on the information without Vladimir's name, which he was using freely anyway.

The call ended, and he collected his bag and exited the room. Fenna met him in the hallway, making her way to a door that led to a stairwell for the ground floor. Situated on the first floor, both felt lazy taking the elevator down one floor. Fenna held the door open for Ted as he approached it.

"Early bird catches the worm," Fenna said.

"What?" Ted said.

"Early bird catches the worm, you know."

"Sorry yeah, I was thinking of other things."

"You get much sleep?"

"A little, you?"

"Enough to call it sleep. Have we got something happening then for the early rise?"

"Sander is here; she will fill us all in."

They reached the bottom of the stairwell, which led to the reception area. Sander was waiting by the reception desk for her bag after checking her suitcase in at reception.

"Sander, nice trip?" Fenna said.

"Yes, thank you. Shall we go into the meeting room? I've just hired it out for us ahead of time," Sander said.

"Yes, let's get this operation back on track. I've got a plan," Ted said as he followed the directions for the meeting rooms.

CHAPTER TWELVE

"IS THE ROOM SECURE?" SANDER ASKED.

"I've asked reception not to intrude. Bartel, can you lock the door, please." Luuk said.

Bartel reached for the lock just under the door handle and turned it. He pushed the handle down and pulled at the door to test the lock; he turned back to Luuk and nodded. The meeting room was big enough to fit about twenty people around an oval table, and a projector screen and multiple portable whiteboards on stands dotted around the room. The hotel manager arranged a coffee table station for the meeting of officers still accustoming to the early rise.

"Thank you all for being up and ready to go early this morning. Ted has debriefed me on the information at the petrol station and our current situation here in Berlin. I know we are in somewhat of limbo here with no trace on the ANPR at the moment. However, back in Amsterdam, we have some new information that could help us here. I hope we can all work together to get ahead of the curve with these criminals. Thank you, Karl, Hans and Emilia, for your work so far and nice to meet you. I was told about your support on the drive over from Berlin City Police."

The national crime squad members nodded the acknow-ledgement from Sander.

"Happy to help. So, what's the update from Dam?" Karl said.

"We have information from the girls in Amsterdam that we managed to save. They are all well, and we have their parents coming today to take them home. We've contacted the authorities in their home nations to see how we can help with counselling and in case we need to revisit them for further questioning. The girls said they were approached by young men, locals to the area. Guys who girls may want to speak to instead of thirty- or forty-year-old Romanian men, who we are aware of."

"We've seen this before. They use them as bait and then take the girls once they've been drugged or intoxicated," Fenna said.

"It's a very complex but highly profitable business, as we know. Unfortunately, we aren't stopping it completely here. This is just a drop in the ocean, but lives are at stake. We don't have many convictions either, but that's got to change at some point, right?" Luuk said.

"Luuk and I have worked a few of these cases across Poland, France and so on. We've never been successful. They bury themselves into the ground, and they have unlimited funds to do so. However, we have our intelligence in this case, and that's the trump card we've never had before," Fenna said.

Ted gave a glance at Bartel, but he was fixated on Fenna and didn't break his glance.

"Yeah. We need to get this right and bring these scumbags to justice," Luuk said.

"You're right, Luuk, but everyone, let's not get emotional with this. Let's keep on track and focused." Ted said.

Everyone was looking at Ted as he spoke, and he tried to deflect the attention away from himself. This was the time to observe the group and find any cracks in their reactions.

"Sander, you have the names of the delta members in the OCG?"

"Yes. We initially had three unknown delta members at the apartment complex, but now we have four known members in the apartment block. Vlado Petrovic, Miroslav Ilic, Vladimir Balan and Zivko Dordevic."

Ted was surveying the room and looking at each officer's reactions. He was intrigued to see Bartel's, who showed a response that mirrored most in the boardroom. The German officers didn't react much because the news wasn't much of a deal to them as it was for those who started the initial operation in The Netherlands. He was confident it wasn't Luuk or Fenna from Europol, and they were rightly confused with the intel. Finn and Zoe had a similar look to Bartel when the news broke; Ted couldn't tell from the responses, which was as he thought would be the case, but it was worth a shot.

"How did we get this information?" Luuk said.

Ted and Sander caught each other's glance as they anticipated this question. There wasn't enough information from the Korps HQ, Europol or the German police for these names to be mustered out of thin air. Ultimately, they were in a hundred-metre hurdle sprint with the OCG, and they were a few hurdles behind. However, Ted discussed a plan with Sander before heading into the boardroom. He had a play, he wanted to confirm his distrust of a small cog of the group's operation.

"The undercover guy?" Bartel asked.

Ted focused on Bartel with a deadly stare. Bartel had guessed the culprit of the information leak concerning the OCG members. He pulled away, keeping his emotions in check, not to give away his suspicions of him.

"Yes, it is," Ted said confidently.

Ted turned his head towards Sander, who was standing at the front of the oval table. The whole room was looking at Ted to expand on his answer. From the first construction, those on operation Hawk knew there was forthcoming information from a source. However, Ted hadn't contributed deeper information beyond the facts already revealed. Some German officers started taking great interest in the conversation as this was the first time they had heard about it. This information, which was something missing from their initial intelligent debrief, intrigued them.

"Miroslav Ilic is my source," Ted said.

The play was out on the table. Ted certainly wasn't ready to throw Vladimir Balan into the fire. He still needed him and wanted to keep him safe, although he had no control over his fate if he was ever exposed as a snitch for the government. A gentlemen's agreement was in place that Vladimir wouldn't reveal his resources, no matter how much torture or pain he may receive for that information.

"Who is he?" Fenna said.

Ted turned his head from Sander to Fenna and then to Finn.

"So, he is actually with them now?" Finn said.

"I won't go into the details. You all know about the intel I've received for our operation at the apartment block. That was from him, and I'm not prepared to discuss more because we have a man's safety on our hands here. Well, my hands," Ted said.

The German officers looked at each other in confusion. So too the operation members.

"We can trust him," Sander said.

"You knew about this?" Bartel said.

"Yes, Bartel. This is how it is. It is for the best of the operation. We know who he is so we can keep him safe and be honest with you."

"Okay, well, I trust you, so I trust him," Zoe said.

"Thank you," Sander said.

"Well, we know we have someone inside helping us. As you said, this is one of the hardest investigations with many lives at stake with all the complexities involved. We have the upper hand on these, which we need to use."

There were a few head nods from the officers around the table, and it was time to move on.

"We have the names of the other three, but only Vlado Petrovic came up with a hit on our system. He has previously worked out of Serbia and Bosnia in fraud and laundering scams. Someone of interest to us and Europol." Sander said.

Fenna and Luuk nodded simultaneously.

"Vlado was the man who paid for the gas and accessories at the petrol station. Vladimir Balan was the guy filling up the tank on the forecourt. We have people working on the other men. Karl, if you can work these photos and names too, I would appreciate that," Sander said

"Certainly, send them over, and I'll get City police on it too," Karl said.

Karl nodded at one of the officials from the City Berlin police as a means of a direct order. Sander turned to the officer from the city police to add another task to his list.

"Sorry, what's your name? We failed to introduce you, sorry," Sander said.

"Officer Phillip Schencker."

"Nice to meet you. Can you also review any missing activity from females or any attacks or reports of stalking from last night and continue to monitor it?" Sander said.

"Of course."

"We will pass you our reports to investigate your system Luuk."

"Thanks," Luuk said.

"So, do we have anything? Do we need to wait on their movement?" Finn said.

"We can't just wait for ANPR to pick up the plates, and they may have changed plates already or are laying low. We need to keep moving and get ahead of the game," Ted interjected.

"One hundred per cent. It was Saturday last night. I know

Berliners know how to party, so we should be hearing about any news this morning, right Hans?" Sander said.

"Yeah, we have the phones covered, of course, and if anything comes through, we will investigate. We have missing reports on priority."

"So, what do we do this morning? Do we wait?" Luuk said.

"Well, I don't know about today," Hans said. "I can tell you Sundays are a little different."

"Certainly. Not just the cities, but all the towns too. There is a 'Quiet law' in Germany, which prohibits 'noisy' work. It's not quite; it's a city, people do things on Sundays. But Sunday nights aren't like Friday night or Saturday night; people work the next day. However, they will still hit the major tourist spots for victims," Fenna said.

"There are flea markets, some museums, there's karaoke and a market in Mauerparkjust north of here. That's a busy place during the day," Emilia said.

That was it. The conversation was out there, and Ted caught the line and dragged the operation right into the lake of opportunity.

"Sounds good, Emilia. When does it start?" Ted said.

"Around 11:00 am until the early evening," Emilia said.

"Okay, we go there late morning. This morning will allow us to get breakfast and check anything that's come in through the night. This will also allow us time to investigate any movement on the plates. In the meantime, we can prepare a plan for the park. We need to go armed, these are dangerous men, but we need to be hidden and blend in with the other tourists."

"So plain clothes please everyone," Sander said.

"Go get ready, get some breakfast and coffee, everyone. It's going to be a long day for us, and maybe night too," Ted said.

Bartel stepped towards the door to unlock it. He held his hand on the lock."

"Anything else we need to know?"

"No, Bartel, not yet," Ted said.

Bartel unlocked the door, and everyone started to file out of the room and turn right down the corridor towards the dining area.

"Good work there," Ted said.

"Thank Emilia," Sander said.

There was a knock on the door. Hans announced himself and asked for permission before entering.

"Come in," Ted said.

Hans opened the door slowly as he already felt awkward about the intrusion.

"Sorry," Hans said.

"How can we help?"

"Karl, Emilia and I were curious out there. Why is it called Operation Hawk?

Ted smiled.

"Good question. Well, my father told me about Aldo Leopold. Before reading books about him, his father told him about Aldo and his father and father. Aldo wrote about wildlife ecology and was an expert on wildlife management. I learnt to love animals, and when I was a child, I was obsessed with Birds of prey. The way they flew so gracefully and the way they could sweep down at virtuous speeds to catch their prey. Leopold once said, 'To the mouse, snow means freedom from want and fear. To a rough-legged hawk, a thaw means freedom from want and fear'.

"So, we are the hawk, and they are the mouse," Hans said.

"Exactly." Ted said

"Okay. I get it now. Buts there's no snow."

"True, Hans," Ted said, laughing.

Hans stepped back through the open door, shutting it as he exited. Ted turned to Sander, and Sander spoke first.

"Let's get that mouse before the snow falls."

CHAPTER THIRTEEN

THE PAVEMENTS AND ROADS LEADING UP TO
Mauerpark were full of people entering and spilling out from
the gated entrance. People were queuing for falafel and
halloumi wraps from the takeaway vans lining the roads.
There were queues of people buying cold drinks, sodas and
beers from the fridges at the corner street shops.

They'd decided to take the U-Bahn to the park to keep up
with the identity of civilians in plain clothing, and they were
opting to travel alone or in pairs on different carriages. It was
close to noon, and the park had been open for nearly an hour
to the public with its food markets of currywurst and flea
markets of vintage luxury.

They'd used the morning to map out the various entry
points and layouts of amenities and walkways of the park. The
team planned to cover the several entrances of the park and
realised that their unit was depleted compared to the vast area
of the park and its multiple exit points. They brought in
several members from the City Berlin police to take on most
of the exit and entry points. They had joined them later that
morning with the operational team for briefing. The plan was
to move from the temporary base of the hotel to a local police

station near the park for their long, long-term base in Berlin. They didn't have any updated information from the ANPR cameras or gain any missing person reports during the morning from the night before, nor anything from Friday night.

Within the core of Mauerpark, Ted took up his location, whilst Fenna, Bartel and Finn took the large area that housed the flea market, a maze of makeshift stalls and gazebos full of antiques, vinyl records and vintage clothes. Hans and Karl took up the bratwurst tents, which they welcomed as they admitted they weren't hungry at breakfast. Sander, Zoe and Emilia patrolled the walkways for any suspicious activity. The order was not to communicate unless something took someone's interest. This was to erase any suspicion of someone watching and alerting the OCG if they were to see tourists talking into their earpieces. Ted took up his spot in the middle of the park. In the centre was a hillside that entered an athletics track over the other side of a hill. Ted walked up the hillside, which covered half of a small amphitheatre. Ted dodged the mass amount of people climbing the mound. Men were selling cold drinks from their ice boxes, to which he politely declined even though the offer was tempting due to the high temperature. He found a seat in the shade of the sun with a tree overhanging his perch. An Englishman was in the middle of the amphitheatre with a microphone and two sound speakers on either side of him. There was also a cart with a rainbow umbrella above it, shadowing his music system from the weather elements. Ted decided to continue moving up the hill for a better vantage point but caught a glance of an elderly German man who started to sing Frank Sinatra's 'My Way'.

He saw a figure coming toward him in his peripheral vision, and he sprang alongside him and touched him forcefully on the shoulder. Ted was engaging in a fight response until he recognised the face of the man, who pulled his hood down.

"Vladimir, what you are doing?"

"Keep it cool; I saw you go up the hill."

Ted eased off on his defences and straightened up, edging close to the tree he was perched under before.

"This is cool, the singing and stuff," Vladimir said, pointing down at the old man singing.

"Look, why are you here? Couldn't you be spotted?"

"I'm taking a break, taking a kit kat as your English people say," Vladimir said with a smile. "I'm safe. No one followed," he continued.

"You sure? This whole thing is blown if you are," Ted said.

"Trust me. Besides, you don't know who the guys look like who are here."

"Okay. Tell me."

"They came last night to our apartment, and Luca told them to go last night and search clubs. They are out in this park this afternoon as it's a busy tourist spot, and they could talk to some girls here, which was their plan."

"Which clubs?"

"They didn't say. They just said they would go out and see what they could do. They knew some bars and clubs, but we didn't ask."

"Do you know their names?"

"I think one was called Jonas."

"Where are you staying?"

"Warehouse apartment just outside the city, but I don't know where the girls are."

Ted thought if he should press on and ask for the address they were staying at, but if he didn't know where the girls were, the other members wouldn't give up the information, meaning they would have lost the girls again, and possibly forever.

"Jonas and this other man are scouting here. That's what they're doing. Looking for new girls?"

"Yeah, that's right"

"So where are they?"

"I will text you. I know what he looks like."

Vladimir reached into his pocket and brought out two throwaway phones. Ted nodded; he was impressed. However, he knew Vladimir was pushing his luck.

"Keep safe, Vladimir."

"I'm paying my debt, remember."

"When this works out. We get you out of this. I don't want you on my conscience."

Vladimir smiled, turned, and made his way down the hill to the pavement level. He began to move through the two-directional traffic of people along the path but joined the crowd heading back towards the flea market area. Ted watched him merge into the queues of people, and then Ted turned back towards the sunshine karaoke. He took a seat on the ground overlooking the man finishing off his rendition of Frank Sinatra. Everyone was applauding, and Ted joined in though he hadn't heard his performance. The older man thanked the crowd and then walked off the performance stage and onto the pavement, making his exit. The Englishman then introduced a middle-aged woman onto the stage, picking her from the crowd of raised hands. Ted was offered a bottle of cold Fitz cola from a man with a cool box, but he shook his head with a polite hand up as a no thank you gesture, and the man moved on. Ted felt a vibration in his pocket, and he reached for his phone to find it was a text from Vladimir.

> Male. White Smith's t-shirt. Blue jeans. Sunglasses. Dark hair. On the path to market.

Ted's body jolted with adrenaline, and he immediately observed the pavement for the description of the man. The path ran alongside the arena, which Ted was overlooking, reaching the outer edge of the flea market area, with other various junctions to different areas of the park. He spotted a few people with blue jeans and different coloured T-shirts, and some with white tops but those in shorts. His next task was to syphon the white T-shirts with a logo that represented the 1980s band The Smiths. Ted was trying to catch sight of the described man but couldn't get an angle on the T-shirt as they were walking away. Ted lifted from his sitting position and made his way down the hill to the pavement. He homed in on the other description details by looking at the glasses and the dark hair. Ted was vigilant as he navigated himself along the path towards the market.

Ted called the team over the communications to update them on a suspicious person.

"I think we have something. Just past the arena, heading towards the market," Ted said.

"What are we looking out for?" Luuk said.

"Dark hair, Blue Jeans, White T-Shirt, Sunglasses. White T-shirt with The Smiths picture on it. The band, The Smiths," Ted said

"Gottcha."

He was conscious of his distance and merged with those around him not wanting to spook anyone. Ted remembered that Vladimir mentioned two guys met them at their apartment, and therefore it was possible to assume the other man was within the park. Suddenly, Ted focused on a man up ahead walking in the direction of the markets, which fit the description.

"Does anyone have a visual?" Ted said.

"Me," Fenna said.

"Me," Luuk said.

"Me too," Sander said.

"Yeah," Bartel said.

"Good, I'm behind him."

Zoe, Finn responded that they were out of reach over the park's north side. The city police held the exit points and were given the updated description. Hans and Karl left their kiosk stand to join the park's west side surveillance.

"Good. Can anyone see the front of the T-shirt? I'm sure this is him, but I can't get a look at the front of the shirt," Ted said.

Immediately another person fitting the same description but with a cap caught the Team's attention. Instead of carrying on ahead, the unknown suspect broke off in an 'L' style junction to the right. Both people carried on around the flea market stalls, leaving them to decide who to pursue.

"There are two fitting the same description," Luuk said.

"Can someone stay on the one without the cap?" Ted said

"On him," Fenna said.

Ted pulled out his phone. He was waiting for another update from Vladimir, and he had been descriptive in his message but needed the final piece for confirmation. At once, his phone screen lit up, and it was a message from Vladimir.

Cap.

Ted became entirely focused on the man who had turned right at the junction. He turned right, too, following the man with the cap on, keeping a safe distance between them.

"There's no logo on his T-Shirt. This isn't him." Fenna said.

"He has a cap on now; I'm following," Ted said.

"I see him, and he has The Smith picture on his front. I'm in front of you; I see him turning right, your left," Luuk said.

The man turned left from Ted's position between two stalls selling vintage blankets and towels and disappeared into the crowds of people lining the open space.

"He's in the market. Does anyone see him? I've lost him in the crowd," Ted said.

"Out of sight at the moment." Luuk said.

The other officers were homing in on the market, who

now had Ted in view. They couldn't provide a visual of the unknown man, stating they had lost the man for the moment. Luuk turned into the market, and Ted followed. The stalls served as a series of walls within the market, providing cover if someone knew they were being followed. Ted and Luuk split up, Ted going left and Luuk going right around the stalls. A few moments passed as they moved in their directions through the crowds. Ted couldn't see the man with the cap on; he thought he may have taken it off, so he added that to his checklist when scanning the tourists.

Luuk radioed over the communication device.

"I see someone with a cap by one of the stalls here."

"Is it him?" Ted said.

"There is a queue in front of the stall. The suspect just moved past them; I can't get a visual on the shirt. There's a lot of people; I'm not sure," Luuk said.

There was a pause as adrenaline built up in Ted's chest. Ted turned around to give up his search and moved towards Luuk, shortcutting through the stalls premise. The stall owner shouted at him in German for entering the private space.

"Do you see him?" Ted said.

"I've got him." Luuk replied.

CHAPTER FOURTEEN

LUUK FOUND A GAP IN ONE OF THE COVERS within the stalls as the man's movement was limited by the crowds. Luuk approached the guy from behind as he re-joined the main corridors. Luuk manoeuvred his body in position to strike the approach. Luuk spotted up ahead, Hans and Karl ready to face the man. Hans nodded to Luuk; it was time to make his move. Luuk grabbed the right-hand shoulder of the guy, who turned his head to see who was behind him. Luuk pushed his knee into the man's standing leg and pulled his shoulder, tilting the guy back. Hans and Karl approached the man from the front to secure him from any resistance. The man looked around early to mid-twenties and started to shout in German as onlookers stood and watched the arrest take place. Hans began to speak back to the unknown man, giving him his Miranda Rights in German. The man didn't seem threatened as he began to wriggle and fight the hold Karl and Luuk had him. It was to no avail; the three men were too strong for him and put the cuffs around his wrists.

"Suspect is secure," Luuk said over the comms.

"Take him in. He's probably going to lawyer up, so let's do it properly." Ted said.

Ted caught up, spotting the arrested suspect in the crowd. He began to navigate his way through the crowd until he heard Fenna communicating over the radio.

"Someone's spotted you; he's moving. Behind you, Luuk."

Luuk looked around and spotted the man running through the crowd, pushing people aside. Ted saw the man running through the crowd just ahead of him.

"I see him. Cover the road exits! He doesn't leave this park," Ted said.

"Do we use force?" Phillip radioed.

"Only if we have to," Ted said.

Ted knew he couldn't lose this second man, he would alert the OCG they were in Berlin and the situation would be worse if he did. A few officers came over the comms radio, stating they were covering the exits to the main road and were ready. Ted dodged people in the crowds, often pushing through the pack crowds to keep his momentum. The man was young and bouncing off people at speed. Ted was in his early thrities and still fit but was more a marathon-style runner than a sprinter. The man turned sharply right into a Turkish towel stand, momentarily disappearing from Ted's view. Ted followed through the stall, with the man reappearing at the end of the passageway, leading to another area for pedestrians.

One of the shop owners accidentally pulled out in front of the man, causing them to crash and tumble onto the sandy floor. The man was on the ground, looking back at Ted, who was closing on him rapidly. The shop owner on the floor was shouting at him in an Asian dialect for crashing into him. The man pushed himself back up from the ground, but the shop owner grabbed his leg. It wasn't enough to stop him from raising to his feet, but it gave Ted time to catch up.

Ted had him within touching distance but couldn't get a grip of his clothing. The man turned left back into the oncoming traffic of people within the market's stalls. Again, he was weaving in and out of people, making it incredibly hard to focus on the attack point and for Ted to maintain the speed to keep up. Ted saw the opening to the exit gate of the park and knew this would be the chance. He had the backup of some of the officers at the entrance, but there was a risk the man could escape. Suddenly Ted had an opportunity; the man stumbled to the ground as he crashed into an older man who turned into his path. Ted threw himself on top of the man, grabbing his shoulders and kneeling on his back. The man on the floor let out a loud grown.

"Stop there right now!" Ted said.

Ted reached around his wrist and grabbed his cuffs, attaching them to both of the man's wrists behind his back. As he cuffed his wrists, Ted noticed a gold Rolex watch; and thought these guys must be getting a good income from their job. He knew this guy was a suspect because he ran, but Vladimir didn't give any indication of the second man's identity.

"Why did you run?" Ted said.

The guy didn't respond to the question or even when Ted repeated the question to him. Onlookers watched as Ted kneeled on the man's back, and he gave the Miranda Rights. Luuk and Fenna appeared from behind the market stall of Turkish towels.

"Good take there," Luuk said.

"Come on, move along. No photos," Fenna instructed the crowd.

The rest of the team started to file into the flea market area, with Zoe ushering people around the suspect. Finn and Sander gathered around Ted, who was still on top of the arrested man. Ted stepped back and grabbed the man by the shoulder to stand him up. He didn't put up a fight, but he didn't help himself up either; it was all Ted's work. The man had sand on his face and in his hair, but he was unphased by it. Ted checked his surroundings after his exertion and took in a deep breath. It was a hot day, and the run in jeans and boots was uncomfortable.

"The officers haven't seen anyone else on the exits, but they are still covering them as we speak," Sander said.

"Yeah, you can never be sure."

Ted saw that Emilia had made a phone call for a few moments and then came off the phone, and Fenna engaged in conversation.

"Want me to take him?" Luuk offered.

Ted nodded and passed the man over to Luuk. The man was looking right into Ted's eyes, motionless but with what looked like a smirk. He was very handsome and Ted could see why the OCG employed people like this to attract girls with a combination of good charm and conversation. It could tempt girls into a false sense of security with these men, even if it weren't to return to an apartment for sexual purposes. They just needed them in an enclosed space. Luuk grabbed the man and spun him around to face out towards the street. In the distance, there was a squadron of flashing blue vehicles ready to take the suspects.

"Hans and Karl are taking Jonas Alem now in a car with another officer to Volkspark Am Weinberg station. They checked his ID, and he is twenty-two years old, a German national," Fenna said.

"Where is the station?"

"It is not far from this park. We will do the same with the second man," Emilia said.

Ted shouted at Luuk to stop as he caught up with them both. Ted reached into the man's pocket and reached for his wallet. Ted had forgotten to check for his name when he was catching his breath in the heat. He opened the wallet and studied his driving licence, closing the wallet's flap and placing it back into the man's pocket.

"Elias Beck," Ted said.

Elias still had no emotion on his face as he stared back at Ted.

"We'll meet you down there, Ted," Luuk said.

Luuk turned towards the Police vehicles on the street outside the park walls. Sander, Fenna and a few other officers followed Luuk, heading back to the station.

Ted's phone buzzed in his pocket, and he reached down and pulled it out and saw it was another message from Vladimir.

> I didn't spot the second guy. They must have arrived separately. Talk soon

"Anything good?" Finn said.

Ted looked up from the message and put the phone back into his jeans pocket.

"Nothing. Just confirming Jonas and Elias are at the station." Ted said. "No problem, we best get down there then."

"Yes, let's go."

Ted watched as Finn followed through the crowd towards the main road exit. Ted spoke over comms and told the team to move back to the police station at Volkpark am Weinberg- but for the officers on the gates to remain.

"Is there CCTV in the park?" Ted said over the communications.

"At street level, but not in the park," Hans replied.

"Okay, may not be anything there, but it's worth a look," Ted said.

Emilia offered to stay to work with the remaining state police officers in surveillance of the park.

"Finn, can you stay with Emilia too. We need a few more bodies here just in case. Radio us if anything happens."

Finn nodded hesitantly and walked off with Emilia through the crowd.

The crowds started to reclaim the vacant space again as the officers left the area.

The shop owner, who Elias knocked over, approached Ted.

"Hey, what was that about?"

"We arrested him thanks to you," Ted replied.

"He just ran into me; I didn't do anything."

"You did enough, thank you."

The Asian man smiled and returned to his stall of vinyl records. Ted didn't hear the music playing when he pursued or arrested Elias. Once the situation had relaxed somewhat at that moment, Ted could listen to the record playing from the stall: "How Soon Is Now" by The Smiths.

He smiled to himself at the irony of the T-shirt Jonas was wearing and that it was linked to the song he was listening to. Ted made a move towards the street outside of the park. Some police vehicles were outside in the layby, with some cars already leaving. He pulled out his phone to check the address of the police station from his location. It was a fifteen-minute walk which he thought would do him good, so he could process how the interviews would go at the station. He looked around on the pavements to see if he could spot Vladimir, but there was no sign of him.

CHAPTER FIFTEEN

TED REACHED THE POLICE STATION WITH A sweaty complexion on his face. He showed his credentials to the reception area when he entered the station. Ted walked over to the water fountain and quickly drank two cups full of cold water from his small polystyrene cup. The operation would be moving swiftly, and there wouldn't be time for rest, so he thought he would have some time to call back home before heading to meet the team. Ted found a quiet corner in the reception area, away from the front entrance.

He pulled out his phone and found his wife's contact details on his phone. He pressed the green button to call her.

"Hello, Ted."

"Hey, how are things?"

"Yeah, good. Just been out to the park with the girls. Having some lunch now at home and then going out to Kalver-passage."

Kalverpassage is a Shopping Centre located in Kalver-straat, Amsterdam's busiest shopping street. Ted knew the scouts for the OCG would work the busy tourist areas in the cities; if there were any still working in Amsterdam after the operation at the apartment.

"Listen, be careful when you go there."

"Why?" She said with stress in her voice.

"You know the case I'm working on?"

"Well yeah, but no. You didn't tell me much about it. You know, secrecy."

"I know, but I'll tell you now. It's an OCG."

"OCG? I don't work with your acronyms, Ted."

"Sorry, an Organised Crime Group. They were working in Amsterdam and now across Europe. They know we are on to them, and they escaped to Berlin."

"Okay, but why are you telling me now?"

"I just want you and the girls to be careful."

"What is it?" the stress raised in her voice.

"They are trafficking young women to sell for sex slavery. Kidnapping them and then trying to traffic them through Europe and sell them on for mass profit."

"Oh my God! That's horrible. What happened to the girls?"

"I can't discuss the details. However, we think that during the non-peak evening times, they are hitting major tourist destinations to search for victims. We don't believe they are looking for children as the girls are much older. Fifteen to twenty years old, approximately. I'm just saying when you go out, please be careful. They may have gone into hiding, but you never know."

"Oh my. I'm not going out this afternoon. I'll just do online shopping."

"I don't want you to not take the girls out because of this. I'm just warning you."

"Do they know you, us?"

"No, they don't, don't worry."

"We're going to stay in. This sounds dangerous, Ted; please be careful."

There was a sound of sadness in her voice, and it sounded like she was getting upset and crying over the phone.

"Listen, Rose, I will."

"I always told you the job would kill you. Down to stress; not that it would physically kill you."

"Rose, I'm not going to... I'll be fine. Are Florence and Ivy around?"

"They're playing upstairs, but I look a mess. They'll know I'm upset."

"No problem, I'll try and call you later when I can?"

"Yeah, sure, please be safe."

"I will. Love you."

"Love you too."

The call disconnected and he felt guilty for sharing the information with her on the OCG, but he knew if she were vigilant, at the very least, it would help in some way. Ted dropped the phone into his pocket. He pulled at the nozzle on the water fountain and drank another drink of water from his cup. When he finished the water, he threw the cup into the bin next to the fountain. Ted walked over to reception as he was unaware of the systematics of the building. He asked a woman on the desk where the operational team's meeting room would be and where Elias and Jonas were being held. The women gave him the directions to the first floor and asked Ted if he had his firearm. Ted was confused with the request but confirmed he did.

"Good, they're putting the building on Red alert due to the nature of the suspects."

"Thanks for the heads up."

Ted checked his firearm consciously, which was in a holster on his waist, and it was there.

CHAPTER SIXTEEN

JONAS AND ELIAS HAD BEEN CHECKED INTO the police station and placed in different interview rooms for questioning. The plan was to interview them separately and see if both would play off each other, not knowing what the other said. It was almost late afternoon, and the suspects were in their rooms for around an hour to ponder their thoughts. Ted wanted to go into the room with Jonas first and have Luuk in with him as backup, and Fenna and Hans would question Elias.

Ted walked through the door to what seemed like the designated squad room from the reception instructions. The room was full of long desks, three stretching from one side of the room to the other with a break in-between for movement. Ted saw Phillip Schencker from the City police debriefing with Luuk and Fenna at the back of one of the rows.

"Hey," Ted said as he approached.

"Hey, just the man. Did you catch a lift? Luuk said.

"I walked. Where are Jonas and Elias?"

"They're in the interview rooms through the doors here."

Within the squad room, there were a few exits points. One was for the corridor that led to the stairs, one was the sergeant's office, and another was another corridor that led to multiple interview rooms, and the entry point backed up onto some jail cells on the ground floor.

Luuk pointed at Phillip and then to Ted.

"Tell him what you just told us." Phillip cleared his throat. As he began to speak, Sander and the rest of the Korps police arrived in the squad room, and Hans and Karl from the National squad entered too.

"Start again," Luuk said as everyone gathered around.

"I was keeping in touch with the control room this afternoon, and I came back to an update. We had two girls say someone followed them home last night. We are following up on these reports, but the girls described them as mid-twenties men."

"Okay, good; we have something to work with when we can get CCTV?" Ted said.

"Of course. But there's more," Phillip said.

Ted took a step closer, and the room engaged. Phillip took a second to compose himself through his nervousness as a young officer in a newly established office.

"We had a women report that two girls from England who were supposed to be checking out of her Air BnB today haven't done so. Their names are Mabel Hepburn and Hafwen Rees, both eighteen. Their suitcases were left unpacked; they didn't exchange or leave a key either. The women knew they were making their way to Copenhagen today, and they've left their passports in the apartment, no phone, no cards but money under the bedsheets."

"Could be connected. Do you think these guys you have could have anything to do with it?" Sander inputted.

"Yes, it could be. The apartment owner said she knew they were going out last night near Alexanderplatz. There are restaurants and clubs near, and I only know one there," Phillip said.

"Okay, possibly make contact with the nightclub or see if

we can check their social media? Do you have pictures of these girls from their passport or Air BnB accounts?" Ted said.

"Yes, the apartment owner has a picture of them both from the Air BnB app, maybe more recent than their passport photos would be."

"Okay, can we get some large photos of those? For our missing person reports?" Luuk said.

"Yeah, sure," Philip said.

"Can you print two more copies of each, and I'll take them into my interview if you can do the same for Fenna and Hans?" Ted said.

"Got it," Phillip said.

"They must have social media; I'll try on these computers now before you go in. You can get Facebook on here, right?" Fenna said.

"Yeah, they haven't blocked that site on here," Philip said.

Fenna pulled out a chair and sat down, rolling the chair forward to position herself in front of the computer. She moved the mouse, and a password-protected screen came up.

"Allow me." Phillip said.

Fenna leaned to the side so Phillip could log in.

"Thank you."

Fenna went to the internet tab, typed in Facebook, and followed the log-in screen.

"By the way, Ted," Hans said.

"Yeah?" he said, looking back at him.

"The ILO for Berlin is on holiday, and we can't reach him."

"I completely forgot about that; thanks for reminding me."

"No problem, he took a holiday to Asia last week; talk about bad timing."

"Yeah, but everyone needs their time off from work. Thanks, Hans."

Fenna logged into her account and proceeded to type in the name of Mabel Hepburn. She scrolled through the related names and cross-referenced the profile pictures using the enlarged image Phillip had printed off. Phillip asked her to type Wales in the location because it showed the person visiting the apartment when Mabel made the booking was from Wales. She clicked the search button again to refine the search and found the first match.

"There," Fenna said.

She double-clicked on the profile, and the page loaded up with Mabel's Facebook page; it was her.

"It looks like it's private. I can't access Mabel's recent posts or pictures. It only shows those from years ago. Oh there is one from last night."

"Hang on, that's House of Weekend Club," Phillip said, pointing at the screen.

"How do you know?"

"I've been, and I recognise the backdrop. The Park Inn Hotel, the TV Tower from the rooftop bar."

"Yeah. This was uploaded last night," Fenna said.

"That's Hafwen in the photo. She's tagged in it; can you access her profile?" Ted said.

Fenna clicked on the name Hafwen Rees and her profile page loaded as she began to scroll the page.

"It's not private." Fenna said.

Ted was pointing at a post Hafwen had uploaded last night.

"The House of Weekend Club in Berlin again," Phillip said, pointing at the screen.

"This is vital, and this could be where they went before going missing," Luuk said.

"Any news on contacting the club?"

"Not yet. They're not open, and there's only an email available on their website," Philip said.

"Are they open today?"

"Not today or tonight."

There was another photo of Mabel and Hafwen on Hafwen's profile page, and it was a photo that looked like someone had taken of them. It was a table shot of the two girls holding a cocktail glass each. Ted's heart raced as he jolted forward to look closer at the screen. He was looking with interest at the picture's background that Hafwen posted. There was another table just across from the girls on the image, which was empty. However, the still photo showed two men approaching the table from the side. He stared at the men's faces; it was Jonas and Elias.

CHAPTER SEVENTEEN

JONAS WAS SITTING SLUMPED FORWARD IN HIS chair with his hands cuffed behind his back. The interview room door opened, and Fenna and Hans entered the room. Fenna was holding a folder stacked with papers. There were only a few pages in the relevant folder, but Ted suggested they go in with blank pieces of paper to make it look like there was a mountain of evidence against them. Jonas sat up, using his arms to guide himself into a comfier position on the metal chair. Fenna took a seat across from Jonas whilst Hans continued around the table to Jonas with a key. Hans was directly behind Jonas, who was trying to turn his body to see what he was doing.

"Don't try anything funny," Hans said.

Jonas nodded tentatively. Hans brought the key to the lock and took the cuffs from behind him. Jonas positioned his arms in front of him and reached for each wrist, squeezing and rubbing them to start blood flow again.

"You understood what I said then. So can we speak in English for my sake and others?" Fenna said.

Jonas nodded again.

"Okay, you were given your rights by Hans and Karl at

Mauerpark?"

Jonas nodded again.

"Can you confirm, Yes, or No? The Camara can see you nodded, but I need you to say it for the tape."

"Yes."

"Okay, good. Where were you last night around 11:00 pm?" Fenna asked.

There was a pause as Jonas's face started to look white, and his eyes sank to the floor. A few seconds passed when Jonas lifted his head back towards the interviewers.

"I want my lawyer." Jonas said.

"Now or after?" Hans said.

"Now."

The team were prepared for the lawyer requestor not to comment on the questions they were being asked. The operational team hoped the evidence might allow them to speak freely, as it would be in their best interests to cooperate.

"So, Jonas Alem. You're a German national with a Turkish father and a German mother. You were born in Bremen and attended Universitat Bremen studying Social Sciences. You moved to Berlin recently..." Hans said.

"I'm not saying another word."

"You're still speaking."

"No comment."

Jonas looked to the floor again, nervously fiddling with his hands.

"You've got no criminal convictions and nothing relating to you with criminal activity in the past. You're clean. How did you get involved in this?" Fenna continued

Jonas lifted his eyes to Fenna.

"No comment."

Ted watched on a monitor from the watch room with Luuk and Karl. Ted was waiting impatiently for the pair to bring out the folder with the photographs in them. He hoped he would crumble as the Berlin Wall did in 1989 and cooperate. On the monitor, Hans turned to Fenna and nodded. Fenna then opened up the folder and picked out two sheets of A4 paper. The paper showed the two girls posing with their drinks from a distance photograph and followed it with the taken selfie. She put the papers on the table, used both hands to turn them 180 degrees, and pushed them across the table in Jonas' view.

"Do you recognise these girls?" Fenna said.

Jonas lifted his eyes to the pages, looking for only a second. Fenna saw shame in his eyes as he looked down again at his hands, and Fenna took it as a sign of guilt.

"I want my lawyer."

"Certainly, you can have your phone in a moment," Fenna pushed

Hans spoke, "Look, this is you in the photo, right? We can help you. If you call your lawyer and he sees this, he will walk straight out of here laughing at you. What I don't understand is you seem a normal guy. You went to University, come from a good family. Why are you involved in this?"

Fenna saw a change of complexion on his face, which displayed desperation.

"I didn't want to do it," Jonas said.

"Do what?" Fenna said.

"This," Jonas said, pointing to the pages on the table.

"You're going to have to explain this to us. Tell us what you know," Fenna said.

"I moved to Berlin for a job, the city has good opportunities.. I shared a house with... who I became friends with, and he said he could get me a job."

"Elias?" Hans said.

Jonas leaned back in his chair and took in a deep breath.

"Yes. He was the guy."

"When did you move to Berlin and start working with Elias?" Fenna said.

"About two months ago. I moved in and started working straight away. Elias said he could get us good money for talking to girls. I was like, what? I asked whether it was research or something. I want to try and get into counselling as I did a module on psychology at University. He said it was kind of like that, and I needed a job, and I was interested."

"What did you do when you spoke to girls?" Fenna said.

"Once I knew what the job was, I wanted out, but he said they would kill me."

"Was this after your first experience?" Fenna said.

"Yes, we went to a club in Kreuzberg and met these two girls from Poland. We spoke to them and drank, and I thought this wasn't research. It's like we were hitting on them. When we got back to their apartment, I noticed they were very drunk quickly, which was odd."

"Then what?"

"I was worried, but Elias said it was fine. He made a call, and then two Eastern European men came and took the girls, taking them in a big car. I freaked out, and I asked where they were going. Then he told me what was going on."

"What did he say?".

"He said we were working for a gang who trafficked women for money. He gave me my payment of four hundred euros that night. I took the money because I needed it, but I couldn't see the positives with the money. I was seeing the girls in my dreams, my nightmares. We did it to so many people," Jonas said with a tear in his eyes.

"How many?" Hans said.

"Maybe fifteen or seventeen after last night."

"Do you remember any names?"

"No, not really. I try to forget them."

"Did you try to get out of this or call the police?"

"I asked Elias, and he said they would kill me, and it was too late now. I was scared, frightened for my life and maybe my family. I wanted to escape, but I was too scared," Jonas said, using his hands to wipe his tears.

"Do you know the European men?"

"I don't know their names or who they are; they wear masks most of the time when they come in and take them."

"Where do they go to?"

"I asked Elias that, but he told me I shouldn't be so nosy, and we didn't need to know. We just do our job, and that's it, get paid."

"Did you get those Rolex watches off the gang?" Fenna said, pointing at his wrist.

"Yes, after the first time, as a gift a few days after," Elias dropped his head to the floor again in guilt.

"Jonas. We want to stop this, and we've tracked his gang from Amsterdam to here, and you can still help us here, okay?"

Jonas nodded slowly and lifted his back upright again. He seemed to be searching for some forgiveness in the two officers' eyes.

"Jonas, look at these girls again. Did you talk to these girls last night?" Hans said.

Jonas nodded at the interviewers.

"Can you say for the tape, please," Fenna said.

"Yes, we did."

There was a knock on the door of the interview room. Fenna looked at Hans and Jonas and told them she wouldn't be a minute. She stated she was pausing the tape and stepped out of the room; Ted waited there in the corridor.

"Good work there," Ted said.

"Thanks, at least we've got our guy. However, I don't know how we will get to the OCG, and these don't know anything," Fenna said.

"I know. I'm going in with Elias now. Just keep going about repeat locations with meeting girls or anything else he can remember. Get his lawyer too. Sander and the team will get some warrants ready to check the apartment's address, which should be straightforward to obtain. We will get a warrant for these two on their phone records, bank accounts and see if it links back to the OCG. I have a feeling the bank accounts won't show much, could be cash in hand sort of job."

"Okay, good luck with Elias," Fenna said.

Ted left Fenna in the interview room and walked down the corridor where Luuk was standing. Ted heard the door behind him go as Fenna returned to the room. Ted held the door handle to the interview room where Elias was held.

"Ready?" Ted said to Luuk.

"Ready."

Ted opened the door for Luuk to enter first so that Ted could have a more extended look at Elias as he approached the table in between them. Elias locked eyes with Ted again as he closed the door behind him. Luuk took the first seat, and Ted sat down next to him.

"You going to uncuff me?" Elias said.

Luuk pressed the tape recording and stated that the recording was in progress, and named the attendees within the room.

"I'm not going to beat around the bush for you, Elias. You've two options here, you go to prison for a long time, or you go to prison for a very long time," Ted said.

"This is bullshit!"

"Calm down," Luuk said as he looked at Ted, confused by his harsh approach.

"Your friend has told us all we need to know. All we need is you," Ted said.

Elias's face grew red and angry. He pulled his eye contact from Ted and looked to the corner of the room.

"You have nothing," Elias said.

"We do, Elias Beck. You seem to be a nobody from the suburbs of Berlin, no degree, no previous convictions except for drunk driving offences two years ago, common offences for a beat-up waste man like you," Ted said.

"Get me a lawyer now!" he shouted.

"You have your right to a lawyer, of course, but as I said, you either help us, or you don't. We have you nailed Elias, and there's no escaping this," Ted said.

Ted turned to Luuk and nodded. Luuk opened a similar file to what Fenna held when talking to Jonas. With this folder, it was much lighter, just including the photos of the girls.

Ted and the team agreed that Elias was the main person in the pair, and Jonas would only need a hint of fear to break him. There would need to be a more direct approach to Elias, as he seemed heartless and unremorseful. Luuk slid the Two pieces of A4 paper on the table, turning them for a better view. Elias was still looking towards one of the room corners, not interested in what was presented to him.

"You were at the House of Weekend Club last night, and you saw these two girls here in the photograph," Ted said.

"Nope." Elias said, still not acknowledging the paper.

"And this is you and Jonas," Ted said.

The confidence in Elias's face seemed to evaporate, and he looked back towards the desk where the paper was. Ted knew this was the time to press on; Elias would either shut up and ride it out with his lawyer or take this seriously.

"Elias, we know you're working for a Hungarian criminal gang," Ted said.

"No comment."

"Sorry, employed by a criminal gang. They tell you what to do, and you follow their orders and pretend you're the big man bossing Jonas around. Is that right?"

"Fuck you."

"Okay, Elias, you don't want to work with us, do you. How does going away for a long-time sound?" Ted said.

"Men will like you in jail. Young, athletic." Luuk added.

Luuk was beginning to understand the approach Ted was taking. The only way Elias was going to be broken down was through fear. Elias was a cocky man who thought nobody could touch him, and he was a small piece of chewing gum in the hierarchy of dangerous power. He would be thrown away if needed at any precise moment by the OCG. He felt protected by them as they probably promised him protection, but that was to keep him working like a rat gathering the cheese for the monsters who were hungry. Ted intensified the fear factor so Elias would crumble and turn into a weak, desperate man.

"Listen, Elias. If the OCG don't know now, they will know later that you've been brought in for questioning. Your face is on these photos, and we are gaining a warrant for the apartment. If there is CCTV with your face on it, you're going to be disposable to the OCG. We can offer some form of protection," Ted said.

Ted searched Elias's face for signs he had succumbed to the unfolding situation.

"Elias, we can protect you if needed. I can't guarantee you won't be charged or prosecuted, but if you can help us here and give us information on the other girls you helped kidnap, we can help the best we can."

There it was. Elias knew the situation was imploding and looked bleak even with a lawyer, and the photos were incriminating enough.

"Okay, I'll talk."

"Okay, good. So, tell us what happened?" Ted said.

"We met them at the club, and we talked, and we drank. We got friendly with them, and we went back to their apartment."

"So you can confirm that you took these girls back to their apartment?" Ted said.

"Yeah."

"Do you get paid for this type of work?"

"Yes. I get paid, and then I give Jonas his cut. Look at this watch. It's a Gold Rolex, after the first job I got his. That's why I did it in the first place, the money. I just became emotionless and hardened by it you know? I just did it and didn't feel any sadness after a while."

"Did you try to get out of it and stop?" Luuk said.

"You don't get out; they control your life. Threaten you

and your family if you ever give them up or say you want to leave. They say they will kill everyone," Elias said

"Okay, so you went back to the girls' apartment last night. Then what?" Ted said.

"We went back; I texted one of the guys the address. Before you ask, I don't know their names; they are different people at different times, and some wear masks."

"Do you have the number?"

"Yes, but it changes a lot. Unknown numbers contact me and those I text, they don't work the next time."

"Okay, burner phones. What happened then?"

"When we were at their place, they were already drunk, drugged and they both went to sleep before we entered the apartment door."

"What was the drug?"

"I don't know how you say it. Temy Paz?"

"Temazepam?"

"Yeah, that."

"Then what?"

"When they start to feel a bit sleepy. They either pass out or give a little fight once they realise what's happening; I have scratches on me from one of them last night outside the apartment: the dark-haired one, Mabel. We just pinned them down against the wall until they fell asleep, which was quick. I upped the dose after last time. I then let the guy know we were ready to go. The guys came in; they quickly carried them out to this van, and we went off. Leaving us somewhere else in the city."

Luuk opened the file again and slid out another piece of paper with five men's faces on it. Vlado Petrovic, Miroslav Ilic, Vladimir Balan, Zivko Dordevic and Luca Manu.

"Any of these the guys?" Luuk said.

Elias studied the photos and started to nod slightly.

"Yeah, these three I recognise."

Elias pointed at Miroslav Ilic, Zivko Dordevic and Vladimir.

"But I don't know the others, as they wear masks, but yeah, maybe they have been," Elias said.

"When did you start working for them?"

"About three months ago."

In Ted's head, he was trying to piece together if this was the same OCG operating out of Amsterdam and Berlin or if he started initially with another gang. He knew the criminals fled Amsterdam to Berlin, but maybe they were already cross-continental with their work.

"Has it always been these people you've worked for?"

"Yeah, it has. This guy here," Elias said whilst pointing back at the suspect sheet. Elias was pointing at Luca Manu's photo. "I think he is the boss. I've not seen his face, but I've spoken to him over the phone, and when I've seen him in disguise, I think that's him."

Ted was annoyed he didn't ask Vladimir who was in charge, but Elias's confession indicated that he was one of the prominent leaders in the gang.

Ted looked at Luuk and tilted his head back towards the door to say the interview was finished. Luuk verbally commenced the end of the interview and switched off the tape.

"Thanks for your time here," Ted said as he rose from his chair.

"Now you got to protect us, man!" Elias pleaded.

Both Ted and Luuk pushed their chairs back under the table, and Luuk collected the papers from the desk and shuffled them back into the folder. Ted walked over to the door, opening it wide, allowing Luuk to exit first.

"Come on. You got to help us now. I helped you, right?" Elias said.

Ted gave him a long hard stare and exited through the door.

CHAPTER EIGHTEEN

A BOLT OF PAIN COURSED THROUGH HIS BODY as the metal pole hit the back of his neck. There was a loud ringing sensation inside his ears, causing sharp pain in the centre of his brain. Vladimir gave out a large moan as he lay curled up on the floor in a ball shape for protection. He heard a loud bang again and flinched with anticipation, but he felt no further pain to match the last blow. However, he could listen to another groan coming from across the room and shouts from the gang members.

"Who is the snitch, motherfucker!" someone shouted.

Vladimir started to process the unfolding scenario under the intense pain he felt. Adrenaline flowed through his body naturally through the fight or flight response he was inhabiting. Vladimir had returned from Mauerpark to the warehouse near an abandoned Tempelhof Airport, which had turned into a public park in 2008 when it closed. The decommissioned airport hangers turned into temporary accommodation for immigrants, which became widely criticised by the public, but the OCG had found shelter nearby to keep their activities secluded. However, none of the girls were held in the facility as it would be too open and public. Once he returned and relaxed in the shabby quarters, he was joined by Miroslav Ilic. Luca Manu confronted them when he entered their quarters. Luca held a gun to them both, forcing them to make their way into the kitchen area. Vladimir was unsure what Luca knew. He wondered if someone saw him at Mauerpark or Angel Club when he talked to Ted, but then equally confused at why Miroslav was being brought into this too, he was straight and not an intelligence informer for any government. Vladimir was bracing himself for the barrage of torture he may endure, although he knew he couldn't give up any information to them, even if it cost him his life.

Vladimir pushed himself up from the ball position, on his hands and knees, with his head facing down to the floor. He felt a hand under his armpit as he was lifted to his feet. His visual was hazy under the blow he had taken to the back of his head. He was carried a few metres and slammed back down again onto a wooden chair in the kitchen. Vladimir saw the figure of the man who had picked him up, and it was Luca. Across the table from him was Miroslav, who had blood coming from his nose. Vladimir's vision was starting to become clearer every second that passed. Vlado Petrovic walked into the kitchen area with a bottle of champagne and a female prostitute. Both of their smiles turned into horror at the scene unfolding.

"Get her out of here!" Luca ordered.

Vlado pushed the girl out of the kitchen and told her to sit down on the sofa in the next room, telling her to do it quicker as she hesitated. Vlado shut the door behind him, leaving the women alone again.

"You are going to have to kill her now," Luca said.

Vlado nodded at his orders and walked back into the lounge area where the pair came from.

Vladimir's vision came back entirely, and he could see Miroslav clearly with a bloody nose and a bruise already forming on the side of his head.

Both men looked up a Zivko, who approached the table from one side of the kitchen area. He reached from his belt and handed a pistol to Luca. Zivko retreated back to his initial position in the corner of the room. There were only four people in the room now Vlado had exited to the lounge; Vladimir knew this was everyone accounted for, as some of the members were at the undisclosed location with the young women.

Vladimir was ready in his mind to face the consequences of his actions. He was playing through his mind how it had come to this point. Ted thought the disclosure of the Amsterdam address may have brought an end to this nightmare he was involved in. He was confident that there was a clog in the mechanism of the investigator's team, the OCG's very own intelligence agent. It was the only way the OCG knew of the incoming officers to the apartment block; or had Ted given him up?

Luca slammed his hand on the table, and both Vladimir and Miroslav jumped in their seats. Luca removed his hand from the table, and underneath laid the pistol. It was situated in the middle of the table and out of the reach of both of them. Miroslav jerked his body forward to reach the gun, but it was too far. Luca blocked his advances, grabbing Miroslav's head and slamming it down on the table with both of his hands.

"Not so easy, Miroslav. We play a little game," Luca said.

Vladimir knew what was coming. Under the circumstances and the pain in his head, he thought, how would this prove who the spy was? If he stayed calm and quiet, he might have a chance. Within this game, you were the definition of lucky if you managed to walk away.

"Russian Roulette," Luca said.

Luca leaned forward over the table, using both hands to keep him propped over the pistol. Luca looked side to side at each participant in the game and nodded at them both.

"One of you is spying for the police scum. Now you will

die." Luca said.

"No way, man, I'm no spy; he is," Miroslav said, pointing at Vladimir.

Vladimir was deep in thought again. He was playing everything through his mind, replaying steps. Vladimir felt a tightening in his chest with a cocktail of negative feelings. Luca lifted his hands and opened his fingers wide to get a grip on the gun from the table. He twisted his hand clockwise and immediately anti-clockwise, and the gun span on the table. Vladimir's heart was beating out of his chest as the gun started to slow down in its direction. The point fell towards Miroslav first, whose face was in complete fear.

"This is bullshit; no way am I a snitch, Luca!" Miroslav shouted.

"Let the gun decide," Luca said.

"Trust me, please," Miroslav begged

Luca picked up the gun and fixed it to the side of his head. Without hesitation, he pulled the trigger. The sound infused the room, and Vladimir blinked. Miroslav remained seated with a relieved face, and his breathing deepened. Miroslav even cracked a small smile as his evil eyes fixed on Vladimir.

"You next, Vladimir," Luca said.

"I'm no snitch, Luca. You will see," Vladimir said.

Luca held the gun against Vladimir's head and looked back at Miroslav

"I know who the snitch is, and I've been told by one of my men working within the police. Do you think I was lucky or was it a guess that we needed to escape from that apartment on Friday?"

"You have a snitch?" Vladimir said.

"Sure, why not."

Luca held the metal barrel against Vladimir's temple, and the heat from the barrel was causing him discomfort. Vladimir closed his eyes as Luca pulled the trigger. Vladimir's body shook from the sound, and he was still alive. He could hear the short footsteps of Luca as he walked away. The pause allowed him to submit to the possibility that this was the end of his life. Through Luca's speech, it was clear that Ted Chester had given his name to the operational team, and the rat in the group had to have fed the name back to the OCG.

Vladimir had Christian roots, and he learnt from his parents to forgive people no matter what they did in their lives. Not to murder, which he hadn't done during his life at any point, although his undercover operation did push his religious beliefs to the limits. Vladimir, at that moment, forgave Ted for what he did and prayed in his head that God would show forgiveness to him. It was an honest mistake to which Vladimir believed Ted didn't know there was a rat in the police force. At that moment, he was ready to face his impending death. Vladimir was young when his parents died in Serbia, and he missed them every day. He remembered their faces when he slept and kept a fading photograph of them in his wallet for a keepsake. In his mind, he was going to heaven to be with his parents, with his momma and papa.

"Is no one going to make this easy and give up? You piece of Shit," Luca said.

Miroslav's cocky look before turned back into fear as he was up next. Vladimir closed his eyes as the gun pressed against Miroslav's head. He could hear Miroslav breathing deep and fast, almost drowning the ears of everyone in the room with his pleas too.

"Come on, please, you got to believe me!"

There was another silence.

"Please!"

The gun fired, and Vladimir's body flinched again. He could still hear the heavy breathing of Miroslav; he was still alive.

Vladimir didn't know much about ammunition in a pistol or how many bullets a specific gun held. However, he knew his chances of each round were dropping fast. His eyes still closed, he could hear Luca take the few steps back towards him and stop. He thought Luca was tormenting him, and his time was next. Vladimir started reciting the lord's prayer in his head as his body and mind were ready.

"Your friends gave you up. Gave your name," Luca said.

Vladimir knew his thoughts were now true. He kept his eyes closed and continued with the prayer without pause. Once he finished, his thoughts turned to old memories, and he began reminiscing about life when he was a child, when things were so carefree, although in the height of the cold war—he loved playing football on the acre field with his father.

"Die, you rat," Luca said.

Vladimir was still in darkness with his eyes shut. He heard Miroslav give out one more plea, and the metal trigger sprang back as the sound jolted his body.

CHAPTER NINETEEN

TED OPENED HIS PHONE SCREEN TO SEE A
missed call from his wife, Rose. He hadn't checked in with her
to video call her and his daughters as he promised. After the
Elias interviews, he debriefed the team in the squad room to
build a case against the two suspects. The group began
planning to visit the apartment where the girls were staying.
The suspects were with the German Police custody sergeants
being read their charges before being placed into their cells
within the station.

Ted found a free interview room that wasn't being used to
call home. Ted felt his phone vibrate in his hand and saw a
message light up on the screen from Rose.

He opened the text message screen and saw it was from
Rose, asking when he was free to video call. Ted typed a
response to say he was from now. Immediately he got a reply
from her.

I'll call now. The girls are excited.

The phone started to vibrate as the video call function
began to call his phone from Rose. Ted clicked the green

button on the screen to accept the call.

"Daddy!" one of his daughters shouted.

He was comforted by the face of one of his daughters on the screen.

"Hello, Florence," Ted said with a wide smile.

"Hi, Daaad," the other daughter said

Both of his daughters were on the screen, looking back at him with excited faces.

"Hello, Ivy!"

"Hello, Ted," Rose, his wife, said.

"Hey, you okay?"

The trio of his family was now on the screen, looking back at him through the video app.

"When are you coming home?" Florence said.

Ted knew that question was coming. He was already blaming himself for not being home, but hearing his daughter ask that question struck him hard.

"Come on, Flo; I've said he is busy with work," Rose replied.

There was a brief pause as the daughters seemed to remember not to ask their dad when he was coming home from mum's request. Ted felt the tight knot in his chest and took a deep breath.

"Soon, I hope, girls. Dad is working hard," Ted replied.

"I know you are, dad," Ivy said.

"Hey, it's your eighth birthday in a few weeks, twins! I'll be back for that, so don't worry."

Both girls cheered with their hands in the air, and Ted had a beaming smile to return to them over the screen. As the girls embraced the news, Rose moved the screen to her face and whispered.

"Are you going to be back by then to sort their present and see them?"

"I hope so, yes," Ted said.

"I hope so too."

The noise from the girls quietened after Ted and Rose's conversation, and rose said they'd moved to another part of the room as the cat had come into the room.

"How's Berlin?" Rose said.

"Good, different type of visit to when we went."

"Yeah, I bet. I'm so worried, Ted, about all of this, and it's so dangerous. I don't know how I would cope if...."

"Rose. Nothing is going to happen. There are lives at stake in the operation, and I need to keep focused. I can't be worrying about you too."

"Well, sorry, Ted, but I can be worried. I have two... we have two daughters who love you very much. They don't want anything to happen to their father."

"Listen, I'll be back soon. I can't say how long, but I will be back for their birthday."

"Are you going to promise this, or is that just a guess? We've sacrificed a lot for this. I have Ted."

"I know you have, Rose. If you can help organise the day, it will be one less thing to worry about. Are the girls still there?"

"No, they've gone into the front room."

"Any ideas on what to get them?"

"I've slipped it into conversations to see what they say. Except them wanting their dad here, Ivy wants some new doll that a few girls have got in school, and Flo wants a drawing and jewellery set."

"Okay nice."

Rose looked behind her to check on the girls and whispered again.

"And they both want a puppy."

"Right. I don't know if Evie is going to like that."

"I thought that. Oh, here they come."

The two girls came back into the video, and both were supporting a black cat on the screen.

"Look, Dad, it's Evie. She says Hi," Ivy said.

"Hello, Evie. She been okay?"

"Yeah, Dad," Ivy said.

The cat fidgeted in her hands and wriggled. Ivy released her grip, and Evie jumped down and out of sight.

"What she been doing?"

"Just sleeping. She wants food," Flo said.

"She's lazy. Hey. How's school been? You learned any more Dutch?"

"Yeah. We find it hard, but we are trying. The teacher is nice to us now, but we still miss home," Ivy said.

The daughters had been struggling with their adjustment to education in The Netherlands. Although they had been at the school for a year, the first few months were very hard. It was a new life for the girls, new friends, a new school, and a new language that came with it. They had both struggled and found the move hard but had slowly built confidence in school and everyday life more recently, and the school staff were adapting to their needs and struggles, which Ted and Rose welcomed.

Ted heard a knock on the door to the interview room, and the door opened slightly. Fenna stepped into the room, then mimed an apology for the intrusion, and Ted put his hand up and shook his head to say it was fine.

"You ready to go?" Fenna whispered.

Ted nodded to her and put up his index finger to indicate he would be one minute.

"Hey. I've got to go now," Ted said.

"Awwh," the two daughters replied.

"Come on, girls, Dad's got to go," Rose said.

"You going to get the bad guys?" Flo said.

"Yeah, going to get the bad guys."

"Okay, girls say goodbye to Dad," Rose said.

"Bye, Daaad!" both girls said.

"Love you lots. Bye, see you soon. I will call you tomorrow," Ted said.

The video returned to Rose's face.

"Love you, be safe, please."

"I will; I love you too."

The video disconnected, and he turned the phone off and placed it into his pocket. He lifted himself off the seat and walked over to the interview room door. He gripped the steel metal door handle and saw Fenna waiting in the corridor.

"Let's get this done so I can go home."

CHAPTER TWENTY

THE APARTMENT WAS IN KREUZBERG, HOME TO
a suburb full of artists and students just south of the Centre of
Berlin. The location offered food stalls, bars, and street art,
with the Landwehr Canal running through the heart of it. The
girl's apartment was on Burknerstraße, just off the main Kottbusser–Damn road, which runs from U Kotbusser Tor station
to Hermannplatz.

When the interviews had finished, Emilia, at Mauerpark,
updated that the park was clear. Under instruction, she was
directed to the apartment as a first responder. Emilia met the
team at the entrance to the ground floor door of the multi-
story apartment. Emilia confirmed no sign of struggle or
forced entry inside the property. Ted thought this would be
true as it would coincide with the admission from the suspects
about returning to the apartment with the girls. Once the gang
members arrived to take the girls away, the suspects could
easily have let them in by releasing the lock on the front door
to the property. The state processed the charges for Jonas and
Elias, but evidence placing them at the scene would help build
a stronger case, not just for their convictions but to seek
connections to the other OCG members. Emilia confirmed

they had the apartment owner's laptop, which contained the CCTV of the apartment's entry point from the street. The camera was in the hallway, looking down at the front door entrance. There was a room to the right of the hallway, home to a young couple. They were both interviewed but stayed over at a friend's house before returning in the morning. The hallway led to a staircase which allowed access to the stairs of the building. As the team made their way up the stairs, they reached the first floor where the girls' rented apartment was situated.

One of the City-state officers held up the yellow tape across the door as the operations team ducked under to enter. The apartment had a small hallway with a bathroom on the left and a bedroom on the right. The hallway opened into a kitchen and lounge area which was open plan. The sofa turned into another bed which was laid out and looked used. The apartment owner was sat on a breakfast stool in the kitchen area, being interviewed by one of the Berlin City Police officers. The apartment seemed used, but again there was no sign of disturbance or intrusion.

"The laptop is over here," Fenna said, pointing to the far corner of the room.

A desk with a chair and various house plants hung down from the desk's edge in the far corner of the apartment.

"Has she seen it?" Ted replied.

"Yeah, she checked the video as soon as it was the designated check-out time. Initially, the cleaner alerted the owner that their belongings were still in the apartment."

Fenna continued to mention the CCTV didn't show the inside of the apartment, only the front door coverage on the ground floor.

"Okay, let's look," Ted said.

Fenna pointed to the laptop, and Luuk took a seat, pulled up to the desk, and flipped the computer open. The computer required a password to access its content, which Fenna provided. Once he typed the secret words in and pressed enter. The screen went black momentarily and lit up with a generic home page. The home screen had different app icons running along the left-hand side. Luuk started to manoeuvre through the start screen and document view to access the CCTV video files. He read the German words as he was very familiar with them because his German mother was born in Hannover before moving to Eindhoven for employment.

"Here we are. Are you ready? The owner set it to the time they arrived," Luuk said.

Luuk looked up to check that the team had a visual of the screen. A window appeared with a still picture of the front door footage from the overhead corridor camera. In the bottom right-hand corner, the time stamp read: **07/07/2019 03:25.**

Luuk hit the play button, and the video footage played with slightly grainy but good quality to reveal the visual representation of the events.

"Here they come," Ted said.

The video showed the front door from the street open, and the first to enter was Mabel, followed by Hafwen. Both were intoxicated as they stumbled through the front door, continuing out of view down the corridor. Just behind them, Jonas and Elias followed them, closing the door and going through the corridor.

"Hold it there," Ted instructed.

"Rewind it a few seconds to when they close the door."

Luuk did as instructed, hovering over the time bar and dragging it back ten seconds to when the girls opened the front apartment door.

"Watch when they close the door," Ted continued.

When Jonas, who was at the back of the group, tracked back to close the door behind him, he pulled out a beer coaster from his jacket pocket. Elias looked back at him, and Jonas, bending down, pointed towards the girls who had continued down the hall. Jonas seemed to say something, but the video didn't pick up the audio. Even a trained lip-reader would struggle as the movement of the mouth wasn't clear with the video quality. Elias caught up with the two girls and suddenly disappeared from the camera's view. Jonas knelt after working the beer mat into the door's opening. He folded the beer mat in half and slid it between the edge of the door and its frame to keep the door open.

Fenna shook her head in disgust. "They knew what they were doing," she said

There was a silence in the room, but Ted nodded his head slightly in agreement. He knew not to fall into a pit of empathy for the suspects, and he knew they were fully involved in the crime.

"Here is our evidence of intent," Fenna continued.

Ted asked if footage of the stairwell was contiguous to the corridor and if Luuk could set up a split-screen or minimise both to compare. Luuk paused the corridor camera and went back onto the document viewer, scrolling through the appropriate files to find the CCTV folder for the stairwell. He fast-forwarded when Mabel and Hafwen first came into view on the stairway. Luuk hit the play button on both videos once the timestamps matched. The corridor camera showed Jonas standing up from the floor and pushing the door to check it wouldn't lock with the cardboard wedge in place. He jogged down the corridor out of view and climbed the stairs. The stairwell video only showed the remaining five or six steps before reaching the first floor. In this frame, the girls deteriorated in their states of consciousness.

Elias had reached both of the girls before they made the final two steps, as the girls began to lose balance. Elias caught them from falling backwards on the stairs and tried to move them forward by propping his shoulders under their arms. Jonas came from behind to support Mabel, allowing Elias to keep Hafwen up on his own. They went out of view on the camera as they presumably entered the apartment.

"What are we looking for now? The front door?" Fenna said.

"I would guess so. There's no other footage here or any witnesses that pass by. They got fortunate with timing the drug to knock them out here."

"Maybe just a few seconds too early," Hans said.

"Yeah, shame they didn't cry for help," Karl said.

"They didn't know what was going on," Ted continued. "The others must arrive soon."

"I'll look now," Luuk said.

Luuk moved the time bar forward on the corridor's video when the front door opened. The movement on the door was a slight push, which allowed the beer mat to drop from its propped position. Luuk brought the time forward on the stairwell video and stopped it so the time-stamp was linear. Jonas looked down the stairs on his phone on the stairwell screen, presumably to the men entering the apartment complex. Jonas went out of view, remaining on the first floor and back into the apartment room.

"This must be it now; I'll just play them both out?" Luuk looked around for confirmation before hitting play.

"Yeah, just play it out," Ted replied.

The corridor video showed two men wearing black gloves, one with a black baseball cap and the other dark green baseball cap covering both of their faces from view. They were both of a similar height and build on the feed.

"Just stop it a second," Ted said.

Luuk stopped both the videos to keep the times together. Ted leaned forward to study the footage from the corridor.

"Zivko Dordevic?" Ted said.

Fenna started to nod.

"Yeah, looks like it," Luuk said.

"Hold on," Karl said.

Karl reached into his back pocket and pulled out a fold of

papers. He unfolded a few pages and searched the collection, pulling out one of them and putting the others into his back pocket. He unfolded the paper and handed it to Luuk, who held up the paper to the screen to compare.

"Looks like him," Luuk said.

Luuk restarted the two videos again, and Zivko, wearing the black cap, went out of view of the camera and towards the stairwell. The other man took a position by the front door, watching the street level. Zivko climbed the stairwell and then went out of view when he reached the top of the stairs. Around a minute passed until Jonas reappeared at the top of the stairs. Suddenly, a cluster of figures filled the stairwell when Elias and Jonas held one of the girl's shoulders each. Zivko was keeping the legs of both girls under his extended arms as he started to descend the stairs. They slowly made their way down the stairs as they slowly sunk out of view. The man at the front door made his way back to the stairwell as the others came into view of the corridor. The man with the green cap grabbed Hafwen's leg to free Zivko's left arm, who readjusted to concentrate on Mabel.

"Hans, have you got the other pictures with you?" Ted said.

"Yeah, I have."

Hans reached back into his pocket and pulled out the papers. He sifted through them and passed them to Ted. He glanced at the video as it was playing, shuffling the picture and matching the identity.

"Miroslav," Ted said.

"Looks like your guy has done this before," Finn said.

"He's got to fit in. You have to do what they say," Luuk said, turning round in his chair.

Finn nodded back to acknowledge the statement.

The video continued as the five of them made their way to the end of the corridor as Miroslav reached out to open the door. They shuffled through the door, leaving Jonas as the last person in the corridor. As they walked through the front door, Jonas looked back at the corridor one last time, closing the door behind him.

"Efficient," Hans said.

"Professionals," Karl said.

"Anything from outside?" Ted said

"Phillip and Zoe are knocking on the doors now to see if there is any CCTV". Hans said.

"I think I saw a camera on the apartment two doors down," Fenna said.

"Great, let's see what they find," Ted replied.

Officer Phillip came into the apartment hallway, quickly navigating his way to the team gathered around the office desk.

"We found a camera just two blocks down from outside."

Ted looked at Hans and nodded. "Good work Phillip."

"We asked if we could look at the camera footage, and we did. We've got a car arriving with two men and then leaving with two more men and two women."

Ted felt a warm relief that the operation wasn't at a dead end.

"We've got them," Ted said.

"Zoe is getting it now from the owner."

"We got the plate?"

"We got it, and I've contacted the station. We will have the ANPR hits shortly."

"Thank you."

The sound of a phone ringtone came from Hans, who reached it from his pocket and accepted the call. After the initial introductions, Hans focused on Ted and nodded in an empathetic state. Ted felt the inside of his chest twist and felt unsteady on his feet. He looked away and placed his hand on the desk, feeling hot, when Luuk looked across from his seat to see if he was okay.

"Ted," Hans shouted over as he disconnected the phone.

Ted's face was beginning to turn white as he felt dizzy, and guilt began to overwhelm him.

"They've found a body."

He placed his palm on the table in front of him and pressed his heavy weight on the desk.

Luuk looked at Ted, and was concerned about his welfare, turning to look at Hans.

"Who?" Luuk added.

"Miroslav's body was found about an hour ago by the Wilhelm Spindler Bridge. southeast of the city, near Union Berlin's stadium," Hans said.

Ted felt the heavy weight in his chest lift and he gained colour to his face. He pushed his body back up from the desk and turned around.

"Miroslav?" Ted said.

"Yes, they sent a few officers down there and sent the still images of evidence to the station to run through the system. One of the officers cross-referenced the photographs we left at the station and identified him."

"How was he found?"

"Someone saw him as they were cycling by the river, called it in, and officers were nearby. They called it in and sent over pictures to the central station who confirmed the match with the pictures we have," Hans said.

Ted was elated inside, but he kept a straight face to remain undetected and still somewhat had disappointment all over his face.

"Sorry, Ted," Hans offered.

Ted nodded at him and lifted himself from leaning on the desk.

"Shit, sorry, Ted," Bartel said.

"Yeah," Ted said as he regained balance in his body

"No more intel now?" Karl said.

"He got us this far, and we need to keep going."

After the news that Miroslav's body was found dead in the

river, this confirmed there was a snitch in the operational team. Ted planned to announce Vladimir as the undercover agent at some stage, announcing his plan was to uncover the snitch in the team. However, he hadn't discovered the very under operative yet, although he had his suspicions with Bartel. The operation was now heading in a different direction after the outcome of the footage. Ted knew he had to uncover the snitch quickly, knowing one more outcome like that apartment in Amsterdam, he would lose the girls forever.

CHAPTER TWENTY-ONE

THE TEAM PIECED TOGETHER THE NEW INTEL from the apartment back in the stations' boardroom. The camera's footage from the apartment down the side street was a significant turn in the investigation and created some focus and a solid lead on the location of the OCG. Zoe spoke to the owner of the CCTV and retrieved the USB stick with the footage of the front door, which showed the vehicle pulling up outside the apartment block and leaving a few minutes later. The footage clearly showed the black SUV, Mercedes-Benz GLC, with fake German licence plates. German licence plates are typically issued officially by the district authorities to motorise the vehicles. In this case, although fake, the plates started with HB, which had the name of Hansestadt Bremen, whose authority was in Bremen City or Bremerhaven.

Nevertheless, there was a positive hit on the Mercedes SUV through an ANPR camera on the 96a near Plänterwald, a small Berlin borough southeast of the city. The timing of the notification was approximately fifteen minutes after leaving the apartment. Ted felt a surge of energy flow through him that was much stronger than the instant police station coffee from the machine. The ANPR hit indicated the direction the

OCG members were hiding out or holding the girls, but even more where the girls may be. The ANPR system picked up another hit on the 96a near Bohnsdorf, which again was southeast of the city a few minutes after the first. This marker point was just before the junction for the 117 or the continuation of the 96a, which passed the Schönefeld Airport heading west. The team searched the comprehensive catalogue of hits for the vehicle which flagged over the last couple of days and the few remaining hits from the early morning hours.

"Here we go!" Karl shouted.

"Where do they go next?" Ted said.

"They take the 117 and merge onto the 113 here," Karl said whilst double screening with a map app on his phone showing the location of their position.

Ted focused on Karl's finger showing the route from the airport. Ted's mind raced with the possibilities of which directions they could have gone next. Were they trying to escape the country?

"Any more hits?" Ted said.

"No, I think it goes cold after this," Karl replied.

"We may need to access roadside CCTV. There are two possibilities here as to where they would have gone. Plates may have changed, but I would say they've changed plates again, but looking at our ANPR locators, there are no other cameras on the main roads until later on. They must have gone off the road, or they are still within this area," Hans said.

"The previous hits from this morning, are they within the city?" Ted said.

"Yes, just around the south of the city. One or two near the Tempelhof Airport but nowhere else."

"If they've not changed the plates, we have this area to search," Ted said whilst circling his finger on an area on Karl's phone.

Ted focused on the map and, in particular, the following route south, which saw the 113 merge into the 13. Further along, the 13 met a cross junction of road 10, which ran east and west. Scenarios began to swirl around Ted's mind. They could have taken the 10 west to Poland or the 13 south to southern Germany if they had changed plates undetected. It was doubtful they'd turned around to head back north towards the city, although the airport was back in that direction. Luuk contacted Schönefeld Airport, and through faxing photographs of the OCG members and those girls, there were no matches to their facial recognition system, which ruled out that possibility.

"I don't think they would have gone back west or gone north. It's got to be south or east, right?" Fenna said.

"Agreed. However, we follow all possibilities, but I have no doubt you're right. Where could they have exited?" Ted replied.

"Suppose they'd managed to make it off the autobahn undetected from other ANPR cameras. There are a few options," Hans said.

Hans zoomed out on the app to check the next exit points from the 13 and 10 cross junction. Hans spotted a few small towns called Mittenwalde, south of the intersection, Wildau to the west and Zeesen further south of Wildau's location.

"Can we check the road camera for these areas to see what we have?" Luuk said.

"We can; I just need to make a quick call in that case," Hans said.

Hans stepped away from the group to make a call, announcing he was getting in touch with the surveillance department for the city to access the cameras near the junction.

"Elias and Jonas still secure? Have we had anything from their phones yet? They may not know we've got them now, but soon they will," Ted said.

"They're secure," Karl said.

Since the CCTV in the apartment showed their role in the

kidnapping, further questioning from the camera outside the apartment block would show them entering the vehicle, and there would be no escape from that fact. The two suspects had lawyered up, but their admissions already created the case against them. The Berlin state police tried to contact the House of Weekend club owners to find further CCTV evidence from the rooftop, but there was no luck with it being a Sunday.

The Dutch Korps officers and Phillip made their way into the control room. Bartel didn't notice Ted's intense look; Ted broke away from his presence as they approached the desk, and Phillip was the first to break the silence.

"The neighbour's camera good?"

"Yeah, it's good. We found the plates on the car, and we're tracking them south of Berlin," Ted replied.

"Great news. Are the two suspects in their cells?" Phillip replied.

"Yeah, they're waiting for their lawyers to arrive," Ted said.

"Okay, anyone want a drink?"

Everyone declined, but he said he needed a coffee. Ted noticed Bartel break away from the group and walk towards the door he had entered. Ted knew this was his time to confront him, possibly updating the OCG on the new information the task force held. Ted followed Bartel as he walked down the corridor and turned right into the staff male toilets. Ted picked up the pace with a slight jog as Bartel went out of sight, and Ted caught the door just before it closed. Ted pushed the door with a heavy force that made a loud bang against the wall.

"What the hell?" Bartel said as he became startled.

"What the fuck you are doing, Bartel?" Ted shouted.

"Nothing," Bartel said whilst holding his phone in his hand.

"Give me your phone."

"What? What is this?"

"Listen, Bartel, give me the phone."

"Fine, here."

Bartel handed over his phone, and Ted attempted to unlock the passcode, but he couldn't. Ted asked for the passcode, and Bartel relayed it back to him. Ted opened the phone and clicked on Bartel's text message app, and scrolled through the messages. Ted clicked through the messages but he didn't see anything that concerned him.

"What's wrong, Ted, tell me?"

Ted flicked back through the messages to review anything he missed. Some of the messages were in English, some in Dutch and some from fellow officers. Ted saw a message from Finn a few days ago, and it was a picture message that he sent to Bartel. Ted froze and felt a tight knot in his stomach.

"The fucking Rolex," Ted said as he gave back the phone.

"The Rolex? What Rolex?"

Before Bartel could finish his sentence, Ted had manoeuvred towards the door and disappeared.

CHAPTER TWENTY-TWO

TED ENTERED THE CONTROL AND FOUND
Fenna sitting down on the floor, leaning back against one of
the work desks. She was holding the side of her face whilst
Hans was knelt on his knees checking on her. She looked
dazed but fully conscious and gave a slight nod to Ted to say
she was okay. Ted observed the room and saw that Finn was
nowhere to be seen as Luuk approached.

"It was Finn, Ted," Luuk said.

"I know. I thought it was Bartel. Where is he?" Ted replied

"He left down the stairwell; Phillip, Zoe and Karl have gone
after him. We've called down to close the station doors before
he escapes."

Ted and Luuk exited the room and turned left down the
stairwell to the ground floor. When they reached the bottom
of the stairs, they still needed to make it across the building
complex through various corridors to exit the front door by
the reception. However, there was a rear fire exit door closer
to their position. He knew this would be where he was
heading. The reception area seemed quiet because there
would be a confrontation if he had gone that way. Like all
officers in the building, Finn was armed and would be looking

to escape by any means. Ted touched his waist to make sure his gun was present, although he could feel the weight of it. Both Ted and Luuk held their weapons ready with one finger hovering over the trigger. They edged through the corridor, which led to a T-style junction. He heard footsteps approaching from the right walkway. His adrenaline levels rose as he raised his weapon to the opening. Suddenly, there was a voice from the corridor.

"It's Karl, don't shoot! It's me, Ted and Luuk".

Karl turned the corner, and they all lowered their weapons. Karl announced that Finn hadn't made it to the reception front door, and Zoe was still at the location, but Phillip and another City State Officer had made their way to the rear exit with no current updates. Additional police officers from the station's various departments started to assemble behind Karl for further instructions.

"Do we have the front exit covered?" Ted stated.

"Yes, they've locked it down, and additional officers are on route. They're searching some of the nearby rooms there too," Karl said.

"Okay, we need to search this corridor and head towards the exit. Find Phillip and Finn."

Finn was vital to them if he was alive. But he had gone rogue, hiding, and armed, and he wouldn't have warmed to the idea of imprisonment that easily. Ted would want him alive to question him and bring another case of justice to the operation, but if the safety of any officers were in question, they would have to kill Finn in self-defence.

They moved through the corridor slowly with their guns aimed up towards the end of the corridor. A pair of officers broke off from the group upon reaching each door, and they opened it and gave it the all-clear. As they were approximately halfway through the corridor, there was a thunder of gunshots. Ted and the group became more alert as they manoeuvred through the passageway, locking eyes on the junction ahead. The junction up ahead reached a wall with a corridor running left to right. Ted held up his left hand whilst keeping his hand on the trigger with his right, signalling to halt as they approached the junction. He turned back to focus on Luuk and Karl. Ted pointed at them and then towards the right exit and pointed to himself for the left. He waited for a second and started counting down from three with his fingers.

"Two. One," Ted said under his breath.

With one swift movement, they turned both corners. Luuk and Karl remained silent, and no gunfire was heard behind him. Ted's view of the left was different, and he saw the fire exit door wide open, bringing in the natural sunlight. Ted advised the group to proceed down both corridors still to confirm Finn wasn't hiding in another room and remain vigilant. Some remaining officers cleared the remaining two doors before reaching the fire door exit and announcing they were clear. From Ted's short time at the Volkspark station, Ted knew that the fire exit led to a car park containing the service cars and the officers' vehicles for the station. There was a large metal gate at one end of the car park, and a person stationed inside a cubical who controlled the entrance. The cubical was outside the gate and halted those who approached. However, the exit was automatic, and if Finn was in a vehicle, this could turn into a vehicle pursuit.

Around ten seconds had passed from the initial gunshots heard in the corridor. Finn and the operational team didn't have their vehicles so Finn could have tried each car or unlocked one of the car doors.

"He's taken my car keys when he hit me," Fenna radioed.

The pace quickened as they approached the fire exit door, and a resurgence of gunfire filled the opening. Tentatively Ted peered through the opening of the door. To his left, Ted saw Phillip crouched down behind the rear of one of the service vehicles. Phillip caught the presence of Ted and the incoming officers and shared a visible sigh of relief. Ted gave him a thumbs up to check he was okay, and Phillip returned the signal. Ted would risk giving up the element of surprise if he peered around the door to seek Finn's location. But there was a flurry of gunfire aimed at Phillip, revealing Finn's position across the car park. The gunshot hit the car's metal but shattered the driver's side door.

"He's wounded," Phillip whispered.

Ted nodded. Ted was impressed with Phillips' pursuit of Finn. It was a risky move going after him on his own, and there was a sense of comfort that he was unharmed. Phillip had managed to disable Finn momentarily with a gunshot wound, which probably stopped his momentum in getting away in a service vehicle. Ted looked back at the officers behind and then looked towards the floor and saw blood trickles which led to the car park. Ted turned around to look out of the door. He knelt to get a lower angle so Finn couldn't see his position. Out on the tarmac of the car park, Ted saw the slight shine of bloody stains flickering in the sunlight. The last bloodstain that was visible dropped between two vehicles.

An outcry of European Police Sirens blocked the exit gates, which cornered Finn's position. Finn had cover from the fire exit and the gated entrance between the two cars where he was situated, but he was trapped in his position

"What now?" Luuk said from behind Ted's position.

"Two ways this ends. Alive or dead, but I think Finn's betting on the latter already."

Ted had an idea that could work. He was confident Finn would be low on ammunition with Phillip's tussle before and including Finn's pot shots in the car park.

"I'm going to fire at him. You make your way into the car park and get to cover."

"Sure," Luuk responded.

Luuk turned to tell Karl and the other officer behind him of the impending plan.

"Phillip? You got much left," Ted said.

"Just enough."

"Okay, ready to fire?"

"Yes. What's the plan?"

"We're coming out."

Phillip nodded and readied his weapon, and Ted started the count down.

"Three... Two... one."

Gunfire echoed in the car park from Phillip and Ted's weapons. Luuk joined in with the firing, all three aiming at the vehicle Finn was concealed behind. Luuk and half a dozen officers made it through the door and stashed themselves alongside a car. Once the cover fire stopped, Luuk and Ted made cover alongside Phillip. The officers stopped exiting the door and remained covered as instructed. The car sirens at the exit gates went silent, giving time to be with one's thoughts, but remained illuminated. The smell of gunpowder and metal filled the yard as Ted checked his weapon to reload his last clip of ammunition. Finn was surrounded, and there would be no escape from law enforcement.

"It's over, Finn. Give it up," Ted shouted out.

There was a continued silence; however, the tension was palpable. After a few additional seconds passed, Ted would continue his plea until Finn filled that silence with his defence.

"I was in trouble, Ted."

"What kind of trouble?"

Finn didn't respond, and Ted remembered that Finn had a wound from the shootout with Phillip, and medical assistance was required before he eventually bled out.

"I know you're wounded Finn; we can get you help."

"I don't need it. It's all over for me now."

Ted knew there were two choices for Finn, and he chose the latter.

"We can help you. What did they offer you? Money?"

"I'm in deep shit financially, and with this I didn't need to hurt anyone or get my hands dirty."

"This wasn't the answer, Finn. Sander could have helped." Ted said whilst shaking his head.

Ted looked back at the fire exit and saw Sander taking cover with a tear in her eyes. She felt sadness that this had happened to someone she trusted and mentored for so many years in the Korps department.

"Did they threaten you? We could help you if they did." Ted said, focusing back on Finn's position.

Again, no response. Ted was wondering if he was battling the pain or losing focus with the loss of blood he was experiencing.

"How did they approach you, Finn?"

"Off duty. They could offer me loads of money to give them information."

Crossing the line from working for the law to handing out intel to OCG groups wasn't the answer to anyone's bleak financial situation. However, Ted had seen it before when he began his role as an ILO in Amsterdam. He worked with the Belgian police force near the border, which involved a case of drug transportation out of The Netherlands across European borders. One of the police officers in Belgium became blind to his role as border force patrol, being handed immense amounts of cash for each HGV that crossed freely.

In Ted's far peripheral vision, he noticed movement from Luuk. He knelt up, this time holding his gun ready. Ted looked at him, bewildered at what he was doing, lifting his left arm.

"What you doing, Luuk?" Ted said.

Luuk leant towards Ted.

"He's getting ready."

Ted glanced towards Finn's position and could now see Finn's head through the car's window. His position was still between the two vehicles, but he knelt up instead of hiding, ready to fight it out. Ted held his finger on the trigger and lifted his gun above the vehicle's roof he was hiding behind.

"Finn. Don't do this." Sander shouted out from the door.

"Sorry, Sander, I really am. Tell my family I love them."

Finn's head raised above the metal roof of the car. His arms rose above the car's metal with his gun, aiming toward Ted and the officers. The exchange only lasted a few seconds, with Finn managing to get off two shots in return that had no direction or purpose. Finn's body jerked backwards onto the vehicle's driver's window and disappeared from view between the cars with a slow descent. Ted and a few officers moved in to secure the area. Ted was the first to arrive, lowering his gun as it was clear the danger was over.

"All Clear," he announced.

Ted looked down at Finn's fallen body with his eyes staring wildly and lifelessly into the sky. Ted noticed the sunlight was gleaming off the face of Finn's Rolex, and the Rolex had a crack on its face and smeared with blood that had exited from the body.

Sander manoeuvred through the crowd of officers to Ted's position. Ted noticed her standing alongside him, too, looking down at his dead body.

"Sorry about Finn, Sander," Ted said.

"We've found out the leak. Now go and get those girls."

CHAPTER TWENTY-THREE

THE FOOTSTEPS OF HIS BOOTS ECHOED through the large warehouse walls, and with each step, a fear of dread entered Mabel's body. The man moved from one side of the warehouse to the other, looking at each girl as he passed them, observing if they were still in chains. Mabel saw the man holding a plastic bag as he approached the first girl's position in the row. This was the only time she welcomed anything from the man who entered to check up on their health a few times a day. The first girl was Hafwen, who didn't even look up to him. He reached his hand into the bag and brought out a plastic water bottle and a small bread roll. It was dinner time as this was the third meal for the day. He did the same to each girl as he approached them, placing down a bottle and a roll for them to eat. He only ever provided them with water and food, and it was never to allow them time to relieve them of their human needs. Their seated position was their lavatory.

Mabel noticed that Hafwen hadn't moved to reach for the water and food. This was the third time it had happened. Mabel needed to eat her food to regain her strength for what may lay ahead. When she threw up this morning, she knew her stomach would be empty, and the lack of energy made her sleepy and vulnerable. Her stomach was dry from the stomach acid which passed through it this morning, leaving a stain next to her on the concrete flooring.

The man continued to pass out the food and water after dropping Mabel's in front of her. Mabel picked up the water and drank half of its contents. She reached down for the bread roll and took a large bite of it. Mabel nearly ate the bread roll in one bite. She then drank more of the room temperature water to wash it down and took her last bite of the roll. She noticed the man was handing out the items to the last girl across from Hafwen. Mabel looked around and saw all the girls were eating and drinking. She crossed eyes with Amanda, looking back at Mabel with an intense stare. Amanda then nodded in Hafwen's direction. Mabel saw Hafwen still hadn't touched her items; Mabel wanted to encourage her to drink but knew the man would hear her. The man turned to look back at the room and noticed Hafwen hadn't touched her food again. He looked at her, waiting for her to see his stare.

"Eat. Drink," the man ordered

There was a silence between Hafwen and the onlooking girls. The man stepped closer to Hafwen, so he was towering over her. Hafwen kept her head low, looking at the food and water in front of her.

"I said eat," he said.

Silence again. He then knelt in front of her and grabbed her jaw up so she could look at him.

"Eat!".

The man raised his right hand and slapped her on the face. She crashed back against the wall behind her from the force of his blow After a few seconds, she regained her position when the man grabbed her hair. Mabel stared in intense horror. The man towered over her again, lifting her slightly off the floor. She let out an agonising scream as the hair pulled from her scalp.

"You need to eat, now."

The man let go of her hair and reached down to hold her throat.

"Eat!"

Suddenly, a noise built up in her mouth. The man's grip on her throat began to loosen, and she opened her mouth. A projection of phlegm left her mouth and covered the man's eyes and nose.

"You bitch!"

The man punched her in the face knocking her back against the wall. Her back hit the wall again, avoiding a laceration to the head. Mabel was full of terror and fear about what was happening. Hafwen had utterly lost the will to live and provoked her capture into doing something to end the torment.

"You mock me! In front of all these girls. Now you must learn."

"Fuck you," Hafwen shouted back.

"Right. Let's go."

"Hafwen!" Mabel shouted.

He reached into his pocket and pulled out a single key. He went around Hafwen and unlocked the handcuffs around one hand of the chain. Hafwen manoeuvred her body to make a sudden movement, but the man was ready. He held her down with his bare hand and then grabbed her under her armpit to stand her up. He readjusted and held onto her as she wriggled. He used his huge arms to move her towards the double doors nearest where she was sitting, and opposite where he had entered.

Hafwen tried to wriggle free and use her small arms to fight back, but his muscular torso engulfed her body and kept her in place. The man pushed the door open, and it swung open, revealing a partial view of the room blocked by the pair.

"I'm sorry, Mabel, I can't do this," she said as the double doors swung closed.

The sounds from the other room were muffled, but the

intense nature was even more harrowing. Sometimes the volume increased through the concrete walls and closed doors. Noises started to come from the man too, but then those noises were faded by Hafwen's begging screams in the other room. The girl who sat opposite Hafwen threw up on the floor next to her, leaving the bread roll differently from how it was before. The noises continued for what seemed a few minutes but felt like hours. Mabel started to feel queasy and dizzy. She took a passing glance from Amanda, who immediately bowed her head to the floor to avoid eye contact.

The noises stopped from the room they entered. Suddenly, a loud bang was followed by another, when the doors pulled back to reveal just the man. His face was red and sweaty from the exhaustion of exercise. He stepped into the large room as the doors closed behind him. He stopped in his footsteps and spat on the floor where Hafwen had previously sat. He continued to walk through the room in a cocky style. He pulled out a tissue from his pocket to clean his concealed blade. As the man passed Mabel, she saw the edge was painted red. He completed the wipe off the blade and threw the tissue to the ground, keeping the knife held in his hand. He reached the doors he originally entered from, turning to look back at the girls in the room.

"Any of you do that, and you will end up like her."

Tears started to stream down Mabel's face.

CHAPTER TWENTY-FOUR

THERE WAS A SOMBRE AND EERIE ATMOSPHERE in the control room after what had happened with Finn. The emergency ambulance services were en route when the pursuit was happening. After the gunfire stopped, the services entered the station, only to confirm Finn's death. A media presence was starting to gather as pedestrians reported the sound of gunfire coming from the police station. The media outlets wouldn't be aware of the full details yet, and officers were sworn not to discuss this outside the police walls. As the operation was gathering pace and the location of the SUV was a priority, it would spook the OCG if they knew there was a shootout at the police station or if it was learnt their informant was dead. However, they wouldn't be able to hold out on the press for much longer, so they needed to move to the area the vehicle was last located.

Senior Officers of the Berlin City police were informed immediately, and the specialist detective branch '*Kriminalpolizei*' questioned and wanted a play-by-play account of Ted's actions and instructions to others which led to Finn's death. Although it was a lengthy process that took nearly an hour, and the other team members' stories matched, the station

CCTV gave vital evidence towards a righteous kill verdict. The overall outcome concluded that the team followed the correct procedures, and they were allowed to continue with their operation without any further investigation.

Ted wanted to obtain an international warrant to check through the contents of Finn's phone and asked Luuk to run a background check on Finn. Sander called HQ in Amsterdam to speak to her deputy about rerunning the security checks when they recruited Finn to spot any possible red flags. At the time of his recruitment, it would be expected that all background checks would be clear, as he was only influenced by the OCG recently.

Although recent activity, including phone and message data and his bank accounts and financial information, would show current changes in his allegiance, Ted wondered why Finn decided to strike now. The phone messages could prove that, but he didn't want to access the data until the warrant was issued and approved. Fenna explained that she saw Finn look nervously around the room after reading something on his mobile device. Fenna took additional notice when it wasn't his regular android phone but a small burner-type device. Fenna continued to narrate the story that after witnessing his body language, he asked the team if anyone wanted a coffee like Phillip did, and that's when Ted followed Bartel. Ted's movements spooked Finn, and Fenna stood by the desk closest to the door when Finn made his way towards it. Fenna confronted him about the message, and the panic on his face turned to anger.

"He tried to walk around me, but I moved when he moved. He pushed me, and I pushed back, and then everyone noticed what was going on. Finn punched me in the temple, and I fell against the desk, and he got me good."

"Want us to get the medics up to look at it?" Phillip asked.

"I just need a bag of ice, and I'll be fine," Fenna said.

Sander approached Ted from across the room, holding her

phone.

"We have some news."

"God, we need it."

"So, we tracked a white van like the ones in Amsterdam. There were loads, but we followed ANPR and worked with the German authorities across our range. Anyway, using distinctive markers and description of the original van, we saw it last on the 10 south of Berlin."

"We got that before, though."

"That's right, but it's not been spotted again. They are definitely in that area."

"We will be deploying there soon after this is all cleared up. Tell them to keep their eyes on it."

"Don't worry, they are."

Sander continued to update Ted on the Amsterdam suspect who picked up girls, like Elias and Jonas had. They'd tracked him down through a girl's accounts of how she met him. The man was seen on CCTV around the Leidseplein area, known as the city's party area. They tracked Erwin Johnson using facial recognition, there was a match from a previous minor offence for intent to supply drugs. The police went to his home address and arrested the twenty-three-year-old from Amsterdam. Erwin had dropped out of university and taken a supermarket job. He was renting just outside the city and sometimes slept on friends' couches when he couldn't make rent; his motive was solely down to money. Like Elias and Jonas, the numbers from which the messages and calls they received were no longer used. Erwin was charged but couldn't provide any information to the OCG, which again led the team to believe that these were 'pawn' pieces to the chessboard members in the OCG.

"I'm sorry again about Finn, Sander."

"I know, and I'm just sorry for his girlfriend and daughter," she said.

"Around Ivy and Florences' age."

Ted was lost in thought. He couldn't imagine his daughters losing their daddy like what had happened with Finn. Ted started to feel sorry for Finn and his position of desperation, but more for the family and the impending news. He broke away from his thoughts as he visioned Rose and the girls hearing the information about Ted's death and how they would react.

"It's sad news."

"I know. I'll sort everything with Finn. I may need to return to Amsterdam with the body and debrief with my bosses over this. I may not be able to carry on with you."

"Okay, I understand. Thank you for everything so far."

"That's my job. Take care, Ted."

They shook hands, and she walked through the room, saying her goodbyes before exiting through the door. Luuk waited for Sander to leave before approaching Ted, and when she had, informed Ted that the warrant had been approved. They were now able to access Finn's bank details and phone messages. The team gathered around one of the working desks searching through the recent messages on the burner phone. The most recent texts from an untraceable number had specific orders to neutralise the threat of Elias and Jonas, which was around the time he had his confrontation with Fenna. The messages also included Finn stating that Miroslav was the snitch inside the OCG. A follow-up message from the same untraceable number announcing the snitch was neutralised. There were other messages which would be investigated at a later point. Still, no addresses were included in the conversations from the OCG member. However, Finn did include the addresses where the operational team were investigating from: The petrol station in Beckum, the hotel in Berlin, the police station, Mauerpark and the impending pursuit of the apartment complex in Amsterdam.

Somebody paid several transactions of up to four thousand euros into Finn's account over the last three weeks. The payer was a Romanian electrical warehouse company that made light bulbs and other equipment just outside Timişoara. The payments were investigated and found to be fake when it was discovered the company had been closed for four years on the Bucharest stock exchange and its operational warehouse ground abandoned. Luuk contacted Poliția Română to see if they could investigate the warehouse and see if it was genuinely neglected or in operation, and they confirmed it was neglect. Luuk further explained he was working with the Romanian authorities. This was common among the Dutch police and Europol due to trafficking, drugs and other criminal activities related to Romanian gang members.

Karl accessed Jonas and Elias's phone records and searched the messages from dubious contacts. Again, there wasn't any inclusion of addresses from the OCG, but there were addresses from the suspect's phones about meeting points. These messages included pictures of the unconscious girls to presumably show their looks, rather than if they were unconscious. Multiple payments were made into their accounts from the same abandoned warehouse in Romania.

Ted noticed Hans had ended his call and approached the desk.

"Some good news on the CCTV."

"Go on."

"They tracked the plates of the SUV on the CCTV in the city as it made its way south, as we know. They dropped off Elias and Jonas around 03:50 am in Plänterwald. But that's not all."

Luuk, Fenna and the operational officers stopped their investigations to listen to Hans.

"We've got them on CCTV in Wildau."

Luuk whistled.

"Nice," Luuk said.

"So, they took the 10 west and then took the first exit. When you exit the junction there, you come to a retail area with many shops, and a car park and ride for the airport".

"I know that area well. I've parked there many times when going on holiday," Phillip said.

"So, the last CCTV hit we have is near Autohof, a car dealership in Wildau. Then nothing else on either route from there," Hans continued.

"This is good. We need to get ourselves out to Wildau now. Is everyone ready to move? Keep some of the City police here to deal with Jonas, Elias and the investigation on the accounts," Ted said.

"I'll get a team on it," Phillip said.

Ted knew that there would be a race against the clock until the OCG knew Finn had failed in his mission. They needed to move fast before it was too late.

CHAPTER TWENTY-FIVE

MOMENTUM BUILT AS THE TEAM MAPPED OUT their next steps, considering the new information given on the SUV's plates. The last capture of the vehicle was outside a car dealership on Chausseestraße in Wildau. Using a map app, they concluded the possible routes the car could have taken. They also researched the CCTV in the area to see if a similar vehicle had passed through with different plates. There wasn't, so Ted and the team were still working on the theory they were still in the area. Including the information from Sander that confirmed that a similarly distinctive van that came from Amsterdam passed Chausseestraße was not to be held as a coincidence any more.

Using the map app, they found a possible location for a composting facility that specialised in processing organic garden waste and turning it into high-quality natural compost. However, like the phoney Romanian address the suspects were receiving payments from, the compost facility hadn't been operational for several months. The team concluded from the van's last CCTV sighting, giving a viable option in terms of a hideout. There were other locations just east of a supermarket, around a two-minute drive away. However, they were legitimate businesses, and the German Government website listed those companies as operational. These warehouses included construction companies such as; fire protection, mechanical engineering and freight forwarding services. However the freight forwarding services were attractive to the officers, they planned to investigate this due to the importance of transportation services in this particular business.

Daylight began to fade as the sun fell beyond the fast open fields on either side of the autobahn. In the distance was the drone of planes taking off at Schönefeld Airport. Along the autobahn, the parade of undercover cars stretched three cars deep. Ted was upfront with Luuk and Hans, followed by Karl riding with Fenna, Phillip and Bartel. The last vehicle contained Emilia, Zoe and two other police officers from the Berlin state police. Fenna was willing to continue after the paramedics, who confirmed Finn had died, checked her over for concussion after the blow to her head. She was fit to work but was instructed to go to the hospital if she felt the slightest headache.

They exited Autobahn 10 for Wildau and headed northeast into the town, passing a vast retail area. They proceeded the same route the SUV took on Chausseestraße when the CCTV captured its movements. The road was relatively short before a corner allowed for a road change to Dorfaue. They had passed the warehouse and saw no activity in the brief second it took to pass. The warehouse had a long stretch of single track running from the main road to its facility. Approximately two hundred metres down Dorfaue was a roundabout with a supermarket on one of its exit points. Here would be the team's spot to regroup, as the next accessible CCTV point was nearby. There was a junction just off the store carpark shortly after another bend with a right turn onto Bergstraße. This road ran southeast from Wildau back towards the Autobahn from another direction. Bergstraße ends at a roundabout with two additional options linking to Karl-Marxstraße. The road ran north to south, with the north option running back into Wildau or south towards Königs Wusterhausen, which was situated south of Autobahn 10 within the Dahme-Spreewald district. Karl-Marxstraße runs parallel to the Dahme river and has no other access point across the river unless you reach the Marine Service Niederlehme, which gives small boat crossings. Contacting ahead of time, they confirmed they didn't offer services to the public and hadn't seen anyone trying to cross who weren't employed staff members of the Marine service. There was CCTV and an ANPR camera on Karl-Marxstraße, but there wasn't any indication they had passed through these possible routes.

The team parked in the far corner of the supermarket for more privacy and remained in their vehicles for cover. Ted had already presented an A1 printout of Wildau and markings for the observations each vehicle would undertake back at the station. Ted explained how the operation would proceed as night commenced, giving additional cover. Zoe's group would observe the freight forwarding facility with Stefan Braun and Klaus Wolf from the City police. Karl's group would remain within the supermarket forecourt as secondary support, and Ted would view the entry point to the facility.

A solo house adjacent to the Autohof car dealership was located across the road from the organic gardening facility. The road leading from the main road to the facility was tarmacked but needed desperate repair. Large birch trees blocked off either side of the facility with its vastness and depth. In their late sixties, an old couple who occupied the solo house had their supper of Käsespätzle and news night TV disturbed. The team explained they were conducting some surveillance in the area and needed the driveway on their home to park up and observe. After Luuk and Hans showed their credentials, the older couple agreed and carried on with their evening partaking in curtain twitching from time to time. The older couple stated they hadn't seen any activity for several months during the day. They usually went to bed around eight-thirty at night and couldn't confirm any activity after these hours. They told the officers they were still awake if needed because they were watching a tribute to German bass singer Franz Crass who died aged eighty-four.

Once the officers were in their spots, everyone radioed in to say they were ready and had their eyes open for any signs of activity. Emilia's group reported that one or two lorries parked inside the freight forwarding facility were currently facing outwards, with workers loading their cargo. Emilia's team couldn't expand anymore due to their viewing of the facility. They could move closer, but this would reveal their position under the industrial estate's street lights.

Karl radioed over the communications link.

"We've got a black Mercedes coming towards your location Ted on Dorfaue. It has Hungarian plates." Hans said over the radio.

"Give us the plate if you have it," Ted said.

Hans gave the plate registration. They would trace the plates, but it may take longer with it being Hungarian.

"I'll get to check it out with the Team," Luuk said.

"Okay, where is it now, Hans?"

"It disappeared about ten seconds ago. Shall we follow?"

"Not yet. Stay put."

"Over."

Ted knew the traffic was light on the main road, and no headlights were approaching the supermarket. Suddenly, a light touched the road's surface and increased its surface area as it came. The vehicle passed their position but didn't seem to be the Mercedes that Hans described.

"Vehicle passed, but it wasn't the Mercedes," Ted said.

"It was a Mercedes E-Class with those plates?" Karl said.

"This was a Volkswagen."

Immediately, another light lit the road's surface, approaching slower than the Volkswagen. The black Mercedes came into view from the driveway turning right into the facility single track road. The rear of the vehicle displayed the plates which matched Hans's description.

"Think your friends will get back soon, Luuk?" Ted said.

"I've sent a message to someone working. He is checking them shortly."

"Mercedes has entered the facility," Ted radioed.

The rear brake lights of the car shone red as it slowed down and turned to park, disappearing behind the row of birch trees.

"Lost visual on the car. Think he's parking," Ted reported. "Can you park on the main road Karl just in case we need you. Just by the junction?"

Karl confirmed he was on his way when a figure appeared from behind the trees. The man was standing at the end of the track looking back down the single road towards the main road, and then turned quickly, manoeuvring to the building. The building's exterior was dark, with no floodlights to give any visuals to the team. The figure merged into the shadow of the building.

"This must be the place," Hans said.

"I think so," Ted said.

Luuk turned to Ted in the car.

"Should we check the freight company for any recent or pending departures to Hungary?"

"Yeah, I'll radio," Ted said.

Ted was about to radio the instructions to approach the freight forwarding facility.

"Should they take Hans, the team, as backup?" Luuk said.

Ted thought about losing the backup on the organic facility when required, but Ted agreed and instructed Karl's group to offer Emilia backup when they approached the facility. Ted asked Phillip to contact the police station if anyone was on patrol nearby to provide support.

"We've got two cars, one on the 113 near the airport and

another on the 110 near Ludwigsfelde," Phillip said.

"Okay, good, tell them to come in silent, one to back up Emilia and one of us. Tell them to position themselves before the junction between here and the supermarket," Ted said.

"Got it."

Luuk nudged Ted on the shoulder and readjusted his position to lean forward. Ted quickly focused on the road leading to the facility, and Hans leaned forward from the rear middle seat and gripped onto the two front headrests. A light illuminated the man for a brief second as the automatic car's lock system was put in place, and then again once the man unlocked the vehicle. He was wearing a smart suit with what looked like shoes to match. Within that second, Luuk noticed he seemed to point beyond the car as if saying something to someone. Four other people moved across the outdoor space from the building and behind the birch trees. Headlights shone across the front of the building. The lights rolled forward, and so did the vehicles. The Mercedes moved out first and turned back towards the main road. A much larger white van followed the car. Ted realised they were now sitting where the car's headlights would shine the brightest as it approached the main road. All three of them ducked down in their seats, keeping their eyes over the top of the dashboard to maintain a visual of the oncoming cars.

"We have movement—the Mercedes and an unknown vehicle. Approximately five persons," Luuk radioed.

"Any news on the police patrol Phillip? We may scare them off if they're on the main road. Tell them to divert to the Supermarket," Ted said.

"We have one patrol car with us at the freight warehouse. We are about to approach now. The other car is taking the exit of autobahn 10 onto Chausseestraße."

The two vehicles were now at the junction for the main road—the headlights from the Mercedes blinding the team's view. The Mercedes exited right from the side road towards autobahn 10. Ted could see the suited man in the driver's seat was alone as he drove out of sight. However, the van pulled up at the junction and ventured back towards the supermarket on Dorfaue. Inside the van were two figures, but it was too dark to describe them.

"Same plates as spotted on the CCTV. This is them," Hans said.

"What now?" Luuk said.

"We follow the van, there are two people unaccounted for in the back of the van, and I'm guessing it's our girls."

Ted followed up with a radio call out to Karl and Emilia's car.

"We have a white van coming your way. It's the van we've been looking for from Amsterdam. Be ready to move."

"Over," Karl replied.

"Phillip? Tell the officers approaching from the autobahn to look out for a Mercedes E-Class approaching and follow them at a distance. Don't spook him."

"Understood."

The radio chirped, and Emilia spoke urgently, "You may want to get over here. We walked over to the entry gates, and they're shouting at us."

Emilia's voice had a sense of urgency over the radio now, and gunfire sounded over the communications.

"Get over here now!"

Ted turned the key in the ignition and pushed down the handbrake, and flew out of the driveway, nearly colliding with an oncoming vehicle from the right.

CHAPTER TWENTY-SIX

THE GUNFIRE WAS DEAFENING THROUGHOUT the industrial estate as Ted's car approached the scene. Ted pulled up sharply behind the three undercover vehicles surrounding the freight compound's exit. Towering green metal fences bordered the facility with no other entrances visible and a train line running along the rear of the compound. Upon exiting their vehicle, Ted's team stayed low and joined Emilia's team, who were hiding behind the boot of their car.

When Emilia initially radioed for backup, Karl's team made their way to the freight facility. Ted told them to backtrack and follow the white van whilst Ted joined in on Emilia's request. Hans was following the van carefully, so as not to spook the occupants or alert other OCG members.

Gunshots from inside the facility came from either side of the two heavy goods vehicles parked within the large shuttered entrance. The returning fire was coming from the operational team hiding behind the cars at an entrance gate.

"I've called for backup," Han's shouted across the gunfire.

"Any news on the Mercedes?" Ted said.

"Nothing yet, but they're following," Hans said.

Ted nodded and checked his weapon to ensure he had enough ammo. He thought he didn't, so he would have to use his ammo wisely.

"What do we do?" Luuk said.

"We need some cover to move in," Fenna said.

Ted studied the systematics laid in front of him. He saw a small door open from the congregated iron wall covering the warehouse facility. Two figures from the large warehouse opening appeared and shot towards the teams' position as they rushed towards a van to escape.

"There's our cover," Ted said.

"Fire?" Luuk said.

"Fire."

The vehicle's engine roared and accelerated hard towards the open gate. The getaway vehicle was battered with a torrent of shots to the windscreen. The glass shattered with spatters of red, painting the remaining screen. Suddenly, the car sharply turned right and smashed into the gates post with both airbags deploying and the loud moaning of the car horn cancelling out the gunfire. The vehicle's position gave the team a wide area of cover, which allowed the team to advance to the crashed vehicle. Luuk used the step outside the passenger side door to lift himself to examine the cab, confirming that both men were dead. Both men had bullet wounds to the forehead, face and shoulders. The airbags' force pushed both men's positions back and left their heads tilted forward.

"White van has entered the industrial estate," Karl radioed.

Ted ducked for cover, leaning against the crashed vehicle's metal.

"Stop them now. We're going to be sitting ducks."

"Will try my best."

The gunfire dwindled in the forecourt of the facility—the distraction of an onrushing vehicle brought attention to both groups. The van and another car were side-by-side in their pursuit and roared up the main industrial estate road that ran through the middle of the warehouses. Both cars ignored the speed bumps as they jerked upwards after every impact, with their headlights flickering up every time. The operational team were indecisive in their cover, as they had possible dangers from both sides of their spot.

The two vehicles were only one hundred metres away when Karl's car steered abruptly into the rear side of the van, performing a pit manoeuvre. The van lost control with a cloud of smoke tailing as it collided with the green fence. Karl's vehicle swiftly stopped a few metres in front, and the officers exited the car. Ted and the covered officers took guard of both the facility and the van to see if the gang members had survived the crash. As Karl's team approached the van, no shots were firing from the cab. Karl approached the driver's door with Phillip, Fenna moving around the back of the truck, and Bartel heading towards the passenger door. There was no movement from the cab as they moved in closer.

Karl placed one hand on the door handle whilst keeping aim at the driver's level, ordering both men to surrender. There was no response, and with that, he slowly pulled at the door handle and peered through the door, firing four shots into the cab. Karl remained standing, but the passenger side door opened as the other man tried to escape. Bartel kept his weapon raised and instructed the man to surrender. The man put his hands above his head and dropped to his knees. The knelt man started muttering something in what seemed to be an Eastern European accent. He then reached for the inside of his jacket pocket. Bartel hesitated for a second to see if the movement was a hoax. It was real; the reflection of the streetlight gleamed upon the metal pistol, and the man was down in one shot to the chest.

Their attention was drawn to the back of the vehicle, where the rest of Karl's team was positioned. The firing started again from within the compound towards Ted's position, returning cover fire for Karl.

"We've gone round to the back. Are we ready?" Karl radioed.

Karl and his team held their weapons up at the van's back door, and Phillip held on to one of the door handles, ready to push down and swing it open. Phillip made a move in one quick motion. Two figures were sitting in the corner of the van, huddling in fear and desperation. The team lowered their weapons.

"What do you see?" Ted radioed.

"We got two girls. Alive," Karl said.

"They seem shook up, but they're all right," Fenna added.

Ted's body was overwhelmed with a surge of relief. He immediately turned his attention to the facility they were trying to invade. The team was trapped behind the crashed van with no opportunity to move in under the defence fire from the men in the facility. Two additional police patrol cars pulled up on the main industrial road, providing backup. Luuk told the newly arrived officers to hold their positions behind their vehicles until they could assess the situation.

"We need emergency services here for the girls. Think they've been injured with the crash, but otherwise, they're okay," Karl radioed.

"Of course, They're on their way," Hans said.

Ted looked at the surroundings and then focused on the team cover's van.

"What should we do here, Ted?" Emilia said

Ted ordered some of the surrounding officers to reach up and help him take the dead men out of the cab so he could reach over to the driver's side seat. His idea was to take the men out onto the ground, jump into the cab, and control the vehicle. Once the men were out of the car, Ted crept into the cab, keeping low. The vehicle's engine was already running, so once he had climbed over to the driver's side, Ted put the bloody gearstick into reverse, slowly turned the car's angle, and backed up towards the facility entrance. There was an onslaught of fire from the facility, which was returned by the officers still covered by the moving van.

The officers assembled at the front of the vehicle as Ted edged it closer to the facility. The sound of a bullet pierced against the metal shutter at the van's rear. The covering officers returned fire from the bonnet of the truck. Slowly Ted turned the van side on, with the driver's side furthest away from the facility entrance. Ted quickly exited the cab and returned to the team, shielded by the van again.

"Nice work Ted," Fenna said.

"What now?" Luuk said.

"We've got a chance here. We need to get to that side door, and that gets us inside. I can do it with Emilia. You okay with that?"

"Sure."

"Luuk, can you and the team push in on the main door?"

"Yeah, will do."

"We also need you to cover us as we reach the door."

"We will cover you with our gunfire. We're going to need more officers."

Luuk ordered some of the officers they told to stand by their vehicles to help join in. So too did Bartel and Phillip, whilst Hans and Fenna supported the girls before the ambulance arrived. Ted spoke to the police officers who had just arrived before making their way for the door. Ted asked them to give cover whilst they moved towards the facility's entrance. The sirens came from the main road, the ambulance arrived, and the gunfire stopped inside the building. It was the time of opportunity.

"Go!" Ted shouted.

The team advanced from behind the van, firing shots towards the targets between the two parked lorries. The police officers shot off multiple bullets to form a shield of cover fire, allowing Ted and Emilia to make their way safely to the side entrance. Furthermore, some of the officers, including Luuk and Hans, managed to advance to the warehouse wall, allowing them to peer around the large opening to fire. Luuk and Hans now had either side covered and began to pin down two small groups of antagonists in the warehouse's interior. The gang started to retreat to a more central area within the warehouse, using pallets and plastic-wrapped boxes of inventory as cover. Luuk managed to shoot down two of the opposition and moved into the warehouse, finding shelter at the front grill of one of the lorries.

Meanwhile, Ted and Emilia entered the side door, which led to a corridor with multiple office rooms branching off its walkway. The offices had see-through glass for each separate room and some with blinds to provide privacy. Ted and Emilia progressed cautiously down the corridor, with Ted checking the left rooms and Emilia the right. All the rooms were clear so far and they had made it to the halfway point of the corridor before reaching an exit door that gave access to the warehouse facility. In the distance, there was the sound of groans and bullets thundering.

Ted sharply turned his body around as the sound of glass shattered behind his right shoulder. He saw a man holding a gun he had fired toward Emilia. Emilia fell back, hitting her back against the corridor wall, and she lost grip of her weapon as it flew backwards upon her impact. Ted fired three bullets at the man, piercing his chest and throwing him back over an office meeting table.

Ted quickly went to Emilia rescue, kneeling on one knee. Ted held her chest, but became confused as she was conscious, and there were no signs of blood.

"Are you okay, Emilia? Where were you hit?" Ted said
"Ouch, that hurt." She groaned with her eyes closed.
"Did you get hit?"
"Yeah, but I've got my vest on."
"That was a close one. I didn't see any of those in the

station," Ted said with a smile of relief.

"Yeah, I take it with me always, Ted. You should invest in one now you have a family."

"I will."

"Area is secure," Luuk said over the radio.

"The warehouse?" Ted replied.

"Yeah, all clear."

"Great work, team."

Emilia smiled back and nodded. "Don't you help a woman up when they're down?"

"Sorry."

Ted reached out his hand, and Emilia grabbed it. Through push and pull, she was back on her feet. Emilia started to unbutton her loose blue shirt, removing it and holding it out for Ted to hold. Ted caught a glimpse of her athletic body covered by armour and a white vest underneath.

"I won't tell anyone if you don't," Emilia said.

"Sorry, you didn't give me any warning."

Next, she unstrapped her compression vest and lifted it off.

"It burns when you keep it on."

She found the entry point on the armour where the bullet had compressed on impact and showed it to Ted. She grabbed the blue shirt off him and threw it back on, and clicked only a few of the buttons back together.

"Let's go see what the damage is."

Ted and Emilia made their way through the door to the warehouse floor and noticed the team in complete control of the vicinity. They both lowered their weapons, but his thoughts moved immediately to the welfare of the two girls found in the back of the van. There were two girls saved, but where were the rest of them?

CHAPTER TWENTY-SEVEN

THE DARKNESS WAS FRIGHTENING, AND THE unknown was even more so. The darkness paralysed Mabel's sight, leaving only the remaining four senses. She could hear the roar of the vehicle's engine and the muffled noise of voices in the connected driver's cab behind her. The sound of low-level cries from the passengers inside the container they were being transported in. The taste of sweat touched her lips as it dripped down her forehead, eyebrows and into her eyes and mouth. She felt the thirst from her lips and throat, even tasting the sweat was welcomed moisture She smelt the linger of urine too, which filled the van's container. She could smell something else but decided it was the smell of fear of the other people.

She felt the harsh irritation of the plastic zip tie around her wrists, bound together in front of her. She was comforted when she felt the bracelet too perfectly intact around her wrist—bringing back memories of her mother. She visioned in the darkness, horse riding along the dunes with her horse Laila. She would go riding on a secluded beach area with her mother, where they were free to canter along the sand as the waves crashed beneath them. Thoughts of guilt overwhelmed her as she remembered the last interaction with her mother before she went away and those last words she conveyed to her. She wanted to escape from the nightmare so she could relive the memories again, but to also tell her mother she didn't mean it and she was sorry. Hafwen had given up on her fight to escape and accepted her fate, but Mabel was ready to fight when the moment came.

Her legs began to go numb under the pressure of sitting down for a long time, including the period sitting on the warehouse floor. She estimated that she had been in the lorry for around eight hours maximum. The vehicle had stopped once for approximately ten minutes which she presumed was a rest break from driving. She hadn't slept the entirety of the time in the cab as guilt and planning overwhelmed her mind. From the journey, she was currently taking in the darkness, she guessed she might be travelling anywhere across the continent. Maybe eastern Poland, Italy, France, or one of the Balkans states, but she wasn't sure of the order they fit.

A few conversations broke out in the darkness, although most seemed to want to be with their thoughts. Mabel wondered if the other girls were reminiscing about better times in their past too. Those conversations that did break out in the darkness were about where they thought they were heading and what the men would do to them. However, it was clear to most of the girls that they had been kidnapped and trafficked. That caused a few girls to panic and hyperventilate in the container before being coached to regulate their breathing before passing out. Mabel couldn't promise the authorities were hunting them down but knew it was only a matter of time before missing person's reports would be published. She also thought that the apartment owner in Berlin, who they were meant to meet for check out, would have issued a report. Although how can you find an invisible person? She could be anywhere in Europe now.

Mabel hadn't spoken to her mother since she left to travel

but was in daily contact with her father. If she weren't to message him how she was doing, he would know there was an issue. She always had a great relationship with her father, stemming from when she was very young. He worked as a police officer, and was now retired, working a varied combination of long day and night shifts. There were times when she was in primary school when she would run to her father, waiting at the school gates when he was able to do so. As she got older, she would go on mountain walks up the Brecon Beacons in South Wales with her father and dog, Pip.

She felt the lorry slow down. The truck had slowed down at several moments during the trip, but not like this. It felt like a service station stop, but voices were coming from outside the container this time. The vehicle's engine shut off, and the sound of the cab's door slamming shut. There were loud voices outside in a foreign language. Those voices slowly drifted towards the back of the lorry where the entry point was for cargo. The bolts on the outside door made a harsh sound against the metal frame of the container. The doors opened, and it was night time outside. The light from a torch blinded her eyes momentarily. She looked away and squeezed her eyes shut, and blinked a few times to try and regain her vision. The torch's light was moving around the vessel wall, then suddenly switched off again, bringing darkness back to where she was sitting.

A man's figure lowered the torch to his side and waved forward to the closest girl sitting next to the door. "Move now," he said, "Everyone up".

The first girl did as instructed and rose from her position with her wrists tied together at the front. Mabel's eyes readjusted to the impact of light on her retina. The man looked back at her with a harsh stare. It was the man who killed Hafwen. She returned a powerful look at him with profound evil in her eyes. She didn't sleep much during the journey as she visioned how she would get revenge for her friend

Hafwen. She ran different scenarios in her mind, which started to haunt her and affect her judgement as desperate desire overruled intelligence. She decided at that moment, as she prolonged the stare, she would wait for her time and wait for the right moment, if that moment ever came.

The nightmare continued for now.

CHAPTER TWENTY-EIGHT

THE GIRLS ENCLOSED INSIDE THE CRASHED van received medical treatment from the paramedics who had arrived. The girls were no older than twenty years old and seemed shook up and distant from the many questions they were asked. The two men shot dead inside the van were identified as Vlado Petrovic and Farkas Arany. Farkas wasn't known to the operation but was found on the German criminal database. Farkas had been arrested in Germany and Romania for multiple frauds and money laundering counts but wasn't on their inventory for the OCG members. Five warehouse members were shot during the exchange of gunfire, six if you include the one that nearly downed Emilia in the office walkway. The deceased had ID documentation on their persons of Romanian or Hungarian nationality.

There would need to be a fast but thorough investigation of the warehouse and the facility. There were no passengers on board within the two parked lorries in the warehouse, which was disappointing, but the two girls' saviours were a joyous grace. In addition, the incoming information from the warehouse invasion may trigger suspicion from the higher-ranking members of the OCG to the intensity of the operations chase. Mobile devices, weapons and ID documents were bagged and seized to evaluate back at the station. The techno genius' would need time to access the electronic sims and hardware data, time which the team may not have.

"Have we got units going over to the organic facility?" Luuk said

"On their way now," Hans replied.

"Once we finish here, we will head over. Tell them to enter and secure it but don't touch anything," Ted said.

Hans moved away from the group and made the call over his phone, relaying the message to the secondary unit at the compost facility. Emilia, Fenna and a few of the Berlin city police officers had interviewed some of the employees hiding out inside one of the raised office containers above the warehouse floor. The employees, who were a mixture of Polish, German, and Turkish immigrants, were bullied and forced to participate in trafficking girls. A few broke down in tears as they knew they had assisted the horrible crimes. Some employees were upset because they had no valid working credentials to work legally in Germany and feared deportation.

One Polish man who was twenty-three years old explained that their boss, Jürgen Hahn, who owned the freight forwarding company by the same name, forced the men to work extra hours for the same daily pay. There were promises of double time for any overtime they did. However, when the payments never arrived, they were bullied into doing the shifts without question because they were illegal workers, there was no employers contract they could refer to. Either they worked the extra shifts or worried about finding a new job that employees would risk taking on illegally or face returning to their homeland. The man wanted to report the activities at the warehouse, but he was scared. He often didn't sleep at night, seeing the girls' faces before the shutters fell, locking them in the lorry.

Another illegal worker mentioned men from Eastern Europe joined the company on shorter selective work patterns. They attended the warehouse and worked when they were transporting the women. None of the workers knew any of the OCG members' names when the overnight transport happened. Jürgen, the company boss wasn't on shift tonight; however, it wasn't hard to find Jürgen's paperwork in the offices listing him as the registered owner of Jürgen Hahn Speditions GmbH & Co. A patrol of officers was on their way to his house shortly after midnight.

Upon further investigation, official records on the history of previous exports were kept on the company's central system. Documents showed the forwarding of technological equipment, medical care, and mechanical machinery to different German destinations and some as far as Italy, Austria, and Poland. There were six thousand documents on freight forwarding services done that year, with the paperwork of its twenty-one legal employees.

Karl appeared from behind one of the stationary lorries on his mobile device and caught Ted's attention.

"Any news on the car?" Ted said

"Just received word now. They're still following on autobahn 13 south, and they're just north of Dresden currently."

"Any guessing where they are going?"

"Well, at the moment, they are taking the main route back to Hungary if we are thinking ahead."

Ted nodded in agreement. He knew that to the southeast were the Eastern European bloc countries. Without a visual, he knew the country south from Dresden was the Czech Republic because he once passed through there on a train from Prague when he was on holiday with his wife.

"If they take the autobahn 13, they will merge onto the four by Dresden Airport. The road goes from right to left, just north of the city. There is an exit onto autobahn 17, and this road takes you south into the Czech Republic. From there, we are not sure, it could be Brno, Bratislava, and then Hungary or anywhere," Karl said.

Ted spoke about Luuk's communications with various European police forces, which they could trust and contact to help support the continued continental pursuit. Luuk responded that he would get the Czech Headquarters against Organised Crime and, depending on the direction of the Mercedes, would contact other forces.

One of the female paramedics made their way through the two lorries towards Ted and the rest in the warehouse interior. The paramedic was dressed in a red and black high vis coat with matching pants and black boots. She was mid-thirties and had her blond hair in a ponytail. She reached out her hand to Fenna, who had introduced her to the girls as the medic arrived.

"Fenna right?" she said.

"Yeah, sorry, I didn't grab your name," Fenna replied.

"Monika. Hi everyone."

Everyone nodded and gave a smile in return.

"So, what did you find?" Ted said.

"They're fine, but I don't know about the long-term effects of this for them mentally".

Monika looked at the floor and then raised her head back up to the group again, this was something she had not witnessed before in her career.

"They've been injected with flunitrazepam or Rohypnol and Ketamine. A large amount, enough for a small horse, but I think the effects are starting to wear off."

"Okay, did they say much?" Luuk said.

"Mariana from Spain, Bilbao. She is Nineteen, and the other is Sofia from Naples, Eighteen. Both study here at the university."

"Are they injured? Hurt?" Fenna added.

"We did a medical examination on them, and through my visual inspection of the vaginal area, I can confirm they have both been raped, maybe a day or two ago. Both girls have also confirmed this to me too. They are very strong and brave girls, especially to admit this. We have collected samples from around the genital area, mouth, and fingernails."

A sombre mood clouded the air and a few seconds passed without a sound from any of the group. Monika broke the silence and said she would take the girls back to the local hospital, which wasn't more than five minutes away; it was the best place for them. She would update her team and pass the information to the local police force as and when she had it. The group thanked Monika for her time, and she exited the warehouse.

Ted's mind drifted momentarily to think about Vladimir, how he was holding up, and if he had passed through this warehouse recently? Miroslav was dead, and Ted was clinging to the hope he was still alive, but Ted may have given Vladimir the lifeline he needed.

A ringtone chimed within the group, and Hans picked up his mobile device from his pocket, turning away to speak. It was a quick call, and his face had changed in a matter of moments. He took in a deep breath as he digested the information to feed back to the group.

"The facility is clear, but it's not pretty."

Ted's chest sank. He had to be prepared for what he was about to witness at the facility

CHAPTER TWENTY-NINE

THE CAR'S HEADLIGHTS LIT UP THE ROAD AS IT approached the facility. The facility's complex was illuminated with the police's silent LED flashing lights and temporary metal tripod lamps set in the forecourt. The team exited their vehicles whilst Fenna stayed behind to take a more in-depth overview of the documentation at Jürgen Hahn warehouse. They were met in the forecourt by a senior police officer from the Zeuthen District Police, the next town north of Wildau. Other police forces from the city-state police were in attendance to offer support. Thorben Kafer was the senior officer at Zeuthen and was on the scene first to secure the area.

After the standard introductions, they made their way through the interior, which contained roomed officers from the front entrance. Potted house plants lined the corridors, but their leaves were weltered and dead due to the abandonment. The paint had begun to crack on the walls, and mould spread on the corridor's roof. The team followed Thorben as he directed them to the briefly described warehouse.

"So, it's not pretty. What is it we are walking into?" Ted said.

Thorben looked back as he spoke but continued to move

forward as he told them. "So, this facility has been abandoned for about a year now; the owner couldn't make a living off organic fertiliser, so he shut it down. No one has taken over here, and you can see from the outside it's not been maintained."

Thorben continued to move forward, shuffling past officers collecting stain samples on the worn carpet.

Thorben continued. "So just down this walkway, and if we turn right, we come to a walkway which leads to an open room. This was used for storage when the company was fully operating. In there, we have found blood samples, among other things. The OCG left nothing, but we have some forensics here collecting DNA and any fingerprints, so please don't touch anything."

"Thanks, Thorben. You say other things, like what?" Ted said.

"It's best if you look yourself."

They reached the end of the walkway, leading to a door with opaque glass in the middle of it. Thorben pointed down at two buckets before the door.

"Please put on these blue plastic overshoes and gloves," Thorben said.

They did as instructed, and Thorben opened the door for them to follow through once everyone was booted up. There was an aroma of must and dampness to the quality of the air. The large room had two large windows from two different points on the right-hand side. The room's walls were covered in sizeable industrial cement blocks with a single pillar in the middle of the room, presumably holding up its fragile roof.

"So, where do we look?" Luuk said, looking towards Thorben.

"Everywhere," the police officer said.

A knot twisted in Ted's stomach as he took in the visuals of the room. There were patches of wet areas at different intervals within the room. Ted looked up to the frail ceiling and saw no visible leaks from the roof. He also knew it hadn't rained for the last two days in Berlin and temperatures were hitting a high of thirty degrees, so it could be assumed it wasn't weather that had made its way into the property. The puddles were located by walls with single circular rings bolted into them. The rings looked similar to a door knocker, but these had started to age and rust. Some still had a short chain with handcuffs attached to them, and some didn't even have the handcuff attached, and the loose chain hung freely.

Ted knelt next to one of the dried patches and opened his nostrils to take in the scent. The pungent smell burnt his nostrils and made him feel sick. Ted noticed a full white-uniformed forensic woman was standing close by with a clipboard.

"What's the smell?" Ted asked.

The woman turned to answer Ted's question.

"Urine. Or more specifically, Ammonia. This is caused by dehydration."

"That's the smell I got."

"I've taken samples of the urine. We've got some blood spots too that we've started to collect. There is some vomit; we are checking these liquids to check for any drugs use. Please remember not to touch anything, please."

Ted raised his hands in surrender to comply.

"You're English?" the woman asked.

"Yes. I'm Ted Chester. I'm an International Liaison Officer from England. We've followed an investigation from Amsterdam to here. What's your name?"

"I'm Julia Lange, Forensic Crime Scene Investigation from Berlin."

There was no offer of a handshake due to the gloves they were wearing so as not to cause cross-contamination. Ted moved on past her towards the pillar in the middle of the room. He took in the three-sixty view of the surroundings. On either side of the large rectangle-shaped room was a closed door guarded by a police officer. One was the team's entry point into the room, but he was intrigued by what was behind the other door. Ted noticed Luuk was looking around frantically as if he was searching for someone until he locked eyes with Ted, asking him to approach. Ted made his way over to Luuk knelt with another forensic investigator and Hans.

"Look at this," Luuk said.

Ted followed the tip of Luuk's pointing finger and felt repulsed by the images in front of him. Again, a circular ring with a silver chain dangling from it and its handcuffs still attached. There was a stench of Ammonia again and something else which the team couldn't detect. There were tiny drops of blood around the size of a one-euro coin, positioned in similar proximity to each other.

"May I?" the forensic man said from behind them.

"Be my guest," Luuk said as he stepped away.

The man walked over to the blood spot, pulled out a cotton bud, and rubbed it in the dried blood. After writing details on the bag's label, he repeated this with different blood spots and placed them inside an evidence bag.

Luuk turned to the white-dressed man.

"What do you think happened here?"

"Hard to tell. Here, someone had a nosebleed, or there was some sort of altercation which caused a bleed."

Luuk nodded and stood up to face the team.

"Do you think this is where they've been holding them before shipping them off around Europe?" Karl said.

"Looks that way," Ted said.

"Any bodies?" Luuk asked Thorben.

"There's something else to show you," Thorben replied.

Thorben requested that the team follow him through the other double doors, which two police officers guarded. The officers opened the doors to allow the team to walk through. The door led them into a small room, around a quarter of the size of the larger space they had left. There were six large metal dumpsters of different sizes lined up against the room's walls. At the end of the room was a slight drop with a silver metal ramp used to load onto recycling lorries. One of the metal dumpers had two people in white forensic suits taking photographs of the contents within. Ted's throat became dry on the approach to the bin, and a spiralling of possibilities entered his mind. Thorben asked the forensic workers to step away for a few minutes to allow the team to inspect the contents of the container.

The soil broke down into its organic matter within the brown dumpster. Roots were sprouting out of the earth, and fungus was starting to peek through. Laying on top of the compost was a young woman in her late teens to twenty years old with long ginger hair. Her eyes were closed as she lay on her side; she had dark red smudges around her mouth and the dark red blood around her cut throat, which was starting to turn black as it dried. There were traces of maggots circulating her body, and blackflies swarmed from when they had entered the container. The summer weather was causing decomposition to react quickly, decomposers became more active, and the rate increased even after a day or two. The cocktail of smells invaded their nostrils, and some of the team had to cover their noses too. The group stood silently as they assessed the severity of what had happened to this young woman.

"Do you want to fill them in on your first inspections?" Thorben said to one of the white suits.

"Of Course. We can see on first look that the woman here has a laceration to the throat."

"This is how Hafwen died?" Ted said.

"Hafwen?" Thorben said.

"This is Hafwen Rees. We followed an abduction back in the city after two girls went missing; this is how we got even to be here or the other facility. It Looks like we were too late."

"We didn't get debriefed about that. How do you know it's her?" Thorben asked.

Hans lifted a sheet of paper out of his jacket pocket, which contained a printed self-picture from the club in Berlin and passed it to Thorben. Thorben examined the sheet, compared it to the woman's lifeless face in the container, and saw the resemblance, although their faces were completely different.

"I see," Thorben said.

"We investigated a missing person report for two women who didn't check out of their rented apartment. We went to the apartment to view the footage and saw the kidnapping. We identified the women on the tape as the two women she reported missing. We tracked the vehicle to Wildau, and this is where we are."

"Right. I've never seen anything like this before."

"Some of us here have done this before, but I'm in the same boat as you, Thorben," Ted said.

Ted turned back to the white-suited man again and asked how she died.

"Her esophagus was cut, and a rupture occurred, and this allowed fluid to leak into the chest and cause severe lung problems and breathing difficulties. From here, you can see the dry blood around her mouth and the darker stain on the soil around her chest area. She was coughing up and leaking blood quite heavily from the cut to the throat."

"We will see what forensics find with the blood and other liquids," Thorben said.

"Other liquids?" Fenna asked.

"Sorry, yes, she…" Thorben said, pointing at the white suit.

"She was raped, and I would estimate just before she died. We have observed bruising to the vagina area, and I've conducted a swab that we believe to be semen. However, we need to confirm this back at the lab."

Ted took a step back. The smell of the container and the description of what she went through before she died made him sick. He began to stumble slowly backwards from the group but remained undetected as the group continued to communicate. He manoeuvred his way to one of the open shutters where lorries reverse to get the flow of air into his lungs, as he steadied himself against the metal railing.

The team stepped back from the dumpster, and the forensic people swarmed into the vacant area to complete their work. As Ted slowly stepped forward again, he understood the grim reality of human trafficking and the idea that they could be easily thrown away like a piece of trash. He wondered if the blood spots on the floor back in the other room would match Hafwen Rees'. Maybe she fought back but was foolish to assume she could win, or they just decided to have their way. However, she would have been a valuable commodity on the face of things. It was unclear what happened to her unless you were there to witness it.

"There's something else too," Thorben said.

Thorben led them down a set of stairs leading to a door that led to an open yard area for vehicles. Immediately on the right was a small box building with a window that had bars on the outside. The window wasn't see-through and looked covered from the outside. Two metal tripod lights illuminated the room from the darkness as they entered. There were Turkish towels laid out in different areas of the room. String ran along in different angles to leverage towels to hang up to be used as wall borders. Within each sector were used water bottles, needles and candles. The Turkish towels which covered the floors provided a layer of mattress and duvet for those occupying the area.

"I have a feeling they didn't sleep here," Luuk said

Thorben shook his head slowly as he stared back at Luuk.

"Did they use them here for sex, the gangs? Or other people?" Fenna said.

"That's unsure at this time. However, the forensic team did find some used condoms, but they've not finished yet with the scene. We found the body and their attention was drawn away."

Ted looked at the window, where black bin bags had been taped up to block the view from either side.

"Thanks, Thorben. We may need you to keep us in the loop with this because we may be moving on," Luuk said.

"Moving on?"

"The gang has escaped, and we are tracking a car south."

A phone vibrated in one of the teams' pockets, and the team looked at each other, except for Karl, who pulled out his phone and answered it. Everyone was looking at Karl, waiting for an update on what they assumed would be the car one of the police patrol cars was following.

"The car is on autobahn 17 heading south to the Czech Republic, about five kilometres from the border," Karl said.

"Give the Czech authorities the heads up. Make sure they know not to stop or engage with the car. We need them to think everything is fine for now. I'm sure they'll figure it out soon enough, but if they get to their destination before that happens, we will deal with it then. Luuk, did you notify the other forces?" Ted said.

"The Czechs know, but I'll update them again," Luuk said.

"I'll get on to the Slovak police, and Hungarian police too," Fenna said.

Ted nodded back. Ted knew this investigation was going to develop. Hafwen's body was a costly reminder of the failings at the Amsterdam complex or reaching the Wildau complexes in much faster times. He knew Hafwen would have been a daughter to two parents, and Ted thought about his daughters and what it would be like to feel that pain. The thought hit him hard, and he missed them even more, but with the force he felt, it gave him the desire to carry on and new energy to fight on.

CHAPTER THIRTY

THE SKY WAS BRIGHTENING A MIXTURE OF RED and orange above Volkspark station as dawn broke, its light seeping through the window. The team had regrouped back at the station and summoned one of the police officers to collect their luggage from their respective hotel rooms. Some of the officers had taken some time to get some much-needed sleep in the police station's waiting room or empty cells, and Ted took some rest in the canteen, sleeping on one of the sofas provided for police officers. The team was waiting for the ANPR camera update for the vehicle they were tracking. Arrangements to board the team on a public plane or chartered fight depended on the final destination of the vehicle.

Once the team had rested, they had the hit of fresh pretzels and instant coffee, which gave them a short-term buzz. They gathered back in the boardroom to piece together the next steps. They knew they would need to proceed to another country to continue the investigation, and they were continuously tracking the car's direction. The Mercedes had crossed into the Czech Republic and had just passed south of Prague on the E50 road. Its projection would continue on this route and pass Brno, proceeding to the E65 towards Bratislava. If the car were to hit Bratislava, they would be two hours out from Budapest and one hour off Vienna, which was the next major city. However, the vehicle could turn off in any direction, so all options were open.

Luuk and Fenna had contacted the police from the Czech Republic and Slovakia to track the vehicle. The initial police vehicle that followed the Mercedes from Berlin gave up shortly after entering the Czech Republic. This wasn't due to not allowing entry to carry on their pursuit but to allow the officers to return home in line with their shift pattern. The new car following in the Olympic relay event was a police station in the northern Czech Republic, Ústi and Labem. Ted contacted the ILOs for Prague, Bratislava, Vienna, and Budapest, and they were all willing to help support once it was established the car was headed for their respective country.

The two men shot in the white van were identified as Vlado Petrovic and Farkas Arany. There were both Hungarian nationals, and using Europol's database Luuk discovered that Vlado was under investigation previously for drugs smuggling. However, the Hungarian authorities dropped the charges due to a lack of evidence pinning him at different points in the investigation's evidence chain. Europol was still investigating him but was waiting for new evidence or leads to help with a conviction. Farkas wasn't known to the Hungarian police for anything other than a DUI three years ago. Farkas had no known connections to the OCG but, like most, may have joined for criminality primarily for profit or sometimes forced, but this was unclear.

Most of the men who were shooting at the team in the warehouse were dead at the scene. However, two did manage to survive through intense medical treatment from another unit of paramedics, taking them to the nearest hospital. Both were stable and under police protection, with officers on their ward doors. The two men were Romanian nationals who had previous extortion, theft, and pimping charges on their criminal records. There were international warrants for their arrests, for extorting money from Romanian nightclubs that ran prostitutes. They had fled when they were both released on bail six months ago. The other men who died at the scene hadn't yet been identified.

"We've had a report of a female body found near Tempelhof Airport, and they found her in a dumpster around the back of the building where they have immigrant accommodation. I don't think it's connected, but I thought I'd let you know," Phillip said.

"Okay. Is it someone living there?" Ted said.

Ted remembered Vladimir mentioning about his accommodating being near the abandoned airport.

"She's a prostitute, but we don't think she was living there."

"Okay, investigate that for us. Cover all ground."

"I will do."

There was an update on the girls taken for treatment as they started their road to recovery. Counsellors the police had employed for officers with PTSD had some experience with rape victims and were being used to help support the two girls. Both families had been informed and were flying to help with the support process. The rape kits had come back as positive, and samples were collected, as well as medical overviews of their genital area. Monika, who was examining them, called Hans to update what the girls had revealed, and Hans placed her on the loudspeaker.

"So, the girls are holding up okay. Better than expected if you think about what's happened to them. I know we've talked about the rape kit. One of the girls, Mariana from Spain, Bilbao, said they were taken to a room with loads of towels. That mean much to you?"

"It does, yes. We found a room at a facility not far from where you treated the girls," Hans said.

"Well, she said they took girls at the same time in groups of two or three. Some of the men who came to visit them had sex with them, and some men they hadn't seen before too. They injected them with a needle, which was heroin, to space them out.

"So, men who weren't OCG would visit?" Ted said.

"She isn't sure who is who, just people she hadn't seen before, she said."

"Okay. If that older couple had CCTV, we would have them all, but they don't." Ted said the last part, more to himself.

"What about the car dealership?" Karl said.

"Yeah, but it doesn't show them entering the property. We could record the cars passing through and note the timed intervals and then get one of the girls to pick out their photo, but that may take some time," Ted said.

"Agreed, we can get the state police on it, though, whilst we keep going?" Luuk said.

The team agreed, and Monika discussed the second girl Sofia, from Naples.

"Sofia said they were the last two left in the warehouse after the rest of the girls were taken out. She wasn't sure they were, but they came back for them later on and then that was when we found them."

"How long in between the girls being taken and them coming back for them?" Ted said.

Monika looked like she was in thought, trying to remember the answer to a problematic maths question.

"Maybe a few hours, if that helps."

"It could do. It means they're already on route to where they are going." Ted said.

"Do you think it's the same direction as the Mercedes?" Luuk said.

"God, it could be," Ted replied

"There's more...."

There was a silence as the team waited for her to continue

over the phone.

"Okay, Was there a deceased person?"

"There was at the warehouse facility. Why do you ask?" Ted said.

"Sofia said girls called Hafwen and Mabel joined the morning before. They were lucky because they didn't go into the rooms due to being a Sunday and maybe a rest day or something. Sofia said one of the girls, Hafwen, wasn't eating her food, and the man told her to eat. She was scared or had given up on hope and spat in the man's face. He dragged her through some doors towards the recycling area. She never came back, and he had blood on his knife."

"That solves what happened then," Karl said.

Ted nodded.

"If we send some pictures through to you, could you show them to Sofia and Mariana to confirm who they saw?" Hans said.

"Certainly."

They thanked Monika for their update, and she said she would try and speak with them right away. A police officer from the state police approached Hans, and they were engaged in a conversation soon after the police officer moved on.

Jürgen Hahn's ready for us in the interview room," Hans said.

"Let's see him," Ted said.

"When you get out, we may have a flight ready for where we need to go, but the nation's police forces can keep watch until we reach there," Luuk said.

"Of course. Hans, try and push Monika for that confirmation on the pictures." Ted said.

Fenna broke into the circle of officers that gathered to listen to Monika's update. She was loud and full of energy.

"We've got news on the Hungarian car from the authorities, and it's registered to Jozsef Matis. He is a successful businessman with multiple companies in Hungary. He is fifty-years-old, starting his company with consumer goods and wines or something, and then developing his portfolio to agriculture machines, Iron, gas, and so on."

"Where are they now?" Ted said.

"Just crossed the Slovakian border."

"Hopefully, we will know more after we talk to Jürgen."

Ted left the group, reached for his coffee cup, and went to tip the cup to drink the remaining liquid. He decided against it, as he didn't need the energy any more.

CHAPTER THIRTY-ONE

JÜRGEN HAHN SAT IN THE INTERVIEW CHAIR alongside his lawyer. The camera was rolling, but the audio was off per the lawyer's request to protect his client. Jürgen was wearing a fleeced jacket and suited pants, with Chelsea boots. Jürgen had been woken up by a knock on the door at one o'clock in the morning. The knock awoke him, his wife, and his Golden Labrador, who barked at the door until Jürgen answered it. Jürgen grabbed the dog's collar and comforted it, it was just a puppy. Once he opened the door, he was shocked to see local law enforcement crowding his front garden in the small suburb of Hohen Neuendorf, just northwest of the centre of Berlin. The wealthy neighbours were curtain-twitching with the arrival of excitement or shame to the sleepy, quiet suburb, which was full of police lights. Jürgen was given his rights on his doorstep and told he was under arrest for assisting of human trafficking. Jürgen showed no resistance and went with the officers willingly to the station for questioning. He was quiet on the ride in, and when he checked into the station, he asked to contact his lawyer, who would be present during his interview.

His lawyer presented a statement once they were in the

interview room. Present in the room was Ted and Luuk, and onlookers behind the CCTV monitors set up. The audiotape was switched on, and the interview commenced.

"We have a prepared statement from Jürgen Hahn. He will not be willing to answer any of your questions at this time. We deny all of your charges and accusations. Any questions you do ask will be responded to with 'no comment', thank you," the lawyer announced.

The lawyer lowered the piece of paper back onto the table, took out two extra copies from his file, and placed them in front of Luuk and Ted to look at, even turning the form around so it was facing the right way for their view.

"And you are?" Ted said, looking at the Lawyer.

"Sorry. My name is Frank Gunter, and I'm representing my client here today," he said.

"I appreciate your prewritten statement, but we would like to ask a few questions which you have the option to answer or not, of course," Luuk said.

There was no response from Jürgen. This was a small test to see if Jürgen was in character and sticking with the prewritten statement or if that statement was his lawyers idea, and he could be easily persuaded to answer their questions.

"For the purposes of the tape and the recordings, can you at least acknowledge that statement from us?" Ted said.

Jürgen looked at his lawyer Frank. Frank exchanged a nod back in agreement.

"Yes, of course," Jürgen said.

"So, Jürgen, can you explain the armed men who were in your freight warehouse tonight?" Luuk said.

"No comment."

"Can you explain why two Eastern Europeans were trafficking two young women in a van from an organics facility to your facility?"

"No comment."

Ted unfolded his file and picked out an image he'd printed off before heading into the interview room. He placed it on the table and turned it the same way Frank did with the pre-prepared statement.

"Please find image one. This is an image of a body found in the same organic facility in Wildau that the white van came from to your warehouse Jürgen. Can you explain this?" Luuk said.

"No comment."

"Are you working with Eastern European gangs in sex trafficking?" Luuk said.

"No comment."

"You're a successful man, aren't you, Jürgen. You took over your father's business and managed to grow it beyond anything he could do. You're now a European continental transport business. More than just inner Germany or just the confinement of eastern Germany when your father Jürgen created it."

There was no response. Ted was expecting more to come from this during the interview.

"Were you approached? Threatened?" Ted said.

Jürgen remained still, but his eyes wandered to the left, towards his lawyer, but without moving his head to make it obvious. Ted had noticed this weakness and pushed on.

"We can protect you, Jürgen, if that's the case."

Now the lawyer was twitching his eyes in Jürgen's direction to spot any movement from him. There was a silence as Ted allowed his words to linger in Jürgen's mind, and Jürgen broke the silence no more than ten seconds later.

"Can I talk to my lawyer, please?" Jürgen said.

"Of course, we will step out for a minute. Let us know when you are ready to carry on." Ted said.

"Will you take the audio feed off?" the lawyer asked

"Of course. Interview suspended," Luuk said whilst switching the tape off.

Ted made a gesture to the camera to cut the feed. Ted and Luuk stepped up from their chairs, took their documents, and stepped outside.

"What you reckon?" Luuk said outside the door.

"I think he will deal. The evidence doesn't look good, and he may be willing to deal with us. He is going to want protection." Ted said.

"We will see what he gives us, but I agree," Luuk said.

Hans and Karl stepped out of the control room to get a moment with Ted and Luuk.

"Looks good. We could see him twitching," Karl said.

"Yes. What can we offer him?" Ted said.

"Witness protection for his wife and family. But the information needs to be good before I go higher with this. I don't know if we can let him off fully for being involved." Karl said.

"Okay, we will offer that in return for anything we can get," Ted said.

A knock came from the inside of the interview room door, and the door opened, the Lawyer stepped out.

"We are ready."

Once they were all seated, Luuk reached for the tape machine and switched the audio button.

"Interview restarts after a short break," Luuk said.

Ted reached out both hands towards the other side of the table to suggest the ball was in their court.

"My client is willing to answer some of your questions to the best of his knowledge. We want something in return for this arrangement, and my client wants witness protection for himself and his family," Frank said.

"I had a brief conversation with one of the German officers who said we could offer that if the information is good and true. We can promise protection for your family, but we will need to see about you. Please, Jürgen, tell us what you know." Ted said.

Jürgen nodded and started by presenting a detailed timeline of how the OCG approached him about a business opportunity. Around a year ago, when Jürgen was in the raised office container within the freight forwarding warehouse, a man approached him about a chance of moving shipments of medical equipment to Hungary. Jürgen advised him to make an appointment with him to discuss this in more detail when he had time available. The man left, disappointed. This man was called Jozsef Matis, who was already known to the operational team and was driving through Slovakia as they spoke, south of Bratislava.

Jürgen continued to say that Jozsef contacted him the next day and made an appointment for the following week and that is when they first met officially. The deal seemed to go successfully, and they drew up the paperwork for weekly transports. One demand from Jozsef was that ventilation was available within the cabins to allow the equipment to breathe. Jürgen helped with that particular request by adding air vents within the roof of the lorry trailers. Something which Jürgen added to Jozsef's monthly invoice. The first couple of transports were low and only managed to take up one-quarter of the trailer's maximum space, which Jürgen found strange due to the enormous transport costs.

One evening when the staff were finalising a delivery, one of the workers came up to the container to explain that two men had appeared and started to help with loading the medical containers for Budapest. Once Jürgen came out of his office to inspect the situation, he saw two men holding guns threatening to kill everyone if they said anything about what was happening. With the men were four young girls, no older than nineteen, being loaded into the back of the lorry. That was when he knew why Jozsef wanted the vents within the trailer. After the men disappeared, the men on duty pondered about reporting it to the authorities that night, and they decided against it because they didn't know what they were dealing with. Jürgen then tried to call Jozsef to discuss why he was abusing his business for such criminal activities. However, there was no answer to his call. Later that night, when Jürgen got home, a Mercedes car with Hungarian plates parked on his drive. Jürgen explained that he turned into his drive and saw the shadow of a man in the driver's seat. Jürgen entered the passenger side of the mystery vehicle and was welcomed with a gun to the temple. Jozsef held the gun and said if they ever told anyone about what was going on with the transportation, he would make sure that he and his wife would be cut up into small pieces and allow their dog to feed on them. Jürgen stated he only found out later that all the depot employees were also visited over that week and given the same threat. Some of the workers quit within the next few weeks, and it was hard to maintain staff retention due to the additional stress and guilt they were absorbing. Some of the staff that left Jürgen's employment died of heart attacks and chronic liver failures. Although Jürgen knew these weren't natural deaths, the deaths were classified as natural causes and were never investigated further.

Jürgen summarised that the OCG members would come in and help with loading their specialist cargo when transporting the girls. The employees would help with the mechanical machinery to complete the loading of the lorries whilst the gang placed the girls into the truck and observed the process. This would happen every other evening or at least twice a week.

At the interview table, Ted and Luuk sat in silence, taking in the narration from Jürgen. The Lawyer was rigorously trying to make his notes as Jürgen's emotional wall completely broke down. It was time to get all they could whilst Jürgen was willing to support them.

"How long has this been going on for?" Ted said.

"A year ago, near enough."

"How many girls do you know came through your facility

from the first day they arrived until the point you are sitting in this interview room now?"

Jürgen looked up like a lost puppy looking for remorse and acceptance.

"Yeah, I do. I wrote it down, and it's in my head every single day."

"How did you keep track of it all. You didn't work every day, did you?"

A tear started to fill Jürgen's right eye. He looked to be holding back his tears, but he let go and broke down when he announced the figure.

"A hundred and fourteen."

Ted waited for the waterworks to stop and gave him time to reset. Ted noticed his lawyer was still rigorously writing.

"Jürgen. This investigation has been moving very quickly, and we won't be here in person, but I assure you, if you cooperate with us and the German police, we can help you, okay?"

"Please take one, Jürgen," Luuk said, extending his arm towards the box of tissues.

"Yes," Jürgen reached for the box next to the recording machine, grabbing a few sheets.

"Why did you make notes on the number of girls? Do you know where the girls and trucks were heading to?" Ted said.

"I felt guilty. Every time they came and put them in the van, I would rack the numbers up on a fucking tally chart in my notebook. When I wasn't in, some of the employees would tell me how many came, and I would note."

"Where is this notepad?" Ted said.

"At my office at home. I'm sure if you get a warrant, you'll find it there."

"What else is in this notepad, Jürgen?" Luuk said.

Jürgen looked up.

"I know where they were taking them too."

Ted and Luuk looked at each other as if secretly celebrating in their heads.

"Where were they taking them, Jürgen?" Ted said.

"Budapest."

"How do you know?"

"When I worked, I heard the gang members talking about something, and they'd always say Budapest every single time. We also had a driver too...."

"Was the driver yours or the gang members?"

"It was ours to start with. He said he drove to some farm area outside Budapest, and then a van came to take them away. He left after a week; he couldn't cope with it and the threats." Jürgen said he died of a "Heart Attack", lifting both his index and middle fingers to mime the Apostrophe.

"Interesting," Ted said, looking at the camera that overlooked them.

"Where there any other people's names you remember?" Luuk added.

"None, just Jozsef. We never got the names of the other people who came."

Ted nodded and reached into his file and brought out a selection of A4-style photographs with mug shots of members of the OCG. He placed them on the table and spun them around for a better view for Jürgen. There were six individualised photographs that he scanned through. Ted pointed to each photo and announced the names of the men to Jürgen.

"Vlado Petrovic -Deceased, Miroslav Ilic -deceased. Zivko Dordevic, Luca Manu, Farkas Arany - deceased and Vladimir Balan".

"These two for sure," Jürgen said whilst pointing at Zivko and Farkas's photos.

"Him. He was like second in command, or boss when Jozsef wasn't around."

"Luca?" Ted said for confirmation.

"Yes. Not seen him for a week or so, though."

"Okay, good. Anyone else?"

"Not sure on this one, though," Jürgen said whilst pointing at Vlado.

"Not him?"

"Don't think I've seen him. The other guys I may know of."

"Okay, the last two?" Ted said whilst pointing at Vladimir and Miroslav.

"Yeah, I've seen them around a few times. Maybe not for a while either."

"Thank you. Are there others you've seen that aren't on these photographs?"

"Yes, there are a few more. If I saw their faces, I'd recognise them."

"You have CCTV at your workplace?"

Jürgen let out a slight burst of laughter and then stopped due to his inappropriate nature.

"Sorry. They erased the CCTV when working in our warehouse, and you know to delete the evidence. I've seen them change the registration plates on my lorries, for god sake. I was driving home from work just after one of the lorries went out, and I saw them in a layby just down the road changing my god damn plates."

"Do you have any CCTV backups?"

"Unfortunately, these people aren't stupid. They deleted that too."

"A few of our officers are with your employees. We thank you for your time, and someone else will take over this conversation and help with your counteroffer. Do you think your other employees will talk?" Ted said.

"Yes. They will be glad it's all over if they get protected, of course."

"Certainly."

"Will you let us know if you catch these horrible people?"

"I'm sure you'll see it on the news inside whatever room you'll be watching it in," Luuk said.

"What does that mean?" Jürgen responded.

"Figure of speech, sorry."

There was a double knock on the interview door, and Luuk and Ted agreed to call for an end to the interview. Ted said to Jürgen and his lawyer that they could get any refreshments on request, and Ted suggested writing up anything else valuable to the case and their defence. Ted and Luuk exited the room and found Hans and Fenna waiting in the corridor.

"So, we are heading to Hungary, right?" Luuk said.

"Jürgen could be right. Jozsef just entered Hungary about two minutes ago," Fenna said.

Ted nodded.

"Anything from the workers?" Ted said.

"A few spoke in the warehouse. All of them are now being asked questions by some officers, and Hans and Karl have stepped in to help. I spoke to one worker who said he heard Hungary being mentioned as Jürgen has said."

"Let's go back to the hotel and get packed. We've got a plane to catch," Ted said.

CHAPTER THIRTY-TWO

CROWDS FILLED EVERY INCH OF BERLIN
Schönefeld Airport, raising the check-in and security route
waiting time. The kiosk and refreshment areas had large
queues of people purchasing lunchtime refreshments and
souvenirs. The airport was closing in a year for a newly
refurbished Berlin-Brandenburg Airport. The new airport was
already delayed by eight years due to ballooning costs. The
new airport would home five terminals and help to shorten
the wait times that the team were currently experiencing.

The seating areas ran alongside a long window theatre of
the runway. Ted sat down on the uncomfortable metal seating
with a flat white and egg sandwich accompanied by mayo,
Lettuce on a cheese topped roll. This was one of his favourite
snacks when he visited one of the chain bakeries in Germany.
Ted was quietly eating his lunch whilst Fenna and Luuk were
reading their files on the case so far. Hans debated his lunch
options and had taken much longer but went for a pot of
Rouladen. This was a German meat dish consisting of bacon,
onions, mustard, and pickles wrapped in thinly sliced cooked
beef. Everyone was intrigued by the smell but passed on a bite
offering when they witnessed it.

The team was slightly depleted due to ongoing investigations in Berlin. Karl and Emilia decided to stay in Berlin to continue interviewing employees and recover any additional documents within the freight forwarding offices. Emilia was particularly interested in offering support to the two victims who were found and investigating the two men held in the hospital. Phillip remained with the city police forces leading the investigation at the warehouse. He also followed up on the dead prostitute discovered near the immigrant complex. She was a Lithuanian national, Janina Banis, living in Berlin, working out of Angel Club. She had bruises on her neck, and her trachea was crushed with no other visible injuries. He sent a team to interview some residents who identified several OCG members in photographs. Next to the large housing complex was a series of abandoned buildings once home to Tempelhof Airport. Inside the building were living quarters described as similar to a squatter environment, a shell from a pistol and blood marks matching Miroslav Ilic was on a wall next to a kitchen table.

Bartel and Zoe would return to Amsterdam after finishing their continued help in Berlin. Ted had phoned Sander to update the situation and the following steps to Budapest. Sander had decided for Finn's body to be returned to Amsterdam and to support his family's funeral after its initial release after the investigation. However, everything was quiet in Amsterdam, with no additional information to report. Sander updated that the two young scouts were arrested and charged with conspiracy to kidnap, with more evidence required to help support a much larger charge with the intent that Bartel and Zoe would support. Before they departed, Ted managed to catch Bartel to apologise for his false accusations about him being the OCG snitch. Bartel accepted the apology, and all was forgiven, leaving amicably as they went their different ways after a friendly handshake. Ted considered announcing to the group that Ted's own undercover operative was Vladimir rather than Miroslav all along, and he was still actively infiltrating the OCG. Under reflection, he decided he would tell the smaller group heading to Budapest instead, and the other officers would discover the truth when the time was right.

One of the suspects in Amsterdam, Erwin Jansen, was remanded in custody for forty-eight hours. Still, CCTV was released, giving enough time to review and find the evidence of Erwin stalking and intending to prey on the girls. The other scout named Sem Neilson, aged twenty-two, committed suicide in his apartment block. There were no signs of a break-in or suspicious activity, and it was currently not going into a murder investigation under the current evidence they had. The CCTV would also help identify that Sem took part in the kidnapping. Like Finn, their bank accounts received income payments from the Romanian electrical warehouse company near Timişoara. However, after the Romanian authorities came back about the company's address, the address was found to be a post-box in the rural countryside, although there was no history or records of the company.

With the team diminished, a new set of members were to join them when they landed in the Hungarian capital. The British ILO for Budapest, Edward Thomas, had been contacted and arranged to meet at Budapest Ferenc Liszt International Airport to pick the team up. The British Ambassador to Hungary, Lewis Hewitt, and senior officers with the Hungarian Rendőrség Police would be accompanying him.

Once the team completed their refreshments, a broadcast over the airport speakers announced that the flight to Budapest was now ready to board and to proceed to the gate. Other officers started to collect their belongings as Ted picked out his phone from his jeans pocket and began to text his wife. He had forgotten to tell her that the case was moving on to another country, and he would be further away than he was already.

Hey. I will be going to Budapest for a few days following the case. How are the kids? X

Ted rose from the rigid metal seat, stretched his body and grabbed his luggage from the gap next to him. He picked up the coffee he had purchased before and downed the contents, which were now cold. He threw the paper cup in the bin whilst pulling a face when it went down his throat. His phone vibrated, and it was his wife with a reply to him.

They're okay. They've had a few bad days with missing home. We are all just missing you, and keep safe. Ring when you get there? x

He knew that his job was affecting his family life and balance. The girls and his wife were beginning to miss life back in the UK. This case was unique in its cross-continental settings, but even the operations within The Netherlands still affected them. Amsterdam was never called home; Rose would never called it that. His wife gave up her life as a Secondary Teacher of Art to move. She planned to take time out to look after the children and allow them to merge into Dutch culture more easily and then apply for British schools, but she wasn't successful in her first attempt. This was his first ILO posting since his investigator role in the UK. The standard procedure would be to change location after two years, and he was just over a year so far in this one. They had first moved to a rural area outside of the city in Naarden. Around seven months later, they moved closer to the centre, to a townhouse near Westerpark, where they had been for four months. This was Ted's passion, and he knew nothing else but to follow crime and try to solve it. In these situations, he couldn't connect with his emotions or become empathic because he knew he needed it to stay balanced to survive. He knew that he wouldn't be able to hide from the conversation forever. Ted replied with a simple message.

See you all soon. Talk when back x

When he slipped his phone back into his pocket, the team started navigating through the crowd of people congregated around the automatic check-in boards. He tapped his jacket pocket twice to check his passport, and the boarding papers were there. As he caught up with the team, Ted's phone vibrated again. He thought it was his wife, but it was a number starting in +44, which he knew was Great Britain.

"Sorry, I need to take this," Ted said as he slowed behind the moving group again.

Ted pressed the answer button and stepped to the side to let others pass.

"Ted. It's Simon. How're things?"

"Hello, Simon, Busy. Just about to get on a plane to follow this investigation."

Simon Taylor was Ted's boss back in the UK, and Simon oversees the regional continental postings for ILOs around Europe.

"Budapest?"

Ted pulled a confused face. He hadn't reported to him about his progress as that would come after with the mountain of paperwork he would need to produce.

"Yeah, how did you know?"

"I called in at the Korps to catch you at the office about twenty minutes ago. But they said you were on your way to Budapest."

"No problem. Is the ILO for Berlin away? It's not an issue. I just wanted to know."

"Sorry Jordan wasn't available for you in Berlin. He is on secondment and wasn't reachable for you."

"It's okay, we managed. Anywhere nice?"

"Asia for three weeks. He's entailed to his annual leave, and he's turned his phone off. Clever guy."

"Sometimes you got to get away."

"How are you getting on with the investigation?"

"Well, we are tracking someone who is travelling to Hungary, and we have a freight service saying that their lorries were going to Hungary with girls in the back. After Amsterdam, we can't lose them again."

"You've flushed out the rats, so I hope you don't have any problems. Sander told me."

"Yeah, we were fighting an upward battle, and that's why we lost them in Amsterdam. We had them all there in that complex. We've had girls die...."

"Don't beat yourself up, Ted. You did everything right. There is nothing we can do. No one knew about Finn."

"I know. Thanks, Simon."

"Anyway, the reason I called. We will arrange a meeting with you when you return, but we have an opening for your two-year switch. That's around six to seven months, right?"

"Yeah, February next year. Go on."

"Athens. Daniel Belfield is moving on too around the same time. Hot too, can go island hopping with the family."

"Okay, great. Sorry, I know this is important, but I'll speak with you when I'm finished here."

"Of course. It's not fully confirmed, but I will let you know. Keep safe, Ted."

"Thanks, you too."

He ended the call and slid his phone back into his jeans pocket. Looking out through the window, he saw the car park of planes and those taxiing along the runways. His mind wondered about the thoughts of his next post, Athens. He had been before with his family and loved the place. Its historical and monumental landmarks, hipster vibe and colour, lively neighbourhoods, and good food. He would typically be excited about the prospect of a new chapter in his life, but two things halted his emotions. One was the importance of the next forty-eight hours in the case and the lives at stake; this wasn't a time to be selfish and think of his future. His family struggled with adapting to life abroad, and he felt guilty and a build-up of anxiety in his chest over the thought of being selfish in this situation again.

Ted broke away from the window and moved towards the gate where his flight was waiting. Once Ted caught up with the group, they were waiting to have their boarding passes and passports checked before walking down the tunnel to the plane. Ted passed a few tailenders in the queue and caught up with Luuk. Luuk turned to check on Ted's whereabouts and clocked him. He grabbed him so he could slot in behind him. Ted had his passport ready to hand to the women at the check-in desk. The steward checked Luuk's and Ted's credentials and Ted noticed the rest of the group had already moved ahead and were disappearing beyond the curve in the tunnel.

"Jozsef has checked into Boscolo Budapest hotel using cash," Luuk said.

"You just find out now?"

"Yeah, whilst you were on the phone. Hotel confirmed it. That was one of the officers from the police station there."

"Is that hotel the one next to New York Café?"

"The famous Café, yeah. You been before?"

"Yeah, once."

"You get around don't you?"

"We used not to have kids."

"They got a hit on the ANPR, and The Rendőrség followed him to the hotel. They're going to keep eyes on him and lay low until we get there."

Ted looked down at his watch then moved his luggage down the walkway.

"Let's hope there are no delays with the flight."

BUDAPEST

CHAPTER THIRTY-THREE

MABEL WOKE UP FROM HER SLEEP OF AROUND twenty minutes. She had closed her eyes momentarily and woke up with a jolt as she heard the sound of metal from another room. A few other girls in the room were startled, wondering where the noise may have come from. A few girls engaged in conversation as they speculated. A section of girls in one corner of the room had looks of panic on their faces. They could see around an entrance out of the gloomy room from their position. The entrance had no doors on them, so a visual of the outer hall could be seen from their view. There were faint noises, which sounded like screams but were muffled. She could see a man entering the room with a girl in her view. Her body was jerking under the strain of his grip. He held a cloth over her face, pressing hard against her mouth to stop her from shouting. The man was someone she hadn't seen before. He threw her down into one of the spaces, which occupied a chain to hold her like the rest. The man tied her up as her voice got louder. Another man appeared from the opening with a needle in his hand. The other man completed tying her up and held her down so the man could give her a shot into her arm. The two men glanced around the room and exited through the entrance. The girl's breathing slowed down, and she started to calm and visually looked tired. Mabel thought this may have been the same drug she received when she woke up with nausea.

The room was similar to Berlin's, but this was much darker with no natural light. A singular bulb was hanging from the ceiling, which was dull and not providing much light. Across from Mabel's position was Amanda, the girl she spoke to briefly back at the other warehouse. Amanda seemed more distant and unapproachable after the events of Hafwen, although Mabel wasn't sure if this was it. She heard some of the girls crying about something that had happened to them before Mabel and Hafwen arrived. Where somebody took the girls somewhere with loads of men, but Mabel hadn't experienced this horrific experience. She started to think that Amanda was angry that they hadn't put her through it yet.

Her eyes were heavy, and she was battling to keep awake. She wanted to remain awake to seek the perfect opportunity to help her situation. She was unaware of where she was, but if she could get a chance to run, she was confident she could be a good match for anyone. In school, and recently in the sixth form, she competed in cross country competitions and knew how to pace herself when running long-distance. Special memories of participating in contests during school hours and spending time with her grandparents, who took her to the different venues with a McDonald's meal as a reward at the end.

Another reason she didn't want to sleep was because she was reliving every step of Hafwen's last moments. She wondered what was going through her mind to provoke the man and if she felt scared, fearful, or wholly done with her outcome. What happened behind the door was what scared her. The man who cruelly ended Hafwen's life ran through her mind every single second of the day. His face imprinted into the inner parts of her eyelids when she closed her eyes and everywhere in the present. She fantasised about what she would do to him if she got the chance.

Mabel's eyes closed and Hafwen's final moments before she was dragged through the double doors by the man played in her dream. Her mind then flickered to the man's face looking over her and stroking her face with a sinister smile. Suddenly her dream uncovered a past event that unfolded earlier that year. She was out in the city at a nightclub in Cardiff with Hafwen and other friends. A man around the same age as the man who ended Hafwen's life approached Mabel, and after declining his advances, the man went away. He soon came back to try his luck again.

"So why did you say no?"

"I'm not interested, sorry."

"You're stuck up, you whore."

"Excuse me?".

"You heard me."

Mabel threw the contents of her glass onto the man's new white oxford shirt, staining it in the process. The intoxicated man stepped toward Mabel and reached for her throat with an angry expression on his face. Mabel took a step to the right, grabbing his hand and dragging it around his back and holding it in place whilst holding his shoulder to stop his movements. The man surrendered, with his pride bruised he left her alone and probably left the nightclub.

Her eyes opened again, and she thought about the moments she reminisced. The man who approached her in the club deserved what he got, but this was a whole different level. She took it as a sign, a sign she would face the man who took Hafwen.

CHAPTER THIRTY-FOUR

THE ONE HOUR AND TWENTY-FIVE-MINUTE journey went without delay. The heat was like Berlin but with a gustier breeze to go with it. Ted selected a window seat on the plane and took an aerial view of Budapest on the descent. The views took in the Danube River and its riverside monuments, such as Buda palace and the Hungarian parliament building. The landing was a little bumpy, and at the end of taxiing to their spot, they exited the plane. Once they went through security and made their way to the automatic doors to the main concourse, they saw a group of people waiting for their arrival—some families with children and some men and women waiting for whoever they may be anticipating. There was a man with a slight build, short brown hair, a kept beard and sunglasses riding on the top of his head. The man was holding a sign displaying: **Ted or Edward?**

"Nice names," Ted said, pointing at the sign on his approach.

"Sorry, my attempt at humour. Ted is short for Edward." The man said.

"I know, but it's just Ted. Nice to meet you, Edward, I assume?"

"Yes, it is."

Edward exchanged pleasantries with Ted, introducing his operational team. Edward said that Lewis, the British Ambassador to Budapest, was waiting by the taxi rank in the car. The group noticed, waiting a few metres away, were four armed Hungarian police officers. They looked straight-faced until they approached to ask if the team wanted any help with their hand luggage, which was politely declined. As they made their way out to the street, a Mercedes V 8-seater vehicle was waiting just in front of the New York-style queue of taxis. The driver immediately exited from his seat and opened the boot taking their luggage. Edward opened the rear passenger door, which revealed seven seats in the back. He manoeuvred to the side and took the front passenger seat instead. The armed police officers left the group and crossed the street to a parked police vehicle. Taking one of the spots inside the Mercedes was Lewis, who exchanged greetings as they took their seats.

"Nice weather we are having," Lewis said.

"Yeah, nice beaches in Buda, are there?" Fenna said.

Lewis laughed.

"No, but I heard there are some nice lakes in Berlin where you've been."

The team smiled but was unsure how to continue the conversation into a more serious matter, and they didn't need to as Lewis pressed on.

"So, let's get straight down to business, we all know who everyone is, and I've been informed of your work so far from Edward this morning." Lewis said

"Yes, but there are other people who haven't travelled with us who have led us here too," Ted said.

"Of Course, you've had a good team with you across borders, and thanks to them, you are here. It's unusual, though, from our experience. Normally when someone enters your space, you don't let them be the bull that enters the China shop. But we don't often have Europol on our team."

"I need to tell you something in the strictest confidence," Ted said.

Edward turned his head around from the front passenger seat, and Lewis leant forward with his arms spread as if to accept his request.

"Of course. Sure," Lewis replied.

"Is the driver someone you can trust?"

The driver looked in the rear view mirror and looked back at the group.

"You can," he said in an Eastern European accent.

"He is one of our guys. Trusted and fully vetted," Edward said.

Ted nodded to the driver, who was still looking at the mirror intermediately as he was driving. The driver returned the gesture. Ted noticed he reached down into a holder by the gear stick, picked up his headphones, and placed an earpiece in each ear. He picked up his phone and touched the screen a few times, and set the phone back down. Ted presumed he was putting on music to mute his ability to hear the group's conversation.

"So, we have an informant inside the OCG."

Lewis rested his body against the leather seat and looked out the window as the vehicle moved along the busy dual carriageway. Edward was still facing the back of the car and was the first to speak.

Luuk, Fenna and Hans had visible looks of confusion, glaring back at Ted.

"How long has he been under?" Edward said.

"About six months."

"Who is he? He reliable?"

"Vladimir Balan, he is, and he has helped us get to where we are today. He's laying low now, though. This is to be kept between us, no one else. None of your officers in Budapest."

Ted turned his body to face the three members, unaware of Vladimir Balan being the undercover operative and not

Miroslav Ilic, who Ted announced back in Berlin.

"I'm sorry. I had to lie to uncover the real snitch in the team, and I couldn't risk Vladimir's life to expose the real person."

Fenna dropped her head to the floor and then back up to face Ted, smiled, and nodded. Hans nodded and looked out of the window to the dual carriage road they were riding along.

"Totally understand, Ted, don't worry," Luuk said with a smile.

Ted proceeded to tell Edward and Lewis about his various meetups with Vladimir at the Angel Club and Mauerpark. Through Mauerpark, they arrested two men, with a missing report of the two girls linking the men's illegal activities. This, in turn, leads them to the Air BnB apartment, Wildau and now Budapest. He also told them about the OCG's informant Finn and Ted's suspicions from Amsterdam that someone was leaking information to the OCG. Announcing to the team under false pretences, Miroslav was the informant inside the OCG. Subsequently, his body was found in the River Spree, confirming Ted's suspicions were correct. He explained the event at the police station with the demise of Finn, and the conversation reached a natural ending point; then Luuk looked forward to Edward.

"Have you heard from your team on Jozsef?"

"Yes, we've had some movement from Jozsef since your flight. He went to the Café downstairs; you know the New York Café? He ate and went back up to his room. We have a team monitoring from the lobby and out-front if he moves," Edward said.

"Okay, good. I hope that he is our chance of getting to the girls before it's too late," Ted said.

"Me too," Fenna said.

"I agree. We have a good team here, and we will give you everything you need. Cars, surveillance which is already in place now, and we have the cameras in our possession also."

"Sounds good," Ted said.

"Who's the team going to be here?" Luuk said.

"Good question. Edward can tell you that," Lewis said.

Lewis held his palm out, facing Edward, who turned in his seat again to look back at the group.

"Well, myself and Lewis. Lewis will be the go-between regarding the politics required to make everything happen. We know that there is British involvement in the victims, so he will be involved with anything relating to the family or Media.

"No information to the media," Luuk said.

"Of course. We won't give them anything they don't need to know. However, we're starting to hear mumbles that the papers back home are picking up on this story. We have other ambassadors from other countries, too, working with us on that, as some have already been reported missing but we are aware that some of those girls may have gone missing in other countries. We have contact with Amsterdam, Berlin, Paris, Brussels, Krakow and more too, communicating on the missing reports."

"Who else do we have on the team," Ted said, pressing on.

"You'll have senior officers from Rendőrség force," Edward said.

Edward kept his position over the divider between the front driver's section and the back and handed over a file. It contained the six other officers' names and photographs with their work history and vetting information to further clarify their officers' trust. The folder included Léna Garay, Keleman Fazekas, Victor Krizan, Andor Laszlo, Bodor Rabey and Anne Petrus.

"Can we trust the government? No offence, and they don't have the greatest of representations," Fenna said, looking up from her copy of the sheet.

In Hungary, partner violence is high, and twenty per cent of women come from a family where the father beat their mothers, which continued with themselves at twenty-five per cent. Most of the issues around this are because the government deny this happens. Hungary had just signed the Istanbul Convention, which aimed to prevent domestic violence against women. Nevertheless, the government has not implemented its terms and lacks intervention, which concerned the team on their arrival about how officers may perceive the situation and simply accept it and dismiss it.

"I understand. There are always complications, especially here, but we approach like you, and we want to make a change in any way we can, which is our priority. To help you," Edward said.

"Thanks, Edward," Ted said.

"Is that the Puskás stadium?" Hans said, pointing out the window

Edward turned to face the front and straightened up in his seat.

"It is. You a football fan?" Edward said.

"Yeah, Werder Bremen. I moved to Berlin two years ago, so I don't get to see them too much now. But Puskás is one of those legends you know", Hans said.

"He is."

"You into football, Ted?" Edward continued.

"Yeah, Liverpool is my club", Ted said.

"Nice, doing well now you've got a good manager".

"I know. Brought back the good years."

"He certainly has."

"Shame it's one of those summers where there's no football until August, and there's no international tournaments. Got to force myself to watch cricket."

"You never play cricket in school?" Edward continued.

"Yeah, I was good; but I can't waste a day watching or playing cricket with a family now. I won't have one to go back to, nor would I have the time. Who do you support?"

"Swansea."

"I was getting a Welsh tone. I like Swansea, a good team."

There was an exchange of smiles as the conversation died. As the vehicle moved along the busy city road, there was silence. Edward pointed out the passenger window towards a side road.

"We're nearly here," Edward said.

CHAPTER THIRTY-FIVE

THE MERCEDES ARRIVED AT THE BUDAPEST, VII. District police headquarters. Their journey continued past the Puskás Stadium and followed a road that led towards the City Park. Városliget, home to Vajdahunyad Castle, Széchenyi Thermal Bath and Budapest Zoo were significant attractions for many. District seven which the police HQ was in, was known as Terézváros and is home to the Hungarian theatres and state opera along its Broadway tree-lined style street. There is a mixture of tourist hot spots, such as Heroes' square and the darker side of 20th-century Hungary inside the House of Terror. Its exhibits display the fascists and communist regimes and a memorial to the victims of these regimes.

The team unloaded their luggage and made their way up to one of the conference suites inside. The exterior of the building wasn't appealing, with its dingy grey paint and unkempt appearance, lacking attention since the 1960s. The only modern colour was the white and blue Rendőrség Audi vehicles flooding the car spaces at the front of the building. The team made their way to the fourth floor, passing through one of the main control centre rooms—and to a long rectangle table with enough seating arrangements for fourteen people in the conference suite. Half of the seats included Rendőrség officers who were joining the operational team. Ted placed his luggage down with the others and walked to the window to view the street below. The view out of the window wasn't aesthetically pleasing, with just a Nail Salon and School forefront to view. Ted turned towards the table and took up an available seat, and the other officers also took theirs. Pleasantries were exchanged at the table as a welcome before Edward started the meeting.

"So, we have Jozsef in the hotel now. He has an entourage at the hotel, so we need to be careful with our positioning and distance if we follow him. I know he didn't have one coming down from you in Berlin, but a car was tailing him for protection when he crossed into Slovakia. So, the Slovak Police Force and NAKA, National Crime Agency Slovakia kept their distance and picked up the Slovakian plates on the tail car registered to a Ján Varga. He's someone the Slovakian and other border forces have been interested in, so too, Europol. He's a hard man, built like a boxer, used for security. He has previous for assault, Fraud, pimping and movement of drugs. We can't prove it, but we believe he is out of jail because someone paid someone high up in the Slovak government to hide evidence; it just magically disappeared, and he was released."

"Great trust here then," Luuk said.

"We have a good team here. It's just us, no one else, and I requested that, so please don't fight among yourselves," Edward said, looking at Ted.

"I understand why you are nervous about this. But It's good that we have people we can trust," Edward continued, looking at the group to reassure confidence. "We know victims are young girls and young women who are forced into prostitution or sex slavery. It seems to be more common across Europe in many different countries, as you know. They are so artful we can't detect, nor can we convict them. But you are close with this group, and that's the most anyone has done been for years," Edward said.

"Most missing cases aren't realistically correct. We get reports to Europol of ten to eleven thousand per year, but there's nearly two hundred thousand! So, you can see why we are nervous because we are so close. You understand what happened in Amsterdam, but as Ted said, I'm on board, and I won't mention it again," Luuk said.

"Thank you. It's a profitable business, and lack of punishment increases its desire. Rich people buy and enslave the girls into it, and they will pay top money for it too. But it's too big to manage to contain. Money is power," Edward said.

"You ever been involved in a case like this, Edward? This is my first," Ted said.

"I was here in 2008 in my first post as an ILO. Since then, I've been to Berlin, Greece, Romania, Belgium, others, and now I'm back. These are the ones you think about the most you know; there are so many who have gone missing over this time. They stay in your mind, in your dreams sometimes, or call it nightmares."

Ted stared at his notepad in front of him, flipping the pen in his hand. He understood what Edward was describing. Since the Amsterdam complex, he had the girls' images in his mind and nightmares when he managed to sleep. Edward continued.

"There's one. Someone called Esmée Bretnache back in 2008. She was a French student. Her belongings were found on Széchenyi Chain Bridge. A couple walked the bridge around midnight and saw her walking ahead when a man followed her. They assumed they were a couple arguing, but then they started sprinting. When the couple got to the Buda side of the bridge, they found a purse and phone by the underpass, which ran under a roundabout. There was no sign of either the man or the woman. Her body was found on an island in Csepel, in the 21st district just south of the city. On investigation, we saw a vehicle following them along the bridge on the CCTV, which the couple hadn't spotted. We got the plates and ran them, but they were stolen and not traced".

"Then, the man following Esmée was traced to the Budapest University of Technology and Economics, a local student twenty-one years old. We released photos, and one of the students recognised him. We arrested him and questioned him, but he did the silent treatment, but you could see the fear in his eyes. We kept him in a cell overnight, and then he hung himself. He used the bedsheets as thin as possible to get them around the thin threading of a bolt in the ceiling. Once we got warrants and checked his bank details, he'd received huge deposits from a company in Romania. This was traced back to a Romanian abattoir business. Naturally, this was followed up with the help of the Romanian police. This location was an abandoned warehouse that was a slaughterhouse but hadn't been used for five years due to protests for it to be stopped. We found five bodies and linked them to reported missing girls from across Europe, some as far back as 2005. They were decaying and starting to liquefy. I've never got over the smell. It was like a sex dungeon with pretty towels used as walls for separate rooms hanging on a string. The gang had long gone, and we lost the lead from there. Everything went cold. The student could have known something, but we had nothing. So, you understand why I want this as much as you do," Edward said.

There was a silence in the room as the officers absorbed the story from Edward's haunting memories. The room had an ambience of togetherness, and each officer seemed to use that pain and convert it into desire.

Luuk spoke next.

"We had a case in Paris, didn't we, Fenna. Listen, we've had many missing cases with different outcomes. But to end on a positive note here, so we all have the belief. There was a similar situation in France with the girls in the Airbnb. We got the car on CCTV taking them away from the scene. We lost them on CCTV after that. However, a car was involved in a traffic accident just by the Arc de Triomphe. Hit and run, didn't stop. We got the plate from the guy who reported it. It turned out that it was the same car that fled, but now with changed plates. We got those new plates on CCTV, and we followed them to a house outside the city. Six girls were kept in there. All as young as sixteen or seventeen. All drugged up too. We saved them all, but we only got the low levels of the bigger OCG. But we managed to save six girls. These girls now, wherever they are, we need to get them fast. We're running out of time."

"As I said, you've done good work. We need to break this open, and that's what we are going to do," Edward said.

"I agree. Jozsef is the key in this now. How's it with the Media, Lewis?" Ted said.

"Stable for now. We know that the British girls' parents reported them missing and could be going public with this soon. Local news and now national news agents are starting to circulate like sharks. I will make a response in due course, but at least we are on the investigation, at least for them."

Ted nodded, and there was a heavy knock on the door.

"Come in," Edward said.

The door opened, and a young female officer stepped in but held the door open as she stood in the doorway.

"Jozsef is checking out," she said.

Edward looked at the female officer and told her thanks. He then turned back to the gathering of people at the table.

"We will get surveillance equipment readied. Get the undercover cars ready." He replied to her. As she exited the door and it shut, Edward looked around to the rest of the table.

"Let's go."

Everyone got up from their seats, swiftly gathered their files, and rapidly exited the room. Each team member thought this could be a pivotal point in the case and a significant break to get those involved and save those lives before they were lost forever. Ted looked around the room as everyone exited, and everyone seemed to have a fire in their eyes, unlike before. For once, he had a good feeling about Budapest.

CHAPTER THIRTY-SIX

JOZSEF LEFT THE BOSCOLO HOTEL WITH THE help of a valet bringing his Mercedes to the front for the privilege of around 9,000 Hungarian Forint. Jozsef was wearing casual clothes as described by the undercover officers on the pavement by Habakuk bár, across the road from the hotel. Once Joszef was driving, he made his way past the first set of lights at the crossroads for Blaha Lujza tér station. He then took Rákóczi út west towards the Danube River. Another vehicle followed, the driver identified as Ján Varga. Officers followed at a two-car distance, noticing that both cars made an illegal turn left at the crossroads for Astoria train station and took Vámház körút south, heading towards the Liberty Bridge. The police had the authority to pull him over for this offence, but the bigger picture was necessary.

The operational team was making a similar direction towards the river along Andrássy út, the Budapest boulevard passing Magyar Állami Operaház. They made a left turn onto a road that led toward Vámház körút, which was a little further back from Jozsef's location. The team travelled in three different vehicles, with Edward, Ted, and two Hungarian officers in one. Fenna, Luuk and Hans were with another officer driving, and the remaining officers completed the last vehicle. The car full of officers followed the hotel and reported them passing the Nagy Vásárcsarnok just before the Liberty Bridge. Nagy is the largest and oldest indoor market in the city, with two floors full of groceries, souvenirs, and hot and cold food.

"He is crossing the Liberty Bridge," Victorone, of the tailing officers, said over the radio.

The Liberty Bridge was green and connected Buda and Pest across the River Danube, Budapest's southernmost public road bridge. Crossing from Pest to Buda, the view from the bridge takes in Gellért Hill, which is 235m high, overlooking the Danube and cityscape. On approach was the view of the Gellért Hill Caves and Liberty Statue, which commemorates those who sacrificed their lives for the independence and prosperity of Hungary.

The Mercedes turned left off the bridge passing the Gellért Thermal Bath on its right, when he suddenly turned into the neighbouring Danubius Hotel Gellert.

"He's turned into Hotel Gellert," Victor radioed again.

"He's either meeting someone or parking there to use the baths. If you pay ahead, you can use the car park for whatever you want, as long as you pay," Edward said.

"What about Ján Varga?" Ted said.

"He's pulled in too and parked."

"Thanks, Victor"

"What do we think?" Fenna said to those in the vehicle.

Edward put his hands together, both his index fingers pointing up to his mouth.

"Did you pack your swim clothes?" Edward said.

"The baths?" Fenna said.

"I think so. It's a common meeting point for business across the city. Especially away from the tourist hotspot in the central park."

"We're going to stick out like a sore thumb in there

without swimwear if we're going to follow," Luuk said.

"Both are entering the Baths, and we're driving up and around again," Victor said.

Anne, one of the supporting officers, heard of the bath's confirmation in the other car.

"We can rent swimwear in there if needed."

"Looks like we will have to," Edward said.

"No weapons. Too risky, and I don't think they'll be armed unless they know someone to let them in. If we go in and declare them, someone may alert them," Ted said.

"Agreed. There are metal detectors too."

Another officer, called Léna, spoke over the radio.

"We had a case recently when uniformed officers come in to follow someone with guns. Someone let them know we were coming, and they escaped over the wall of the outdoor spa."

"How are we doing this then?" Luuk said.

The plan was for Ted, Edward, and Luuk to enter the baths with Anne and Fenna, who would enter as a separate group. Hans and the remaining officers circled the surrounding roads, spotting a side street just a few metres beyond the hotel with off-street parking on Kemenes U. Edward parked the car there, leaving their service weapons with the other officers who were remaining on the street. The team entered the baths from the right of the building on Kelenhegyi Way.

The complex was built in 1918 in an Art Nouveau style. Before the reign of the ottoman empire, baths were built on the site and deemed for their magical healing springs. More recently, the baths underwent renovation in 2008 and are visited daily by thousands. The team paid for entry and rented swimwear from reception for their retrospective genders, got towels and a compulsory cap for the swimming pool.

The complex layout included thermal baths and small water pools from Gellért Hill mineral hot springs. The smell of the water was because of its calcium, magnesium, chloride, sulphate, and other elements. The complex also included changing room facilities, saunas and plunge pools, an outdoor open-air swimming pool and a Finnish-style sauna with a cold pool. The famous main hall with the gallery has a large pool with walkways, a glass roof built in the same art-nouveau style and surroundings, and the baths are decorated with beautiful mosaic tiles.

Once the team was dressed, they implanted their small-sized earpieces for Bluetooth communication in the changing rooms. They split off around the complex, with Luuk taking the outside area, and Fenna and Anne made their way to the large indoor swimming pool. Ted and Edward made their way to the two heat pools situated at the back of the complex, recording at 30 degrees and 35 degrees with an adjacent plunge pool.

"If you spot either of the individuals, let us know. We all know their faces?" Ted enquired.

"Yes. Will know when we see them," Luuk said.

"Yes. Will do," Fenna said.

Ted and Edward made their way through the maze of changing cubicles, past the shared thermal pool, beyond the main indoor swimming pool, and through to the thermal pools. On Casual inspection of their route, they didn't spot either of the men on their way. As they submerged their bodies in the warm spring water, they positioned themselves near the wall to visualise the room.

"He's not outside," Luuk said. "He's not in the swimming pool either," Fenna said.

"Not in the thermals." Ted replied.

"Have you tried the plunge pool?" Anne said.

Anne further explained over the radio that there was an extra room behind the two thermal rooms that included showers and one plunge pool.

"We'll go check," Edward said.

There was a silence over the radio as Ted and Edward saw

two men come out from the gap in the wall where the plunge pool was. One man was Jozsef, and the other wasn't Ján. However, Ján appeared to become the third man in the group, following in his smart clothing, which looked tailored. The other unknown man was mid-thirties and of Eastern European looks, slim build but a muscle tone to his arms, legs, and torso.

"We have him. He is moving from the thermals back towards the main swimming pool." Edward said.

"We're in the pool ready," Fenna said.

Edward and Ted held their position in the thermal bath, not to raise suspicion, no matter how anxious they were to follow. Luuk announced he was making his way into the main building but would take his position in the shared thermal baths to observe from a distance. The men made their way to the main swimming pool under the glass roof. They walked along the pool edge and took a perch on one of the benches with room for two. Fenna and Anne made their way to the side of the pool where the men were sitting. They were using the double pillar as cover from sight.

"They're sat down on a bench by the pool, and they're speaking Hungarian," Fenna said.

"I'll translate," Anne said.

Around ten seconds passed as Anne took in the first parts of the conversation.

"Jozsef said for the other man to join him at Borkonyha tonight."

"What's that?" Ted said.

"A restaurant near St Stephen's Basilica. He said they're meeting a buyer from Russia, Rublyovka region, who is looking to buy two of the girls for 100,000 euros. The pretty ones."

Rublyovka is a group of elite towns located west of Moscow. It homes politicians, generals, celebrities, and some not-so-spiritually wealthy Russian Orthodox church officials.

In these areas, the critical ambition is privacy and security.

"The other man said he would join Jozsef. The other man asked if the problem is over."

Ted put his finger over his earpiece to listen more intently to the 'problem'.

"Jozsef said it was under control, but they messed up in Berlin. They will have to find a new way to transport the girls down because that was compromised."

Anne continued to say that the unknown man wasn't happy with the situation and Joszef could have jeopardised the whole business. The man said if there was one more problem, he would deal with the issue himself, and Jozsef would be in a body bag. Jozsef apologised profusely and said the girls were completely safe and won't be discovered. Anne carried on with her translation, announcing the unknown man would do a lap in the pool and then head to the dressing room to get changed. The man got up, made his way to the main swimming pool, and followed the other swimmers looping in the same direction. Jozsef, from his seated position, nodded at Ján and warily lifted from his seat as he made his way into the pool to reciprocate the unknown man's movements. Jozsef entered the pool, Ján watched them both submerge into the pool, surveying the whole room in his suit.

Fenna and Anne moved from their standing position and followed the pool's circle of swimmers. Edward and Ted decided to move into the main room, starting their walk along the walkway beside the pool. Luuk remained in the thermal pool, watching Ján, who was now walking towards the thermal pool. Luuk got a look at him and turned his head to the right just in case Ján returned a glance. Ján turned through the open door, which led towards the changing rooms. Luuk got up from the mosaic seat in the pool and made his way out of the pool to follow.

"Ján's on the move," he said.

CHAPTER THIRTY-SEVEN

TED AND ED MADE THEIR WAY TO THE SHARED
thermal baths to replace Luuk's previous position. Ted could
see the main indoor swimming pool in front of him with its
blue water and surrounding pillars. Overlooking the pool was
another floor with white railed balconies draped with green
plants.

"The unknown man is making his way out of the pool,"
Fenna said.

Everyone watched the man walk through the large hall
away from the pool. He was of average build and had a
receding hairline that he was clinging to in his middle age. The
man took the small steps out of the pool and collected his towel
from the bench, and he used it to dry his hair and torso as he
made his way through the open door towards the changing
room.

"Heading towards the changing room," Fenna said.

"Keep yourself covered in there, Luuk. He's coming in,"
Ted said.

"Will do. Ján's checking out the changing rooms and looks
like he's looking for someone," Luuk said.

"Hopefully, it's not you."

Ted and Edward remained in the pool, with Fenna and Anne ready to exit the pool if needed. Jozsef was still swimming in the invisible circuit everyone seemed to follow in the pool.

"Stay in girls, just for now," Edward said.

"Copy," Fenna said.

Meanwhile, Luuk found a long bench near his locker in the changing rooms. He was using a towel to pose as if he was drying off from a swim. The grey tiles lined the floor, positioned perfectly with each square like a jigsaw puzzle. The tiling followed vertically, with red doors separating each changing room, either open or closed. The changing rooms were quiet for the late afternoon, with it being a weekday and local visitors working, their lunchtime breaks were over.

Ján crossed Luuk's path, locking eyes only for a second as Ján walked on and disappeared beyond the back of one of the cabins, continuing down the walkway. Luuk had the urge to stand up and follow, but he knew the unknown man was entering the space too, and the team wanted to see how it would play out. Luuk remained calm and patient about how this was going to unfold, he had a worrying feeling and the empty room added to his anxiety. Luuk thought he heard the noise of a door creaking open and then closing, suspecting that someone had entered a cubicle down the walkway. Another noise came from the locker between the pool and Luuk's positions. Luuk witnessed the unknown man pass him with his belongings which he must have collected from one of the lockers. The man looked straight ahead as he disappeared behind the cabin, too, just like Ján. Luuk pondered his next move. He asked himself why Ján was in there?

"Jozsef still in the pool?" Luuk whispered into the communications.

"Confirmed. Everything okay?" Ted said.

"I don't know."

Luuk stood up and peered around the corner of the tiled

wall to get a view of the walkway. There was no sign of Ján, but the unknown man stopped as he discovered his changing cubicle.

"You need back up?" Ted said.

Luuk remained silent, not to spook anyone. He looked back at the next locker section behind him. It was empty apart from two older men discussing something with their towels wrapped around their waists. The older man exited Luuk's view as they moved towards their lockers. Luuk looked back at the walkway, and the unknown man pushed the red door open and took a step forward. Suddenly Ján appeared from the cabin directly across from the man, taking a slight glance back towards Luuk. Luuk ducked back but kept the two men in view. The attacker didn't notice the partial features of Luuk's face along the tile edge. The attacker walked cautiously, but with purpose in each step he took towards the unknown man. Ján raised his left hand and curved it around the unidentified man's face to his mouth, covering his mouth. Luuk saw a reflection in Ján's right hand, holding a knife. Ján went back and forth on the lower part of the man's back. With the blows, Ján pushed the man into the cubical, and the door shut with a few rattles to the metal frame, opening and shutting until it closed. There was no sound down the walkway or the cubical where the attack had just occurred. Ján had been professional, quick, and thorough with his approach.

"Ján attacked the unknown man in a cubical. Possibly dead." Luuk whispered.

"We can't approach. Move out and exit. I repeat, do not approach," Edward said.

"Jozsef is getting out," Fenna said.

"Let's get out. We can investigate the scene later with the police. We can't spook them, don't get caught, Luuk," Ted said.

Luuk left his position and grabbed his belongings, making his way through another passageway that reached one more set of changing rooms. Luuk looked back at his trail and saw no one behind him. Luuk focused on possible hiding places in front of him, a row of cubicles for changing. He turned back one more time and saw Ján had turned in the same direction Luuk had taken and followed. Luuk kept his composure and straightened his view, surveying the nearest available room. Ahead of him was an open red door which he zoned in on. He could hear behind him Ján's shoe patter on the tiled floor. Luuk reached the door and pushed it open, grabbing its edge and shutting it as he entered, locking it in a swift motion. He stepped back and took a seat on the bench, placing his belongings to the side.

Luuk watched the tiled ground for any movement between the gap under the door. The shadow of Ján's legs flowed through the crack and stopped for a brief second at the entry point to the door. Luuk's heart beat fast, and he entered fight mode. He stood up inside the cubical in his shorts and was ready to face the man if needed. However, the shadow disappeared and continued in the same direction as he was heading. The hesitation confirmed Luuk had been made, or Ján was contemplating if Luuk heard what had occurred in the room. Luuk sat back down on the bench, taking in each breath with appreciation.

"Luuk, you there?" Ted said.

"Ján's on his way out. I don't know if he made me or not," Luuk said.

"How?"

"He followed me. I went into a cubical, and he stopped by the door but then continued after a second. He didn't see me by the cubicle he attacked the man in. I think he just saw me when he was leaving."

"Okay. We will find you. Hans, are you there?" Ted said.

"Yes, we heard it all."

"Anything outside on the streets?"

"Nothing."

"Okay, we're coming out. We will let this be a natural

discovery; we can't risk it. We need you ready to follow Ján when he exits, and we've got Jozsef."

"Got it."

Luuk announced he would get dressed and make his way outside as the others decided to exit the swimming area to enter the changing rooms.

"I think they've found the body," Luuk said.

"I hear it," Ted said.

CHAPTER THIRTY-EIGHT

MABEL HARDLY SLEPT ON THE HARD CON-
crete floor which was underneath her. It was cold and uncomfortable without any soft blankets or quilts to rest on. She was wearing the same clothes from the night she was abducted. She looked around at the dark grey room complete with a big, rusted metal pipe running across the ceiling, with small routes coming down parts of the wall. She looked up above her and saw the pipe to which her left hand was chained. Around the room were a collection of girls she had seen back in the warehouse in Wildau, except for one or two new ones who had been the latest additions. Amanda's face was utterly drained and full of fear. Mabel had tried to communicate with her as she did with Mabel when she first arrived, but Amanda was unresponsive.

A chain was hanging freely from one of the pipes across from her. The man who Mabel despised took her away. He had been taking other girls and then bringing them back a few moments later, and she knew it was her turn soon. The girls didn't seem too distressed about what had happened in the other room, but they still looked upset. The man returned with the girl, stuttering back to her chained position on the floor.

This was the only delight they had since arriving here for circulating blood around their legs from all the sitting they were doing. The man chained the girl up and forced her down to the floor to become seated again. The man turned and looked towards Mabel. She stared back at him, not into his eyes, but into his soul. The detest of fire in her eyes could almost scold him in a stare; he knew that she had a craving to retaliate.

"Where are you taking us?" One of the girls shouted out.

The man turned to the girl sitting down just like the rest. He looked down at her from across the room and smirked.

"What are you doing with us?" she shouted again.

"Selling you to the highest bidder."

Mabel looked around the room to read the reaction. Mabel was already connecting the dots to the scenario, but it was visible that some were still naïve to the thought. Their faces changed dramatically in that response; and some were crying silently, and the girl became quiet.

The man walked over to Mabel and grabbed her upper arm, bringing her to her feet. He picked out a key from his pocket to unlock the chain she was attached to. Holding her up, he grabbed onto the ball joint of her shoulder to move her ahead of him. There was a slight hesitation in her footsteps, which became more flowing once he struck her on the back of her head. She lost her footing briefly, but he held her up so she could carry on. He led her through a double door away from the room of disconsolate girls. The opening led to another room with two other possible routes. There were a series of room divider curtains in sequence across two sides of the space in the room. Two men she had seen before sat at what looked like a card-playing table in one of the rooms. He ushered her to the right to a partially closed door full of light, much lighter from the surrounding rooms and where she was being held. She approached the door, and the man pushed it open and pushed her through the opening.

Upon entering, another man was standing behind a tripod video camera positioned in the corner of the room. Mabel was ushered towards the centre of the room, and was placed on a black taped X on the floor. The harsh lightbulb from the ceiling illuminated her within the room. The man touched her waist as Mabel cringed, turning her to face the camera. He then stood back behind the camera with the other man to take a position.

"Spin," the man said behind the camera.

She stood still, confused by the word.

"I said spin."

She connected the dots from when the man said about selling them to the highest bidder. This was a photo shoot, so they could be placed in a catalogue similar to the inventory of items you can find in Argos.

"This one ain't listening to us, Zivko."

Zivko raised his hand to strike the cameraman but then dropped it and spoke in his language. The cameraman looked scared after his slip up on revealing his name.

"Spin around now!" Zivko said.

She took the order and started to move slowly in a circle, creating the required spin. She completed one whole spin but was ordered to spin again. Once she completed the next spin, Zivko stepped towards her and brought her forward to the camera. He stood in front of her and grabbed her chin, dragging her along.

"Look at the camera and smile," Zivko said.

She had the urge to provoke him and spit on him at that moment, just as Hafwen did, she knew what happened to Hafwen though and fought the urge. She smiled at the camera with a smile that was so fake.

"Do it again," the cameraman said.

Mabel smiled again with more intent, which was some-what sarcastic.

"Done."

Zivko pushed her back towards the black marking and ordered her to undress.

"What?" Mabel said.

"Get naked now for the picture, or I cut you," Zivko said.

Mabel pondered whether she would fight her cause at that moment but decided to put herself through the degrading shame. Her clothes were in a pile in front of her naked body, and she held her hands over her private areas before Zivko ordered her to move them so they could take a picture.

"I said move your hands, now!"

Mabel dropped her arms to her side, exposing her naked skin.

"That's great," the cameraman said with his lips pressed together as he smiled.

Zivko told Mabel to get dressed again, and she did as fast as she could. She felt even more dirty and ashamed than she did already, having to soak in her own expelled liquids.

After she dressed, Zivko grabbed her by her shoulders again and pulled her back into the dark. As she manoeuvred through the divided room, she viewed the two people playing cards that she had seen before. One of the men looked up at her, and she detected a sympathetic warmth. She wasn't sure if it was the drugs that had been surging in her bloodstream or if the lack of sleep was causing her to feel that from the man. As Zivko turned her body towards the room where she was being held, she held a glare at the man's sad eyes and then lost them. Mabel reached her spot, and after Zivko chained her to the pipe, they exchanged another moment of eye contact. He was so unaware of the thoughts flowing through her mind. He didn't need to instruct her to sit after chaining her; she slowly lowered herself locking eyes with him all the way. He broke away first and headed for the neighbouring girl to collect. Once Zivko unchained the girl and led her through the exiting door, one of the girls across spoke up.

"Did they take your picture?"

"Yeah, they did."

"They told me to get naked. Did they do that to you too?"

"Yeah."

"I'm so scared. We're being sold!" the girl said before breaking down in tears.

The other girls in the room were silent as the girl cried. The reality of the situation was hitting the girls in the room, but it had hit Mabel the moment Hafwen was murdered. She knew she would remain enslaved or captured for a lifetime, and her sense of revenge engulfed her. She couldn't be sure if there ever would be a rescue party for the girls or if they genuinely were on their own already. She just needed that right moment. She now had a name to the person she hated the most. Zivko.

"I'm going to get out of here or die trying," she replied.

CHAPTER THIRTY-NINE

A CROWD OF RENDŐRSÉG VEHICLES FILLED
the Gellért Hotel fore-court and side road to the baths. The
operation team exited the building, passing the influx of
officers arriving. Ján had departed a few minutes earlier and
managed to get his car out of the hotel complex before the
horde of police officers arrived. Hans, who was parked a few
streets away, was ready to follow him on his exit. Hans
updated the exiting team from the baths on his movements
over the communications link.

Edward hesitated and broke back from the group exiting
the baths.

"I'll stay here for this and oversee it. I'll meet up later and
plan for the restaurant meeting."

"Jozsef got out of the pool and headed for the changing
room. Luuk, are you still on him?" Fenna said.

"I'm on him in the changing rooms," Luuk said.

"Okay. Has anyone got eyes on Ján?" Ted said over the
comms.

"We've got eyes on Ján going into the car; shall we
continue to follow? He's taking the Raoul Wallenberg rkp
along the river north on the Buda side," Hans said.

"Yes, keep on him," Ted said.

"On the move now. He's passed Elizabeth Bridge. Still Buda side."

"Bodor, are you still outside the baths? Can you pick me up, and I'll ride with you?" said Ted.

"Certainly, at the front?" asked Bodor.

"Yes, I'm here," Ted replied.

The unmarked car pulled up outside the hotel entrance. The car mazed through the incoming and parked police vehicles. Ted got into the back with Keleman, with Bodor and Andor up front in the driver and passenger seats, respectively.

"The man died in there?" Keleman said.

"He did. Edward is dealing with it. Let's see where Ján is going."

The black Mercedes car Ján was driving made its way along the Buda side of the river, keeping on the parallel road along the Danube. The vehicle continued north as it passed Margaret Bridge south of Margaret Island. The car turned off the main river road onto the side roads through Újlak and Óbuda until it met the junction for the main road, which crossed from east to west across the north of the city. The Mercedes navigated its way right, crossing the Árpád Bridge, the northernmost bridge in the city. The vehicle turned right at the bridge's midpoint, which led onto the island. In the middle of the Danube, the island sits covered with recreational areas and landscape parks such as Japanese Gardens, a miniature zoo, fountains, and a water tower.

The road that led onto the island was a two-way road with surrounding trees blocking out the sunlight on the island's ground—creating a cool breeze far different from the city heat circling the city. The Mercedes continued for a period until it reached an entrance to a car park which was nearly full of visitors checking out its green spaces.

Ted's vehicle was not far from the turning onto the island. However, Hans's vehicle kept a close tail on Ján as he was in one of the car spaces, facing out onto one side of the split river facing the Pest side of the city.

"He's getting out," Hans continued with his narration. "Moving through a path towards the river. I'm following on foot now."

Ted's phone vibrated in his pocket, and he pulled it out and saw Edward's number on the screen.

"Hello," said Ted.

"That Ján did a professional job. He's pretty good. Multiple stab wounds to the back of the guy and a clean insertion to the neck. Good news for us; we know the victim after running his photograph through the system," Edward said.

"Who was it?" Ted enquired.

"He's a Hungarian businessman called Ervin Becskei who's been investigated for fraud. He went under the radar for around two years, using false names and false identities to hide his movements. He managed real estate transactions, with the buyers losing their money and never becoming owners of their purchases. Or he would ask for upfront payments," said Edward.

"Is he a part of the operation?" asked Ted.

"Possibly. We will gain a warrant and check his phone," Edward said.

"Why did they kill him?" asked Ted.

"For power, maybe. You heard him say if Joszef messed up he would be dead. Joszef didn't like that threat," said Edward.

"Maybe. I just don't know who is the boss and who isn't," said Ted.

"Another off the street. Pity he can't talk to us," said Edward.

"I don't know how much he would have said anyway," Ted stated.

"True. Any updates on Ján?" asked Edward.

"He's on Margaret Island. Hans is out on patrol watching him; we're just pulling into the car park now. Any reason why he would be here?" said Ted.

"Not sure. It's just water surrounding it and green space. Maybe meeting someone?" Edward said.

"He's heading towards a white jetty," Hans said over the communications link.

"Got to go, Ed. Keep me posted," Ted said as he disconnected the call.

The jetty had wooden stairs from the edge of the land to a wooden lined walkway connected to a floating white structure. A blue gate closed off the walkway, but Ján pushed through the unlocked door entering the floating design. Ján surveyed the area, and with this, Hans ducked behind a row of bushes to hide but still observe. Hans took out his phone and started to take pictures of Ján on the jetty. He sent them through to Ted, whose vehicle was parked in one of the rows of cars.

"He's thrown something into the river," Hans said.

"The knife," Ted said.

"Yeah, it looked like it. He's coming back."

Ján made his way off the floating design and back onto the park's paths underneath the towering trees.

"There's a second guy. Shit! I'm stuck here," Hans said.

The second man approached the north path, which ran along with the river Danube. They started to engage in a conversation whilst surveying their location.

"I haven't got my papers. But I think I recognise the guy." Hans said.

Ted's heart raced. He stepped out of the back passenger door, keeping low as he closed the car's door, drowning out the questions from the officers inside. He knelt towards the front of two parallel vehicles to maintain coverage. The second man had his back turned, facing Ján, and it was hard to distinguish the man's identity. Suddenly they turned their bodies again to search for anyone who may be watching. The two men were side-on, and Ted could see the face of the second man. Relief overwhelmed him, his body feeling light as if somebody had lifted the weight from him. Vladimir spoke to Ján and appeared to pass him something. It was too small to see what the content was, but they seemed to finish, and Ján was the first one to break away

"Who's the second man?" Hans asked.

"It's Vladimir. My guy."

"Do we arrest them?"

"We could, but that's Ján not leading us anywhere. He could spot us and let off some signal on his mobile, and it's too risky. We hold off," Ted said.

"Could we at least follow Vladimir?"

"Leave him be."

Ted said his instruction first before thinking about it in his head. He knew Vladimir wouldn't report to the OCG that he was being followed, and he wasn't sure if Vladimir knew they were even on the island watching Ján. There was a vibration in his pocket, and he pulled out his phone, it was a message from an unknown number.

Please don't follow me.

Ted looked up from his phone to see if he could spot Vladimir, but he was nowhere to be seen. He re-read the message and knew it was the right call to leave him be.

"Jozsef made his way out. We don't know how. The hotel court is blocked, so he's walking across the road making a phone call," Luuk said over the communications.

"Get one of the officers to follow him, and he's probably just going back to the hotel. If so, let him rest. We will see him later," Ted said.

"Ján answered his phone. He's nearly back at the car, and he could be on the phone with Jozsef?" Hans said.

A few seconds passed by as Ján was still on the phone.

"He's just ended his call," Luuk said. "Same here," Hans

said.

Ján entered the Mercedes car and drove off through the parked cars and onto the main route out of the island. He sped off, leaving a cloud of smoke from the wheel spin.

"Luuk, make sure Jozsef does return to the hotel. Let's go back to the station and re-group for tonight. Hans and Léna, you'll need your best clothes on this evening," Ted said.

Ted reached for the door handle of the car, stretching his body on his tiptoes. Ahead in the distance was a gap in the trees' greenery. He thought he saw Vladimir walking along the river path, but it wasn't him; he had gone.

CHAPTER FORTY

BORKONYHA WINE KITCHEN ON SAS STREET IS
within District V of the city and only a few minutes' walk from
St Stephen's Basilica. The sun was already setting behind the
tall row of terrace apartment buildings and offices. The team
was in the police station as the evening approached, marking
another day in the investigation.

Jozsef and Ján returned to their hotel and re-entered their
respective rooms inside. Officers monitored movements from
inside and outside the hotel and were on hand to alert the
operational officers. After Edward and the team investigated
the incident at Gellért Baths, they further explored the CCTV.
They were particularly interested in the entrance camera from
where Ján made his way through the reception area and into
the changing facilities. On further enhancement, they discovered that he gave a security guard his bag to check when he
entered the metal detectors. After interviewing the guard, he
denied that he was given any payment to allow Ján to enter
without detection. The officers found no money in the guard's
possession, nor were his bank statements completed with any
transactions. It seemed to be a case of mis-judgement when
checking the bags and not moving the bag through the metal

detector. Ervin Becskei's phone was littered with contact information from associates from various other partners or buyers. The phone was seized and would be further analysed and its data extracted to ascertain Ervin's part in the illegal activities.

The plan for the Borkonyha's restaurant was to send in Hans and Léna for dinner with microphones under their clothes. Accompanying this would be a tiny earpiece in-ear hidden from view. The restaurant was classed as high-end, serving local wines and dishes, becoming popular for locals and tourists alike. Ahead of the reservation time, Joszef had set with Borkonyha, Hans arranged to meet with the manager to clear the table for the pretend couple, which would be next to Joszef. The manager accommodated them and manoeuvred the original booking of that table to another restaurant area. Ideally, the table needed to be near Joszef's so Léna could pick up any Hungarian if they spoke in that language or Russian, which was her mother's tongue. Joszef had a reservation for nine o'clock, and Hans booked the table for the fifteen-minute earlier slot. The tables were situated at one end of the restaurant near an innovative mirror-lined wall that reflects the rest of the dining room.

Other team members would be using the communications link to listen to the conversations or updates from the restaurant or its exterior areas. Further along Sas Street was an opening to the main road. Across from the road was Elizabeth Square, an open space within the district. Within the square was Budapest Óriáskereke, which is the Ferris Wheel of Budapest. Ted and Fenna remained posted at their location to communicate and hear the restaurant exchange. Luuk and Edward were admiring St Stephen's Basilica but remained in view of Sas Street to observe if there were any suspicious activities. Another two vehicles on the main street contained the remaining police officers helping in the investigation. As the pretend couple were working, they were treated to a fine dining experience whilst the officers fed off street vendors. A variation of Lángos, which is deep-fried flatbread had a covering of sour cream and grated cheese, were picked by some, and some went for a more hearty option; chicken paprikash and Goulash

After Hans and Léna took their seats in the restaurant, a waitress offered water and took both of their orders. Hans and Léna ordered the Cabbage Soup with Veal and Buckwheat. Hans with Fresh fish, leeks, casserole potatoes for his main meal, Goat cheese pasta, sage, and pumpkin for Léna. Both with a bottle of local red wine to accompany the dinner under the waitress' recommendation. After the waitress departed, they continued to discuss the small talk they would construct to keep themselves both in character. Through the mirror reflection, which looked back onto the entrance to the restaurant, Hans spotted Jozsef and another man walking in. They spoke to the waiter, and he guided them to their table. The men sat down across from Hans' table and settled into their chairs. The waiter placed napkins on their laps and offered water from the table jug to the two men, who accepted. They were speaking Hungarian, which Léna could translate as planned for this scenario.

Over the communication link, the restaurant's noise morphed into one constant sound of chatter. The only vocal understanding through the link was the pre-arranged conversations about family, fake history, and fake aspirations together. The wine arrived then with the Cabbage soup, and they started to drink and eat. The two men would have been in the conversation as time passed, but Léna wasn't relaying the information back to the team. Once the starting course was finished and the waitress collected their empty bowls, Léna spoke to Hans directly.

"I'm going to the ladies."

Léna didn't feel comfortable giving feedback in English on what she heard over the communication in case they could hear and easily translate what Lena was saying they were discussing. Hans nodded and took a sip of his wine, pushing the earpiece into his ear to hear the anticipated conversation. Once Léna made her way through to the ladies' restroom, she found a cubicle to rest in after seeing the room empty.

"The Russian man said, where is your bodyguard? You said you'd have one with you. The Russian seemed a bit nervous he didn't have one. Jozsef said he got a message from Ján to say he couldn't make it; he was sorting something out. The two men were discussing the purchase of two girls. Jozsef said, "Did you receive the link with the pictures?" And Jozsef asked which ones he wanted. The Russian guy said there were lots to choose from, but he wanted two, Jennifer and Mabel. Jozsef said the cost would be 35,444,400 Hungarian Forint to be made by bank transfer. Jozsef said he could expect to have them ready by tomorrow evening to be collected from the city.

The Russian guy asked for the address, but Jozsef said he would contact him with the details. Somewhere northeast of the city, twenty minutes out, Jozsef said. There wasn't much after that, and he said he would transfer the money and Jozsef would make the proper arrangements. Jozsef asked how he would transport her back to Moscow, but the Russian guy laughed it off and didn't answer. Saying if you aren't going to tell me the address yet, I won't tell you this either. They then changed the subject and started talking about Budapest and other restaurants in the city and other places they've visited around the world, and which country had the best girls. I won't go into the rest."

"We've got the girl here from Berlin then, Mabel. Luuk and Fenna, can you see if any recent Jennifer's who have gone missing on your database?" Ted said.

"Of course, I'll make contact," Luuk said.

"That's 100,000 Euros like they said in the baths," Edward said.

"Lot of money," Léna said.

"Thanks, Léna. Go back and see what else you can hear. Make it natural and leave it when you finish your meal. We have eyes on the restaurant for when they move. Does anyone know the area northeast of the city?" Ted said.

"Will do," Léna said.

One of the police officers, Victor, came over the communication frequency.

"Újpalota area is where the girls could be."

"That fit with his brief description?" Ted said.

"Yes, I just checked a map now. It fits."

Újpalota is a housing estate in the 15th district of the city. In the 1970s it had inhabitants from the country's poorer neighbourhoods of Budapest, demolishing its housing slum and providing families with hot water and heating and improved living conditions.

"Okay, thank you, Victor," Ted said.

"What do we do now?" Edward said.

"Keep eyes on the restaurant for Jozsef's movements."

"What about the Russian man?

"I've got an ILO in Moscow who I'll contact about his movements. Can we have a car follow him, Victor?" Ted said.

"We will."

The main dish of Fish and goat's cheese pasta arrived as Hans and Léna continued their fake conversations. They finished their meal and left the restaurant around half nine, with the two men tucking into their main meals and sipping their remaining red wine. Once the officers exited the restaurant, they headed towards Elizabeth Square, and Léna confirmed no additional exchange was made about the girls as their conversations continued.

"I just asked for an update on Ján, and he is travelling northwest through District XIV towards Újpalota," Keleman said over the communications.

"Tell them to keep on him and keep us updated," Ted said.

"Reckon he is going to the site?" Edward said.

259

"I hope so. I think that's why he wasn't here tonight. He was checking up on the girls. I think he's a larger fish than we initially thought."

CHAPTER FORTY-ONE

JÁN MADE HIS WAY TOWARDS DISTRICT XIV IN Újpalota, navigating the streets. Tall, outdated apartment blocks covered the area, with streetlights and the windows of the apartment blocks lighting up the darkness. The surveillance of Ján's vehicle became more arduous in the dark due to the headlights on show from the tailing cars. Keleman and Léna kept a distance but managed to navigate through the maze of apartment blocks to an exposed disused road that led to a dead-end near an old disused storage facility. They pulled up to a parked car before the side road began and killed the lights. They saw the car ahead pull into the facility, and then those lights went dead, leaving the facility's area in darkness.

Shortly after the two men finished their meal at Borkonyha, they walked to the main street, where they took separate taxis and departed from each other. Victor, Bodor and Anne followed the Russian's movements and checked into a five-star luxury Corinthia Hotel. Another team confirmed that Jozsef took the route back to his hotel and checked in shortly after eleven o'clock. Edward managed to get a picture of the two men as they walked out of the restaurant together. He shared that media image with Ted, who forwarded it to his

British Moscow contact, James Clair. James was slightly older than Ted and worked with him as a mentor in the first few months as an ILO in Amsterdam, with Ted replacing him in that posting. James phoned him back almost immediately as Ted and the team approached their vehicles from the restaurant's area. James said the man was a former Russian general, Nikolay Sidorov. No criminal records but had retired to live a peaceful life in the suburbs of Moscow. James suggested he would investigate this thoroughly, although political powers may disrupt any approach to Nikolay from him and any senior officers. Ted and James agreed they would let Nikolay return to Russia and arrest him for his involvement in sex trafficking once he returned to Moscow Airport.

Fenna also received an update from Europol on route to Újpalota. On Sunday morning, the Budapest police received a missing person report on Jennifer McCormack. Jennifer had been reported missing by her friend in Budapest. They were out on Saturday night, and in the early hours of Sunday morning she didn't return to the hotel. They were out in a much-visited Szimpla Kert ruin bar that strives for tourists at night-time, especially on Friday and Saturday nights. Her friend returned to their hotel around 02:30 am and left Jennifer with a group of people they had met. Jennifer wasn't tired and said she wouldn't be too long, and got friendly with a guy who attended the university on a year's exchange from Bulgaria. No one at the ruin bar could account for where she went when the club turned on its light around four o'clock. CCTV showed Jennifer leaving the bar with the Bulgarian guy, but the case went cold after that, with no further CCTV in the surrounding areas. However, around the time the team was at Gellért Baths, a taxi driver called Adojan Nemeth made a call about a fare he took in the early hours of Sunday morning with a female and male. He drove them to an address off Késmárk Utca in Újpalota. This area is very industrial and full of different warehousing units such as insulation material, computers, home furniture and storage garages. He thought it was a bizarre drop-off point as most residential apartment blocks were in different locations. The taxi driver described the girl as very sleepy and deteriorated in her state. The taxi man continued to tell the man was holding her up as they exited the taxi. Adojan came into the police station for questioning and confirmed on a photograph that the girl he took was indeed Jennifer through the CCTV evidence.

Keleman and Léna had parked on Raktárház utca which was a side road off Késmárk Utca. They killed their headlights between an Office equipment supplier building and a trucking company's warehouse unit. They both updated the inbound officers on the movements of the facility up ahead, and they received the order instructing them not to move before the officers arrived. Once the other team members caught up, they parked on Késmárk Utca next to an apartment on the side road leading up to the facility.

The plan was to make their way up the side road on foot, heavy with weapons but quiet. The side road had some street lighting, so the team made their way to the facility using the surrounding buildings as coverage, moving around the back and re-entering the road closer to the facility complex. The forecourt was dark with minimal light when they approached, allowing the team to be near with good protection. In the front yard of the facility, a man was patrolling the area, taking steps towards the shut gate and then returning to the facility. When the man was walking back towards the facility, the team pondered their next move.

"Do we have eyes on the other side of the facility?" Ted said.

"We do; there are two out in the back yard. No major movements yet," Hans said.

There was a silence as the officers began to think of their subsequent movements. They knew the gate entrance would be locked, but it was hard to plan how to work their way inside without visualising the facility.

"Okay, when he turns back, I'll go over. I'll take him down and then open the gate. I can't see a lock on it, and it's just a sliding bolt by the looks of it," Edward said.

"Are you not a little old for that? You need support?" Ted said.

"I've done it many times before. I'll be fine. But if he hears me, take him down."

Edward and Ted moved to the front of the group, taking cover around the bush-covered part of the metal gated fence. Ted knelt at the foot of the gate and placed both hands palm up on top of his knee. Edward placed his right boot on it and lifted up the fence using his hands. Ted stood up, pushing Edwards' body upwards as he climbed it. Once Edward had a grip on the top of the fence, Ted's focus turned to the man in the yard. Ted raised his weapon in the man's direction but remained covered behind the foliage. Edward made his way to the top of the gate and swung his leg over the top, narrowly missing the pointed spikes which ran a few centimetres apart. The guard was reaching the entrance point of the facility when he would typically backtrack and take in the view of the gated entrance.

Edward dropped with a thump as his black boots connected with the ground. He manoeuvred himself behind a recycling wheelie bin for cover. The guard, in his turn, heard the noise and raised his weapon towards Edward's position. He moved forward with pace, shouting.

"Who is that? Show yourself!"

"On three, Ed," Ted said through the fence.

Edward nodded back at him from his crouched position.

"One... two... three."

Edward lifted himself from behind the bin with his gun raised in an attack position. Behind the gate, Ted had aimed at the target keeping his hands steady and ready to fire as the guard approached the recycling area. They both fired at the man until he dropped to the floor, waiting a few seconds before confirming he was down. They knew the gunshots would alert those within the facility. Edward turned to slide the bolt across, thus allowing the gate to be opened from inside. Ted reached for the entrance gate and opened it; so he and the other officers could make their way through. They held their attack position as they moved slowly through the forecourt, using vehicles, bins, and pallets as cover.

"There is a movement out the back here. They've heard the gunshots," Hans radioed.

"Can you get in?" Ted said.

"No, it's padlocked. We've moved in position, and we are taking cover behind the vehicles."

"Okay, hold it down."

Suddenly a shower of gunfire flew out from the facility's door, aiming at the advancing officers in the forecourt. Edward and Ted stepped forward between the palleted boxes witnessing two men at the front entrance.

"I'll get the left," Ted said.

Instantly they were both down, falling forward off the stepped platform onto the tarmac ground in a few shots. The next set of men invaded the area of the doors, holding cover further back behind two metal pillars on either side of the entrance. These two men managed to get a shot on target, and one of the gang's bullets struck Andor in the shoulder behind the vehicles.

"Officer down, need medical back up immediately," Keleman said.

Keleman darted from his position to where Andor was lying down with his back against the vehicle.

"It's going to be okay. Let's get you out of here," he said to Andor. He radioed in to the communications.

"Cover me!"

The succession of bullets from the officers increased as Keleman grabbed Andor by the strap on his bulletproof vest and dragged him back towards the gate. The cover fire was good, and he managed to get him to the side street outside of the facility's fence. The sirens of police cars and an oncoming ambulance up the side street drowned out some of the gunfire. From the police cars, the newly arrived officers took over at the gated entrance giving any cover fire for the paramedic to attend to Andor.

"They're getting the girls into vans," Hans radioed over the communications.

"We need to move quickly," Edward said.

CHAPTER FORTY-TWO

MASS PANIC OVERWHELMED EVERY SECTION
of the room and beyond its walkways. The frightened girls
were chained up still, and beyond the walls were loud voices
from the hallway and outside. Mabel heard the sound of
gunshots in the distance and saw a few men running,
shouting, with weapons in their possession. Within that
moment, she was optimistic about what was unfolding beyond
the prison room. She was weak and influenced by topped-up
drugs coursing through her veins from around two hours ago.
Before the skirmish, the men seemed to be readying for
travelling as they loaded and cleared out parts of the
warehouse. There was now no more time for the men to top
up the medicine concoction in the median cubital vein, and as
every minute passed, the drugs started to wear off.

Some of the girls jumped in their positions with every
shot, and some were scowling to cover themselves. Men were
still running backwards and forwards past the walkway
holding weapons and shouting in their native tongues. After
the initial hysteria, the men began to not leave their prisoners
unattended for too long. Three men came in and started to
unchain two girls at a time and lead them back out into the

walkway and right towards the curtain-divided room. She thought they must have been heading towards the other door, which wasn't used for photography. Girls were struggling and trying to wriggle free from the captors, but verbal ordering and a few physical hits from the men put them into their place, and the girls submitted. However, that only allowed the emotional trauma to catch up with the standing girls as some were starting to sob and plead as they left through the door, one being Amanda.

After a minute, those men returned to take the next set of chained girls until only Mabel and another girl were left. When one of the men returned, he shouted in Hungarian to another man who wasn't in view. The man who raised his voice ran towards the front of the facility, and the second man appeared in sight, Zivko. The stare was menacing, and he had evil intent in them. Zivko made his way over to the other girl, unchained her, and lifted her to her feet. She was hesitant in her stance and stood firm when he tried to push her over to Mabel's position. Mabel watched every single step he was taking, like a hawk.

Zivko managed to manoeuvre the other girl over to Mabel's sitting position, standing directly above her. He reached up to the lock between the metal ring and the chain. Mabel grabbed onto her chain with her left hand at the highest point, and once the lock clicked, Mabel had the advantage. Her legs were already free, and she lifted her left leg as high as she could and with as much force as she could gain and kicked into his genital area. He dropped on to his knees with a thud, letting go of his grip on the other girl. As he fell, Mabel rose from her position using the last energy reserves in her body.

She manoeuvred her way around the back of him and lifted the chain over the back of his head to his front, pulling it tight against his neck. He made a loud noise from his mouth as the metal chain made him choke and inhale nothing into his lungs. Zivko moved his hands from his groin area to his neck and started to gain some strength as the fight response of adrenaline coursed through his body. Zivko began to move his legs to leverage a standing position. The other girl stood over him and pushed him down, using both of her hands on top of his shoulders to stop him from moving his legs into an upright position to lift his body upwards. Mabel raised her leg to the point between his shoulder blades and leant back with her body. He made an exhaling noise which sounded like more air leaving his body. He was panicking; he tried to reach behind with his hands and reach up to the girls holding him down from the shoulder. He was losing this battle of survival. There was no remorse in Mabel's body, and she was thoroughly compelled to keep holding onto the chain until she couldn't hold onto it any more. Zivko neared his last breaths, and the strength from his body was getting stronger. However, it wasn't enough. Mabel gained additional power from the harrowing thoughts of what he did to Hafwen. There was no way back now; even if another one of the men came in and saw her killing the man and tried to intervene, she wouldn't let go.

The force from Zivko started to weaken as the seconds progressed with the chain wrapped around his neck. The girl holding onto his shoulders had begun to let go and watch him struggle. Zivko gave up trying to get to his feet; he couldn't. He tried to reach around with his arms to get a hold of Mabel for the last time. He was failing at every attempt, and the choking noise from his mouth became softer and quieter with every moment. Zivko's body went limp, and his heavy body dropped against the chain. The weight of his body was too much for her to hold up. Mabel let go of the chain, and Zivko's body dropped forward flat on the floor with a thump.

His body was still, and a sense of relief filled her body. Adrenaline was competing with the lack of energy she had left, and she wasn't sure who was winning. Mabel dropped to the floor and sat down with her head forward as she took in deep breaths. The adrenaline was starting to wear off, and the lack of energy crept in. She was exhausted and couldn't muster the energy to stand back up again. She had exerted all her energy on gaining revenge and she had no more to save herself.

Suddenly a man appeared through the walkway, holding a gun. It was the man she saw playing cards at the table. Looking more closely she noticed he had a small cross tattoo on the right-hand side of his right eye. He saw the terror in their eyes as he approached them within the room. He spread his arms in a submission fashion.

"I'm not going to hurt you," the man said.

Mabel didn't have the strength to put up a fight any more and remained silent in her position, accepting the inevitable. She thought the gang would take her like the others.

"Why wouldn't you," the other girl said.

"I'm a good guy," he said with his arms stretched out. "I'm undercover."

"I don't believe you," she said again.

From the walkway, another man came into the room.

"What are you doing! Get these in the van. We are in the van ready to go; we've got two men holding the front," he said.

"Everyone's in the van?" the tattooed man said.

"Yeah, let's go! What are you waiting for?" the other man shouted.

The man with the cross tattoo turned and raised his gun in the direction of the man.

"It was you, you..."

The man with the cross fired his weapon into the man's chest. The other man fell backwards through the walkway into the next room, holding his chest. He was still alive through the impact and rolling from side to side, letting out a moan. The tattooed man walked over to him and finished him off by shooting him in the head. The man's body stopped still on the floor.

"Do you believe me now?" he said, looking back at the two

girls.

Mabel stared at the tattooed guy and nodded her head.

"What's your name?"

"Call me Vladimir. Outside are officers coming to get you."

Vladimir looked across the room and saw Zivko murdered with the chain.

"Nice," Vladimir said, nodding his head at the dead body.

"So, what are you going to do to us?" Mabel said.

"Here, get in there," pointing at a door within the room.

The man pointed to a door at the end of the room. A room the girls never saw open and never knew what was in there. The man opened the door so that the girls could see the inside. It was a store cupboard with shelves that had storage boxes on them. The man reached in and turned the light on using the hanging cord.

"Get in," he said, pointing at the empty room.

The girls hesitated to go in.

"Are you sure it's officers outside? What about all the other girls?" Mabel said.

"People are looking for you, I promise. Now get in quick. Here is the key for the door, and lock it now."

"Thank you," they both said.

"What about the other girls?" Mabel said.

"We will try for them."

They both stepped into the room, and the man put the keys into Mabel's hands. Vladimir reached up to the dangling cord and hit the lights. The light from the room they were chained in was the last bit of light they saw as he closed the door on them.

CHAPTER FORTY-THREE

VLADIMIR QUICKLY GLANCED AT HIS SURR-
oundings to find anything he could. He saw a half-torn piece
of paper on a table in a side room and a pencil across the other
side of the room. He looked around to make sure no one was
in the room with him. He heard shouting and gunfire towards
the front of the complex; it was getting closer. He placed the
piece of paper in his palm and wrote one word on the paper
and a small cross in the top right-hand corner. He folded it up,
placed it in the gap by the bottom of the door, looked back at
the utility door, and saw it remained shut.

He felt some form of relief that he had saved two people,
and that's all he could do without risking his own life for now.
Upon entering the hallway, he followed another man running
across the walkway to the back of the warehouse. Waiting was
a van with one OCG in the driver's seat, ushering them
frantically to get in. He jumped up into one of the vans, sitting
on a wooden box bench that ran along the side of the van
against a metal frame. Three other men in the truck looked
intensely at him. Six girls were sat huddled in the corner
against the van's wall that separated them from the driver.

"Where are the girls? Luca said.

"The officers were coming in, and they got to the room first, and Zivko and the girls."

"Fuck. They followed us. Jozsef messed up!"

"I don't know what happened."

There was shouting outside, which translated to someone saying they were ready and to go, telling everyone to keep low. There was a loud bang on the side of the van wall and quick footsteps. Then one of the men jumped up into the back of the open entrance, banging on the side of the van. Vladimir looked back at the building from which they had escaped. He knew he was paying his debt but hoped this long exhausting journey would be over eventually. Vladimir knew leaving the note would be risky if anyone was still around during the evacuation, but he was confident the officers would swarm the building soon. If the escape plan worked and they had escaped, they had another location for the operation to follow. He wasn't going to use his phone, it was too risky, and he hoped it worked for the remaining girls.

The van started to roll forward and jolted with the driver's harsh acceleration, jerking everyone to sit down to the side. The guy who jumped into the back of the truck held onto the metal bar of the open shutter. He then used his weight to bring down the back door, and it slammed shut, leaving everyone in darkness. As the van rolled forward for a few hundred metres through the yard, gunfire met the metal with rapid-fire. The van swerved to the left, picking up speed, and jerked everyone again from their seated position to either fall on the floor or slide to the side. The sound of banging metal against the van's frame started to fade and become a distance noise. They were clear of danger, but those innocent people weren't clear of safety.

CHAPTER FORTY-FOUR

THE FRONT OFFICERS PUSHED FORWARD ON the attack, moving to the last available cover at the front of the facility. Using their fire as cover, they managed to reach the entry point. They sat near cover, checking their ammo, using the last available container of spare ammo. The volleys of bullets from inside the building projected towards the advancing officers, which left a weak link in the chain for their cover. Fenna aimed over the pallet shooting at one of the men exposed from his position. In a two-shot movement, the man fell backwards, dropping his gun on the floor. The entry of the bullet wound was to the chest and neck, with blood spurting out from the second impact.

Luuk lifted his weapon to the other man and aimed at his chest with three shots. He fell back against the wall and slid down against it until he was resting in an upright position against a metal pole. Edward announced it was clear to engage, and they slowly kept aim on the entrance point as they then begun to cautiously move through it and through the corridor.

"All clear at the front. Moving in through the corridor," Luuk said over the comms.

Meanwhile, an escaping van started to accelerate towards the locked gate at the back of the facility. Léna and Hans raised from their covered position to stand in front of the entrance whilst the van headed towards them. The officers opened fire on the incoming vehicle, and the driver started to duck his head as he drove into the gate. The sound was booming as the front of the van impacted the metal gate. The gate managed to break open on impact allowing it to open outwards, away from the facility. Although the bullets partially cracked the window, the gunfire didn't impact the driver's ability. The sound of scraping metal came from the van as Hans and Léna moved out of the way of the incoming vehicle. As the van passed the officers, gunfire pelted at them from the passenger's door. Hans and Léna were both hit by the oncoming bullets as the van sped through the industrial road. Hans took two shots in the chest, knocking him backwards, with a shot in the right leg as he impacted the floor. Léna took a shot in the chest, and one just under her armpit as the force of the bullet knocked her backwards.

"I'm shot. Van on the move," Hans said, letting out a loud groan at the end.

"Officers down," Léna expelled.

"We need an ambulance now," Anne said over communications as she appeared from cover to help.

"Keep eyes on the van. Don't lose it!" Victor said into the radio.

"Got visual," Bodor said.

The sound of another roaring vehicle approached from the back yard, and it was the second van making its exit from the facility. The officers shot at the van, but it didn't stop, and it nearly hit Hans, who was trying desperately to crawl backwards away from its path as it drove by.

"Second van exited," Victor said.

Officer Bodor announced he and another vehicle were in pursuit of the vans.

"Don't lose them!" Ted said.

"I'm going to help with the pursuit. Can you handle it inside?" Edward said. "We're going to see if anyone's been left behind, and I'll be right on it with you," Ted said.

Edward backtracked through the forecourt they had cleared, taking officers gathered around the gate to join the pursuit of the escaping vehicles. Before entering the last room where the girls were held, Ted and Luuk entered the walkway and adjacent rooms. Upon entry, Ted noticed the two bodies on the floor, men. Ted thought it was a peculiar outcome, as Ted and Luuk were the first members of the operational team to reach this room. Therefore, no officers had been in the facility to confront the OCG inside. They had succumbed to their fate another way, he thought. Just inside the room was the body of a man lying on his back with his eyes wide open, staring at the ceiling. There was a pool of blood starting to smother the floor around him. Ted crouched down to get a better visual of the body. A red stain which he presumed was a gunshot to the chest, was the fatal blow. He reached inside the man's pocket and found a wallet. He slipped out a card, being an EU driving licence.

"Demitri Kolorav. Not one we have on our list."

"Who shot him?" Luuk said, lowering his gun as he said it.

"I don't know," Ted said, lifting himself and holstering his gun.

"What about him?" Luuk said, pointing across the room.

Ted and Luuk made their way to the other body in the room. There was no sign of blood on the initial inspection and no wound visible. The man was lying on his front with a silver chain stretched out under the man's chest. Ted knelt to get a better observation of the corpse.

"Help me lift him a bit," Ted said.

Ted reached down, holding one side of his shoulder, and Luuk held the other, lifting his torso into an upright position to get an ID on the face. A bruising was starting to form around his neck, which gave possible confirmation of strangulation.

"This is Zivko Dordevic," Luuk said. "It's like an assassination of members here," he continued.

"It is odd. Let's be quick and move out to the pursuit."

Ted thought if he were going to find the body of an OCG member, it would have been Vladimir, and he was glad it wasn't.

A ruffling noise came from the door just behind Zivko's body. Ted and Luuk glanced at each other and raised their bodies to attack mode. They raised their weapons towards the door and readied for what may be behind it. They were only a few steps away from the door, and Luuk took the left-hand side where the door opened and Ted on the other.

"Come out with hands on your head. We are armed, and we will shoot," Luuk shouted.

There was another noise coming from within. It sounded like voices.

"Come out now, or we will come in," said Luuk.

"Hold on, Luuk," Ted said to him, raising his hand. "Come out; we won't hurt you. We are the police."

There was a noise from the door that sounded like a lock turning. The metal handle on the outside started to move down, and the door opened.

Luuk was the first to take in the mystery behind the door.

"Come out," Luuk said in a friendly tone, still holding his gun towards them, then lowering it.

The two girls steadily came out of the door, Luuk lowering his weapon, and then Ted did once he saw who was behind it. The two girls looked exhausted and dirty, with greasy hair and dirty faces. They looked around the room and at the two bodies on the floor. At that moment, through the walkway came Fenna and a few other police officers. Fenna was amazed at the discovery of the two girls, standing there in disbelief. A smile almost broke on her face, which was rare from the team's experiences so far.

"We need paramedics here ASAP to check the girls once they've dealt with outside," Ted said.

"I'm on it," Fenna said.

"How are Andor, Hans and Léna?" Ted said.

"They'll live. Vests saved their lives. Hans needs his leg looking at though," she said.

"Good," Ted said with a smile.

Fenna stepped back to search for the medical assistant who was on standby.

"It's okay, and it's over now," Luuk said.

One of the girls exited the door and ran to Luuk and gripped him tightly, hugging him for dear life. Mabel dropped to her knees and took in a deep breath as she closed her eyes with her head looking upwards in relief.

"What's your name?" Luuk said to the girl who ran to him.

"Jennifer."

"McCormack?"

She looked at him with a face that finally accepted she was safe. She just nodded back at him, still embraced.

Ted stood over the girl who was on her knees.

"You're Mabel, aren't you?"

She looked up at him in shock. She started to shake her head and open her mouth to speak.

"We've come a long way for you," Ted said.

"But how did you find us?"

"We'll tell you all about it soon, but let's get you looked at by the medics," Ted said.

"A man with a cross on his eye helped us."

Ted nodded at her, and she rose to her feet, aided by Ted's arm. He nodded again to himself in acknowledgement of what she said. The paramedics attended to both girls as Ted and Luuk stepped back from them, and they made their way back to the walkway.

"They okay?" Fenna said.

"They will be now. We've got to go now," Ted said.

"Sure, I'll come with you."

Ted looked down at the open door where they were standing and bent down to pick up what he saw. He lifted the crumpled paper off the floor and checked both sides, and he fixated on one side of the paper. He looked up from the writing and scanned back towards the team in front of him.

"Here. We've got to go now before it's too late," Ted said.

He offered the piece of paper to them. Luuk took it, studied the word written on the paper, and passed it to Fenna. Luuk looked up at Ted with anticipation.

"This Vladimir?"

"Yeah." Ted said.

"He came good for you."

"Not for me. For us all. Let's go."

The three offers jogged back through the walkway and into the open space as dawn was breaking again. The OCG had got away again, but the team radioed they were on the tail of both vehicles. They were hoping not to lose them this time. As the vehicle's engine started, Ted remembered the word on the piece of paper. He didn't need to keep it as a possession to retain its content, and it was just one word. It was a word that gave him fear but also hope, and it was their last chance, their last stand.

Timișoara.

CHAPTER FORTY-FIVE

THE SECOND EXITING VAN MADE ITS WAY north out of Újpalota and through District XV. The pursuit began on the M3, whose first incoming junction was for the Mo surrounding road around Budapest. The pursuit was by a vehicle with the officers Bodor and Keleman in it. The van weaved in and out of the narrow residential area, missing cars navigating the streets as the dark turned into daylight. The van swung out onto the busy main road just missing oncoming vehicles flashing their headlights and sounding their horns. The police cars' sirens caught the attention of other vehicles, moving away from the pursuit as the vehicle tried to catch up.

"Is back up on the way?" Keleman said.

"We're minutes out," Anne said.

The vehicle was fast approaching the junction for the Mo. The shutters at the back of the van lifted and two men started firing bullets into the car's windscreen. The window shattered and glass covered both officers' chests, necks, and heads. The vehicle swerved from left to right at speed, allowing the car to gather traction and flip over twice and rest itself on its roof. The van took the second exit on the junction, performing a loop and remerging on the new freeway road heading southeast of the city.

"Officer Keleman. Officer Keleman?" Anne said. "Are you okay?" she continued.

"What's happening?" Edward said over the radio.

"We heard gunshots and loud noise of metal, and now nothing," Anne said.

"Can you see them?" Edward said.

Anne's vehicle took in the view of the wrecked police car.

"Oh My God. The car tipped over on its roof. There's no sign of the van."

"Make sure they're okay, Anne. We can get CCTV on the motorway and follow them. Let's get some officers on the M0 road searching for the van," Edward said.

"News on the other van?" Ted said over the radio.

"Following them southwest on the M3 towards City Park," Edward said.

"We're on our way," Ted replied.

The sun rose as the van reached the road where the M3 ended. The junction gave the option of a route that ran northwest to southeast around the city. The north exit went towards Árpád Bridge, near Margaret Island. Straight across at the junction led towards Kós Károly stny, a road that led through the middle of City Park. The road was full of trees on either side and green grass verges. Large raised beds full of colourful flowers separated the pavement and the road.

The van swerved from left to right, crossing the two-way road near just missing both sets of directional traffic. The early commuters were getting an early morning scare on their way to and from work. The car horns echoed the park road as the two vehicles drove at approximately eighty kilometres per hour. Edward in the chasing vehicle couldn't get enough acceleration to keep up with the van whilst dodging the incoming traffic. They were fast approaching the vehicle bridge that crossed City Park lake, connecting the park to Heroes Square momentum. The level of danger would multiply ten-fold if the chase continued into the city's heart and its morning traffic and pedestrians.

Edward finally decreased the distance between himself and the van. They began to cross the bridge, and the bumper of Edward's vehicle was just in line with the truck's back wheel. It was dangerous, but he managed to turn the wheel left into the back of the van. The van scraped along the low blue metal railings that protected vehicles from going off the bridge. The two vehicles were on the empty bridge, and the van fought back. The van turned right, and its front side turned into Edward's car. Edward turned the wheel left on impact to maintain balance. Edward turned the wheel right, moving away from the van and then, with one quick steer of the wheel, he turned back into the van. The van scraped along the blue rails again. A blue street lantern stood on a concrete block that separated a small part of the blue rails at different points in the bridge. The concrete block stuck out ever so slightly, the driver's side bumper jolted, and the driver lost control of the vehicle within that moment, losing speed. The driver's side tyre was blown and lost its synthetic rubber, with the metal rubbing against the tarmac road, causing sparks from the friction.

The two vehicles were side by side again, heading towards the junction for Heroes' Square. The van couldn't turn left with much conviction due to the blown-out tyre, so the driver pulled the van to the right and back into Edward's driver's side again. The two vehicles crossed the central pedestrian walkway at the roundabout. A large walkway ran between the monument's frame, which depicted the two horses and chariot on each of its highest points; the vehicles entered the pedestrian square within the heart of the monument. Edward had the upper hand. In his driver's mirror, he saw the lights and heard the sirens of police cars coming from the road from City Park. This was the moment he knew it had to end, but he needed to be precise with his calculations for the safety of those inside the van. The Heroes Monument with a high tower in its middle was ahead of him, resting on a stone base. The driver of the van knew he couldn't turn left; he could only turn right, and Edward eased off a fraction to allow the van to pull into him. He didn't want the van to hit the monument ahead, or that could be disastrous for the occupants inside.

They were metres away from passing the momentum and the edge of the stone base when Edward swung the steering well to the left. The driver's side wheels left the ground from the impact, turning the momentum of the van to the left and gravity brought the van back down again. Edward slammed on the brakes to stop the car in the middle of the square. He got out of the driver's side door, holding his gun up to the stationary van as he approached it. The line of police vehicles crossed the bridge, made their way onto the square, and positioned their cars to surround the van.

"Approach with caution. We have civilians in there," Edward shouted across the square.

He got close enough to the van's cab to see that the driver's head was resting against the side window with blood smeared on the window. Once he got to the driver's door, he looked back down towards the back of the van, and there was still no movement. He held the gun up to the driver's door and opened it, keeping aim on the driver. He raised his left hand to stop the driver from falling out of the cab. He perched a leg onto the step to propel himself up. There was no one else in the vehicle. He stepped back down to ground level and shut the door to the cab again.

He saw another vehicle approaching the open area stop, and Ted and Luuk exited.

"I'm heading towards the back," Edward said.

"Covering the near side," Ted said.

Ted was approaching and Luuk and a few officers went to the back shutter. The shutter was down but looked damaged and loose from the crash's impact. Edward warned the other officers to step to the side and remain there once the door opened. Edward reached for the handle, lifted it, and ducked down behind the metal bar just above the licence plate.

There was no noise of gunfire as the shutter reached the top of the structure of the van. Edward looked up towards Ted, who had moved round to view the back of the van. Ted was holding his gun up as Edward lifted himself up and saw the aftermath of the accident. Luckily it paid to be strapped into chains once the accident occurred. With a quick count, six girls were still in their positions on the wooden benches along the sides of the van. Another man was on the floor with a cut on his forehead, blood flowing on the van floor, face down and motionless.

Ján stood there with a cut on his forehead and held a gun to another girl's head.

"Get me a car to get out of here, or she dies," Ján said

"You know that's not going to happen," Ted said

"Okay, well, she dies."

"Wait," Luuk said, "we can do that."

"What are you..." Ted said.

Luuk held his hand up to Ted.

"We can do that, but let the girl go, okay?"

"No way, car first. I'm not stupid."

"Where are you from, girl?" Luuk said.

"Shut up. No speaking," Ján said.

She hesitated but managed to speak up, "Germany," in a whimpering voice.

"I said shut up," Ján said.

"Sich Vorbeugen," Luuk said.

She didn't hesitate. She leant her torso forward as far she could under the control of Ján's strength. As soon as she reached as far as she could, the power of the man's grip loosened, and she fell forward. An echo thundered around the van's cabin and a loud thud as Ján dropped to the floor.

When Luuk gave the order, the girl moved her body. Ted

saw the space between Ján and the girl once Luuk gave her the instruction and had no hesitation in pulling the trigger. Ján lost all control once the bullet entered his skull, and the splatter of blood sprayed on the cabin wall and over one of the girls nearest to the shutter door. They held their guns towards his body, but after a few seconds of no movement, the confirmation of pooling blood around his head was enough. The officers lifted themselves into the back of the truck to comfort the girls. Ted's thoughts swiftly changed to the two officers involved in the car flip.

"News on Keleman and Bodor?" Ted said.

"They didn't make it. I think they were already dead before the car flipped" Anne said over the radio.

Ted took himself away from the team with his hands on his head, looking up to the sky. Ted was hoping that no one else would die, but the confirmation of the Hungarian officers' deaths brought great sorrow from the satisfying results on Heroes Square. There was no sign of Vladimir in the van, so he assumed he was in the other van heading south from the city.

"Too many good people gone," Ted shouted as he turned to a full circle.

"We've not finished yet; let us finish this together. Your man has left us a breadcrumb, and we need to follow it," Luuk said.

Ted looked up and saw the girls stepping out of the back of the van with smiles and tears of joy. Their faces reminded him of his daughters back home, who he missed dearly. Ted visioned Keleman and Bodors' final moments in pursuit of the vehicle and, if anything, could have been done differently to change the destiny of their lives. He knew the end was near, they had come so far across the continent already, and the time for respect and admiration would come. They had one last journey to make.

TIMIŞOARA

CHAPTER FORTY-SIX

AFTER THE EVACUATION OF THE OCG MEMBERS
and the girls back in Budapest, Jozsef knew he was on the run,
and the police were moving in on him, stalking him like prey.
He needed to escape the city and make a reasonable attempt
to continue his profitable business. He left Wildau that night,
and his journey flowed through the heart of Europe to
Budapest and was about to end in Romania.

The operational team watched Jozsef in the Botanic Park
in Timişoara. The note left on the floor back in Budapest had
given the location where the OCG was heading. Using the
Hungarian Police force's intelligence systems, they managed
to spot on local CCTV the van escaping the city and moving
south of the town on the Mo and southeast on the E75 heading
towards Romania. The strategy was to follow the vehicle but
at a distance and lead the operational team to them. In
addition to the CCTV and ANPR observations, there were
unmarked police vehicles following them on the road which
crossed from Hungary to Romania.

Just north of Timişoara, there is a small town called Arad,
where the white van led the followers. There was a temporary
blow to the pursuit of the van, as it was suspected the OCG

knew of the tail. As the vehicle turned left down one of the town's main streets in Arad, it passed an entrance to a construction yard. As it made its way through the small roads, the following vehicles kept up keeping their distance with another civilian car between them. Suddenly an articulated lorry pulled out of a yard and into the lane. It overshot its exit and blocked the road horizontally, creating a barrier across the street. The move from the OCG made the operation know they knew they were followed from the complex in Budapest. The lorry pulled out and had large Jürgen Hahn's writing alongside in significant blue italics. The Arad construction yard was where the girls were transported to from Berlin. One of the Romanian workers who was driving that lorry confessed he would be paid a wealthy one-off sum if he pulled his lorry into the middle of the road when instructed to do so. It was discovered on the freight forwarding documents that the day before the raid happened there, there was a documented journey from Wildau to Arad, delivering machinery.

The initial van was lost but abandoned in a rural spot by a working farmhouse. The farm owner, a fifty-five-year-old who had lived on this farm all his life, spotted it and reported it to the local police force after seeing men and girls being moved into another van.

The officers documented Jozsef's movements, tracking him to a hotel in Timişoara. A dedicated team watched every step he made from the hotel in Budapest. Edward took over command of this operational opportunity. The officer observed him eating lunch on his own in the sunshine at a local café in the city, oblivious to his much-wanted status. He had dinner meetings at upmarket restaurants in the city. The plan was to take him down in the open and wait for that opportunity to arise. An open area would allow the team to listen to his side of phone conversations or meetings with various people if they so happened. If the evidence were clear on the recorded conversation, they would move in. However, the team were aware they didn't have the location of the second van, and the girls were still captive.

The morning after his first day within the city, he moved to the Botanic Park just northwest of the centre near a building used as a city clinic that towered over the park. There was a bench on which Jozsef sat down on the right-hand side. He sat perched forward, rubbing his hands and rocking back and forth, looking nervous. The team started to position themselves at different points within the park and surrounding buildings. Jozsef sat for a least five minutes, which gave some of the team time to be at various vantage points from windows of nearby buildings, offering a hawk-eye view from above.

Operation Hawk's team had grown as they made their way into Romania. The team in Budapest made the three-hour journey by car, and, on arrival, they met the IOL for Bucharest, Christopher Edwards. He provided as many officers as required for the operation. Jozsef had been a significant problem in the criminal system, and authorities had previously searched for him, but he evaded capture by using his wealth and power to suppress evidence. The new IOL had set new directions within the police force to eradicate anti-corruption in the party and smoke out the rats in the department.

The operational crew covered all surrounding grounds of the park. The team would know about whoever was going into or exiting the park.

"We've got Luca Manu approaching from the south side of the park, alongside the medical centre," Edward said over the communication radio.

"I can see him," Luuk said. "We've got another man approaching Jozsef from the fountain," he added.

Another man was walking down the path towards Jozsef's position. He was around his mid-forties and dressed in a tailored navy suit and was of slight build with balding hair from the scalp of his head. One of the plain-clothed Romanian officers walked past holding a rolled-up newspaper with a live microphone sellotaped into the inside of the pages, and he threw it into the open bin next to the bench. Jozsef looked up for a moment as he walked past, but then was again with his thoughts, waiting anxiously for what seemed like someone to meet him.

The police officer made a diversion onto the adjacent pavement to avoid the oncoming person. Luca was approaching the bench from another direction and reached the bench.

"Luca! You made it," Joszef said.

Luca remained silent, crossing his arms in front of him as the other suited man approached the bench.

"Hello," Jozsef said to the suited man.

"You got here in one piece then," the suited man said as he sat down on the bench.

"Yes, we ran into some problems."

"It's not good, Jozsef; you've cost us a lot of money. You nearly compromised the whole operation. You had the police chasing you across Europe. We've lost many men and business!"

"I'm sorry, Cristian."

"Sorry is not good enough. Are the girls secure?"

"Yes, completely safe. We lost the tail on the van in Arad."

"Have you got the address?"

"Yes, here."

Jozsef took out a card from the inside pocket of his suit and handed it to the man. There was a silence after Jozsef gave the card. The microphone picked up the sound of birds in the trees and other passers-by having their conversations. Christopher radioed from a vantage point across the street:

"Cristian Lazarescu is the other guy."

"Who is he?" Ted said.

"Major kingpin in this type of operation. I wasn't sure about his face; he looks like he's had facial reconstruction. We thought he was dead. We had a tip-off from someone in Istanbul and used that description, and it's got to be him, it's too similar not to be."

Christopher stopped as the conversation continued on the park bench.

"I've got buyers ready to purchase so we will be moving today. I met one last night who made a purchase, and I've got two more meetings tonight," Jozsef said.

"You've sold one already?"

"Two in fact. Big money. Their off to the UAE as we speak on a private jet."

"You won't be getting your commission on these Jozsef, and you've cost me too much."

"I did my best, goddamn it."

"Not good enough."

Jozsef looked straight ahead. His face turned to anger.

"Luca," Cristian said.

Jozsef raised his eyebrows in confusion.

"Luca? How do you know Luca? I didn't tell you his..."A croaking sound came from Jozsef's mouth as Luca reached his massive forearm around his neck. Luca grabbed his free arm and held Jozsef's head as he snapped his neck. Jozsef's body went limp, and Luca slowly laid him back against the bench as if he were asleep.

"That's for my friend Ervin." Cristian said as he raised from his seat, adjusting and straightening his suit.

"Is everyone ready?" Ted said.

The team on the ground confirmed they were ready to move in at any given moment. Ted thought about the consequences of this final moment in the investigation. They had the conversation recorded, and he was taking a risk in hoping the address was on the card.

Ted gave the order to move in, and the team swooped in from all angles surrounding the two men who were beginning to move away from the bench. Luca was the first to notice and started to reach for his gun. Cristian heard the gunshot and turned around in fright. He saw Luca's body slam backwards against the bin, knocking it over as more bullets entered his body. Luca dropped the gun as he started to lose his life and rest on the ground in his final position. Cristian turned back to the direction he was walking and saw three officers holding weapons in front of him. He held his hands up in surrender and accepted there was no way of escape.

Cristian lowered his right hand to reach into his suit inside pocket.

"Hey! Don't think about it," Fenna said.

"Don't shoot; it's not a gun," Luuk said.

He had reached into his pocket to get the card that Jozsef had passed to him. He crumpled it up in his hand and began to lift it towards his open mouth. He felt a firm grip on his wrist as he reached the opening of his mouth. Ted had appeared from behind the bench and watched his position in the bushes. Ted managed to wrestle with Cristian and gain purchase on the card, stopping Cristian from chewing and dissolving the contents of the address. Cristian let out a big cry as the officers approached him, placing him on his knees and putting handcuffs on him.

The team in the offices made their way to ground level in the park.

"Quick hands there, Ted," Edward said on approach.

"Thanks, I just hope this is the address," Ted said, holding up the crumpled card.

"Me too."

Ted saw Christopher approaching their position.

"Here's the address he had," Ted said.

Christopher took the piece of card and studied it.

"This is an address north of the city near the airport. Let's get a team ready."

Ted nodded to him as Christopher gathered some of the officers around.

"This could be it. Good work, Ted," Edward said.

Ted felt a moment of relief surge through his body. He

turned away from the arrested man and looked outwards at the main road alongside the park. He noticed the café's entrance point across the busy main street. Within the door frame of the café was a man looking back at him. He couldn't tell who the man was because the black cap's lip was resting and sitting down, covering his eyes. Ted became uneasy as his thoughts of being spotted charged his mind, and deep worry coursed through him.

"Edward."

Ted started to stroll along the path which led to the main gate, leading back towards the café. Ted was worried the man would alert the OCG at the address that the officers were coming for them again.

"What is it, Ted?"

The man lifted his right hand, grabbing the front lip of his cap and lifting it away from his face. They both stared at each other at that moment, and their eyes did not deviate from each other. The man broke away first and nodded his head towards Ted, and Ted did likewise back at the man.

"It's nothing, sorry."

The man put his black cap back on and started navigating the pavements, becoming another person within the crowd. He then took one of the alleyway entrances alongside one of the buildings and disappeared.

AMSTERDAM

CHAPTER FORTY-SEVEN

THE ROW OF GIRLS LAID LIFELESS ALONG THE hard cemented ground. The room was dark, with the fading light hanging from the ceiling. He took one step in front of the other as the never ending row of bodies continued along the dirty warehouse wall. There was blood drying around the hole in the forehead just above the nose. Their eyes were closed as if there was some sort of care or even regret from those who had done the deed. He started to fidget with what he was witnessing, and his heart rate increased as he reached the end of the row of bodies. The light in the room started to become brighter, to the point it was blinding his vision of the room. He tried to put his hands above his eyes to block out the light, but it became brighter, he had to try something else. He turned away from the bodies and felt a fist to his face. He convulsed as his body was startled by the shock. His eyes opened to see a black figure towering over him. The paw was dangling over him from the edge of the couch. It was his cat, and he had fallen asleep on the sofa after arriving home from Romania. The cat looked down at him, purring as it dropped its paw to its normal sitting position on the edge of the sofa. The cat opened its mouth and let out a yawn. It jumped off the edge of the sofa and wandered across the carpet.

"Me too, Evie. Me too."

Ted rubbed his eyes and stretched out his left hand to check the time on his watch. It was 10:54 am, and he had managed an hour and a half of sleep before he was awakened prematurely by the cat. He arrived back in Amsterdam yesterday evening, a day after the raid of the facility in Timișoara. Before Cristian could destroy the address in the park, he had retrieved it. Most of the operational team made their way to the address just north of the city, as the remaining team dealt with Cristian and the bodies in the park. They managed to save all thirteen girls who were inside the facility. Unfortunately, they were too late for the two girls who had been shipped to the UAE on the private jet. One of the girls they saved in Budapest, Mabel, commented that none of the girls the team rescued in Timișoara was Amanda Coleman, who she knew from being captured. The other girl who was transported was identified as Toni Laurent, who had been reported missing by her French parents after not returning from her trip to Berlin. During Mabel's stay in the hospital, she was given Toni's photograph, which was provided by her parents, allowing Mabel to compare to the array of women she spent her captivity among. Mabel confirmed that Toni was captured in Berlin and was one of the girls transported into the van when the gang evacuated the complex in Budapest. Neither Toni nor Amanda was in the vehicle stopped at Hero's Square, so they assumed they were in the van that escaped southeast of the city after taking down the police vehicle before the motorway. The airport authorities in Dubai weren't helpful, which was usually a sign of bribery. Ted was waiting on contact from Luuk and Fenna at Eurpol on their discussions with Interpol, who were joining the task force for its post-operational journey. Interpol was particularly interested in the case and its foreign connections with other countries and senior figures and the area of investigation in the UAE. Ted returned to Amsterdam in the afternoon the day before to debrief with Sander and other Korp's officials and Luuk, returning to his HQ in The Hague. The debrief included a conference call with officials from Germany, Hungary, and Romania to run through the procedures they took. Agreed also was that nothing would be released to media outlets in various countries. So no potential trials at The Hague would be tarnished before starting the procedures for Cristian and other captured members in Romania. Another conversation that was important to Ted was the safety of Vladimir Balan, and he had appeared and disappeared on the street across from the Botanic Park. Throughout the night, he made his case to the Korps officials and other cross country authorities about the safe tracking of Vladimir and reassurances that he would gain a new identity. His cooperation was merited to the safety of so many girls before being lost within the depths of its dark reality. This was agreed upon, and arrangements were made for his guaranteed protection and relocation. Ted reached for his phone on the coffee table next to the sofa. He was in the study, which opened up into the lounge and kitchen areas. He saw a notification on his emails and clicked on the app to check the content of his inbox. It was from Luuk, giving an update on last night and, more specifically, Vladimir.

Hi Ted,

Lewis Hewitt picked up Vladimir last night on the Hungarian border. They took him to the British Embassy and arranged the documentation for him. He's safe and well. He asked about you. Cristian is being transferred to the Netherlands tomorrow to start the charging process, but I'm sure he will lawyer up. The girls saved from Berlin, Budapest and Timișoara are now in contact with their parents, and preparations are being arranged to return them home. There will be final *questions and medical checks that need arranging for them, but they will be fine. They're going to need counselling of some sort; damn, we all are.*

Interpol is joining the force to conduct their investigations in the UAE, but it is not looking good. We've lost the trail.

The gang members we caught won't be getting away with this. We will go hard with the charges when they recover, even those two in the hospital. It's just about being patient now and carefully piecing all the evidence together, but the hard work has been done.

Nikolay Sidorov. Your ILO James Clair will probably be in touch, but they arrested him at Moscow Airport. They have him in custody, but let's see how long that lasts as they fight against not just his lawyers but the political power behind him.

I know you don't like praise, but you did well. We all did.

This is just the start; let's hope justice is served.

I thought I'd email you because I knew you'd be sleeping. I'm going to catch some Zeds too.

See you soon, my friend.
Luuk.

Ted felt a surge of relief flow through his body which gave him a boost of energy that he needed to function after one hour of sleep. He flicked off the email app and onto his message app and sent a message to his wife to tell her he had gotten home just after she left for the school run. He was slightly concerned about where she was as it was nearly two hours since she would have been home after dropping their daughters off. He thought it would be his wife who would have woken him up from the sofa, not the cat, but at least the cat missed him, he thought. He sent the text and put his phone down by his side. It made a message noise instantly, and he believed that Rose had messaged back; as soon as he messaged he was home. He picked the phone up and looked at the screen. It was a message from an unknown number; he retyped his pin to see the message.

Thank you, my friend. I will never forget you. Alexandru

He nodded to himself; he knew he had succeeded with Vladimir and felt a huge weight lift from his chest. He put his phone down again and sat up from his prone position with both his elbows on his knees, rubbing his eyes for the last time before getting up. He needed sleep, but he didn't want to re-enter the nightmare he had just endured. He didn't know if this was the start of a spiral of PTSD or was just because he had the names and faces of those girls who didn't make it in his mind from the night before, during the debrief. He shook off the thought and pushed down on his knees to rise from the sofa. He heard the lock on the front door, and it opened in the hallway. The door shut, and Rose entered the lounge in front of him.

"Hey," Ted said, standing now from the sofa. Rose was startled as she came in with bags of groceries after dropping the children off at school.

She dropped the bags on the floor and started to walk over to Ted's standing position. Ted was about to move towards her when he stopped, and his phone made a sound from the sofa. From the illuminated screen, he saw it was an email from Simon Taylor. He saw the subject line underneath the name that read one word.

Athens.

Ted turned back towards his wife who was stretching her arms for a hug.

"What was that?" she asked.

"Nothing," Ted said as they embraced.

"You're home!" she said with a smile, leaning back to get a visual of Ted's face.

"Yeah, I'm home."

EPILOGUE

MABEL WAS GIVEN MEDICAL TREATMENT FIRST
at the local hospital, including an IV and the facility to shower
and take in food at the station to build her energy. After this
Mabel attended the police station where the operational team
worked. Officers interviewed her on her steps from arriving
in Berlin to her discovery in the storage cupboard. They
brought her back to the initial night when she met Jonas and
Elias by inviting her into a lineup window. She pointed out
Jonas and Elias as the individuals who drugged her and helped
with assisting their capture. Mabel identified the OCG she saw
during her captivity through paper printouts, helping support
the mountain of evidence the cross-border forces were
collecting. The officers said those OCG members who died
instead of being captured would also be convicted. Mabel also
identified Amanda Coleman and Toni Laurent as those that
weren't found, and those faces crowded her mind daily as she
imagined the severe pain they were enduring.

Mabel reunited with her mother and father in Budapest;
they flew over on a charter flight from Cardiff Airport once
they knew of her discovery. Mabel was warmly embraced by
her father, knowing she was now genuinely safe and acknow-

ledging her true safety in his arms, like when she ran out of the primary school gates as a child. Though there was one moment that Mabel was so longing for when she found herself drugged and chained in that abandoned warehouse; she finally got to apologise to her mother for how things were left between them before she left for her trip away. Both were sympathetic in their first moments, but those emotions changed to happiness once those embraces were genuine and no longer just desired thoughts.

Since returning to her hometown in South Wales, she has attended counselling sessions reliving her ordeal's, haunting and painful memories. By helping to suppress the pain, her counsellor supported her to work through her thoughts and PTSD. She was very much haunted and tormented by the ideas of what her fate could have been. She felt survivor's guilt for not knowing what happened to those transported into the van in Budapest. She felt colossal guilt from living when Hafwen's future was dashed so cruelly, with no chance of saving her. She had constant dreams of the moments she endured and Hafwen's last memory and torment. She saw the face of Zivko everywhere she went in the present and in her nightmares—something which would be imprinted into every man she met for a long time. Her counsellor suggested that she take part in positive experiences and proposed Mabel explore activities and influences that make her happy. Mabel was always one with water and had been since she was a little girl, attending her local beach to swim in the surf, and as she stood on the beach, she heard the crashing waves, which brought serenity to her mind for the first time in weeks.

Mabel was attending the ceremony of Hafwen at Ogmore-by-sea after her funeral in the nearby town's church. The open ceremony included the scattering of ashes into the Bristol Channel off the coast, where Hafwen adored being in her spare time. As the ashes disappeared into the sea breeze, Mabel looked up from her position on the beach and saw a flock of seagulls soaring free above the ocean. Ahead of her into the deeper water, she saw people riding the waves on their boards as she prepared to do the same. The surfers disappeared behind the tide for a brief second and reappeared as they completed the wave. When she was younger, she used to be one of those people, coming down to the beach with her family, friends, and Hafwen on Sunday mornings. Naturally, she would enjoy going to the beach in the summer, but something was quintessential about going in the autumn and winter months, which were fast approaching. This would be the last time she would stand on this beach for a while before going off to university to start her higher education studies. Further ahead, when she completed her studies, she was already planning to enter a career in law enforcement and become one of those officers who opened the door to her freedom.

She stretched her arms into the air towards the warm sunlight and lifted her head towards the sky. Using her hands to block out the sun, she noticed another bird flying in the sky, keeping camouflage in between the screeching seagulls. The elegant bird broke rank behind her; it was a Hawk, and it hovered above the long grassy dunes.

She turned her body to block out the sun's rays and dropped her arm, giving a full view of the bird in flight. From that movement, she could look at the beautiful creature flicking its wings and keeping its head still in its waiting position. She took one last look at the hawk before it swooped down behind the bank; the Eye of the hawk caught its prey.

AFTERWORD

We hope those who have gone missing
are found or find peace.

ACKNOWLEDGMENTS

THE AUTHOR GRATEFULLY ACKNOWLEDGES those who helped in the editorial works of this book. The cast led by Alex Kale was an indispensable part of the process and included Daniel Gutstein and Shelly Lee. I'm grateful to Erin Larson head of the interior design team and Cameron Finch the book publicity director. I'm appreciative to the Art department led by Ronaldo Alves for creating its vision and offering an inspiring cover that brings the story to life from the front page. A special mention to Chris Beale who gave extra delicate touches to the manuscript to give its final edges.

Anyone who helped inspire the story and bring its characters to the page is gratefully acknowledged.

Thank you.

NINE LIVES

TED CHESTER WILL RETURN FOR THE SEQUEL to *Eye of the Hawk*. Ted joins another group of police authorities sooner than anticipated as he takes on a new case in the Greek Capital, Athens. Ted discovers the truth to his abrupt arrival and finds lives are at risk, even his own.

ABOUT ATMOSPHERE PRESS

Atmosphere Press is an independent, full-service publisher for excellent books in all genres and for all audiences. Learn more about what we do at atmospherepress.com.

We encourage you to check out some of Atmosphere's latest releases, which are available at Amazon.com and via order from your local bookstore:

Dancing with David, a novel by Siegfried Johnson

The Friendship Quilts, a novel by June Calender

My Significant Nobody, a novel by Stevie D. Parker

Nine Days, a novel by Judy Lannon

Shining New Testament: The Cloning of Jay Christ, a novel by Cliff Williamson

Shadows of Robyst, a novel by K. E. Maroudas

Home Within a Landscape, a novel by Alexey L. Kovalev

Motherhood, a novel by Siamak Vakili

Death, The Pharmacist, a novel by D. Ike Horst

Mystery of the Lost Years, a novel by Bobby J. Bixler

Bone Deep Bonds, a novel by B. G. Arnold

Terriers in the Jungle, a novel by Georja Umano

Into the Emerald Dream, a novel by Autumn Allen

His Name Was Ellis, a novel by Joseph Libonati

The Cup, a novel by D. P. Hardwick

The Empathy Academy, a novel by Dustin Grinnell

Tholocco's Wake, a novel by W. W. VanOverbeke

Dying to Live, a novel by Barbara Macpherson Reyelts

Looking for Lawson, a novel by Mark Kirby

Yosef's Path: Lessons from my Father, a novel by Jane
   Leclere Doyle

Surrogate Colony, a novel by Boshra Rasti

Orleans Parish, a novel by Chad Pentler

ABOUT THE AUTHOR

Neal R Sutton was born in Billinge, UK, and before he started writing fictional crime novels on the side, Neal received a graduate degree in Sports and Physical Education at Liverpool Hope University, whilst contributing to the International Journal of Social Sciences Studies. Graduating, he then taught primary aged children, Sport and Physical Education. He enjoys a pint of beer among friends or watching his fav-ourite football team. He enjoys listening to a wide range of music and reading Michael Connolly. He lives in Warrington with his partner, Son and Cat, and *Eye of the Hawk* is his first novel.

Website: ww.nealrsutton.com
Twitter: @NealRSutton

Printed in Great Britain
by Amazon

83272356R00185